HOTEL LADD

Dianne Venetta

HOTEL LADD
Book #3

Ladd Springs Series:

LADD SPRINGS ~ #1
LADD FORTUNE ~ #2
HOTEL LADD ~ #3
LADD HAVEN ~ #4
LOSING LADD ~ #5

Other novels by Dianne Venetta

Romantic Women's Fiction
The Gables Trilogy:
JENNIFER'S GARDEN
LUST ON THE ROCKS
WHISPER PRIVILEGES

Women's Fiction
CONDEMN ME NOT

ISBN 9780988487154

Hotel Ladd
Copyright 2013 by Dianne Venetta
ISBN: 978-0-9884871-5-4
Publisher: BloominThyme Press
Editor: Best Foot Forward
Cover Design: Jaxadora Design

Acknowledgements

Tennessee has some of the most beautiful horse country in the world. In fact, Shelby County is said to boast more horses per capita than any other county in the United States. If you've ever been to Tennessee, you'd understand why. Not only are there pastures galore, but Tennesseans know their horses. From Memphis to Knoxville, Nashville to Chattanooga, equestrian lovers are alive and well and flourishing in the state.

I discovered this interesting fact, among others, during my Facebook Release Party for Ladd Springs. As part of the fun, readers were asked to supply names for an upcoming horse in the series. Selections were put up for a vote and I'm proud to announce that Martha Schlegel won with her submission of "Vegas" -- a beauty you'll get to know in this book and continue to love throughout the duration of the series. Congratulations, Martha!

Many thanks to Martha—one of my Bloomin' Warriors—and to all who participated in the week long release party filled with Tennessee trivia, giveaways and fun. Best of all, it was a great way to connect with my readers.
Can't wait for the next one!

Dedication

This book is dedicated to my street team.

Bloomin' Warriors rock!

Meet the cast of characters of Hotel Ladd...

Ernie & Albert Ladd ~ Brothers of Ladd Springs

Susannah Ladd Wilkins~ Sister to Ernie & Albert (deceased)

Jeremiah Ladd ~ Ernie's forsaken son

Annie & Casey Owens ~ Jeremiah's ex and her daughter

Calvin Foster ~ Home from Arizona, son of town banker

Candi Sweeney ~ Annie's best friend

Jillian Devane ~ Hotel developer, competitor to Nick Harris

Malcolm Ward ~ Hotel developer, partner to Nick Harris

Lacy Owens Ward ~ Wife to Malcolm, sister to Annie

Delaney Wilkins ~ Ernie's niece

Felicity Wilkins ~ Delaney's daughter

Nick Harris ~ Founder, Harris Hotels

Travis and Troy Parker ~ Neighbors & friends of Felicity

Jack Foster ~ Brother to Cal, Delaney's ex-husband

Beau, Clint & Gerald ~ Cal's brothers, father

Fran Jones ~ Owner of Fran's Diner, aunt to Annie & Lacy

Hank Dakota ~ Town lawyer working with Annie

Chapter One

Annie Owens fiddled with the business card in hand, the matte finished paper growing worn from her constant handling. Colored green and tan with flecks of natural fiber, the earth-friendly tone of the company card was clearly communicated. *Eco-Domani*. Annie's gaze slid down to the name embossed in the lower right corner. Jillian Devane, President and CEO.

"What are you gonna do?" Candi Sweeney asked, a nervous edge creeping into her voice.

"I don't know," Annie murmured.

"She seemed real intent on talking to you."

Annie nodded, dropping her gaze to two half-eaten sub sandwiches on the coffee table before them, food Candi had graciously picked up on her way over after work. Her friend understood this was a significant development. Annie had to do *something*.

Six months ago Delaney Wilkins had signed over half of Ladd Springs to Annie's daughter, Casey. Ladd Springs, the mecca of rivers and streams, mountains and trails and springs—natural springs that were unique to the property— had been held by the Ladd family for generations. Delaney's uncle, Ernie Ladd, had recently passed away, willing the entire tract to Delaney's daughter, Felicity. Because she was blood kin.

Well, so was Casey. Ernie's son, Jeremiah Ladd, was Casey's father, making her equally entitled to the land. The logic was simple. It was Ladd land and she was a Ladd. Unfortunately, Annie had to prove the fact first, a process Jeremiah fought her every step of the way. But after battling him for years, she finally won when he showed up in town six months ago looking for his piece of the land. Ernie had refused him outright. He was willing it to Felicity and no one else. In the end, Jeremiah landed himself in jail for an unpaid gambling debt, Ernie died and Felicity received title to the property. Annie had secured her paternity test and proved once and for all, Casey was Jeremiah's daughter making it impossible for Delaney to ignore her rights. Eighteen long years and a paternity test had proven it beyond a shadow of a doubt. Annie's daughter was a Ladd. It was the reason Delaney acquiesced and signed over half of the property to Casey.

But the property consisted of hundreds of acres. If she were to keep the property, Annie had to think, plan, strategize—but it was the details regarding what to do that were tripping her up. This was out of her league. She didn't do financial calculations. She did fingernails! A flurry of angst peppered her chest. Flipping her gaze out through the back windows of her apartment, Annie latched onto a range of mountains. Saturated by a late afternoon sun, the Blue Ridge Mountains were ablaze with orange, red and gold, clumps of green tucked here and there in between. Beyond, the sky had cooled to a bluish-lavender. Fall was upon them, dropping temperatures into the upper thirties for the third day in a row. There was even talk of snow.

Seated on the couch in the living room of the two-bedroom apartment she and her daughter called home, Annie looked to Candi. Concern scored her dark brown eyes, her heart-shaped face framed by stick-straight hair that fell in flat-ironed points across her shoulders. Naturally brown, highlighted by chunks of blonde, her hair was perfection. Candi was a hairstylist, her best friend, the only one who understood what was at stake. "Annie? Are you listening?"

Caught by a sudden chill, a shiver raced through Annie. What was she going to do? She knew what she *wanted* to do. She wanted to call Ms. Devane. She wanted to speak with her about the financial potential of her share of Ladd Springs. Casey's share, Annie corrected. Over six hundred acres of pristine forest snaked with rivers and streams and loaded with springs she now owned. Trouble was, now that Casey retained title to half the property, Annie had to figure a way to afford it. That part wasn't as simple.

"Do you think this woman can help?" Candi pressed, hanging on the edge of her seat. She'd been Annie's closest ally throughout and truth be known, the reason Annie and Casey held title to the property. If Candi hadn't called Jeremiah back home from Atlanta, none of this would have happened. Casey would not have title to the property and Annie would not be in a position to earn money from it.

"Maybe."

"She seemed real eager to talk to you when she gave me that card." Upon receiving it, Candi had immediately rushed to Trendz, the salon where Annie worked as a nail tech and delivered both business card and message. *Please have Ms. Owens call me at her earliest convenience. I will make it financially worth her time.*

Seems Jillian Devane had a proposition for her.

Staring at the card in hand, Annie wasn't stupid. She'd heard the woman was in town to get revenge on Nick Harris, boyfriend to Delaney Wilkins and the owner of Harris Hotels. His company was currently transforming Ladd Springs—the other half of Ladd Springs that belonged to Delaney's daughter, Felicity—into an upscale hotel and spa resort for the very wealthy. Nick had signed a 99-year lease to use the land, land that old man Ernie Ladd had refused to sell, instead willing it to Felicity as a life estate. When Ernie died, the land became free and clear to be developed.

"Do you think Jillian Devane wants to build a hotel like Nick?"

Visions of an exclusive wooded retreat for elite guests swam through Annie's mind, guests who would pay top dollar to lose themselves in the mountains of Tennessee, the forests, the natural beauty of the Appalachians. Felicity was barely eighteen and stood to earn a fortune from her deal with Nick Harris while Annie and Casey had nothing but bills as a result of owning their share of the property.

"I don't know. Maybe," she hemmed. Annie knew full well Ms. Devane was interested in building a hotel. In fact, according to Annie's sister Lacy—her direct conduit to all things Ladd Springs—Ms. Devane had looked into purchasing land an hour north of here for that very reason. She wanted to ruin Nick's new hotel by building one of her own. Married to Nick's partner Malcolm Ward, Lacy had the inside scoop and dished it out readily to Annie—because Annie had forgiven the past problems between them.

Leaning forward, Candi grabbed a cheddar-coated chip from a shiny blue plastic bag. "Have you asked Cal about it?"

Annie looked at her friend, ignoring the loud crunching from her mouth. "I don't want to bother him with it."

"Why not? He helped you get the loan to pay the back taxes, didn't he?"

"He did," she acknowledged. Which was easy. His father, Gerald Foster, owned a bank in town and pulled the strings. Not that Cal didn't mean well, he did. Calvin Foster helped, because he was a decent man. As part of the Foster clan, he was a man of means, a man who'd been calling on her ever since his return from Arizona six months ago.

Annie grew up with the Foster brothers. They were four good-looking boys, wild and crazy and always out for a good time with the ladies, although Cal had been the most tame among them. His brother Jack married Delaney, and for a while, they seemed like the perfect couple. It wasn't until Delaney up and left him that everyone in town learned the truth. Jack was abusive. He was a drinker. A mean drunk, at that. After Delaney moved back home with Felicity, Jack left town and Annie hadn't heard a word about him since. Brothers Beau and Clint had remained in town, married, had children, held rank as respectable men in the community. Beau ran the Foster family ranch, acres upon acres of premiere pasture and mountains while Clint worked with his father at the bank, the biggest and most prestigious for miles around. Despite the rowdy reputation forged by the sons, the Fosters were a respectable bunch. They had looks, money, smarts...

Victoria Foster would accept nothing less. A socialite from Chattanooga, Cal's mother came from money and would not allow her move to the small town alter a single aspect of her lifestyle. The Foster estate was grand, the land was beautiful, the four sons were unruly—a fact Mrs. Foster refused to permit injure her standing in the community. It was one of the reasons Gerald Foster was so anti-drinking today. Zero tolerance was his motto, for his boys and his staff.

Although Annie had grown up with Cal, knew him from high school, knew his family through church, she had never thought of him romantically. He was nice-looking enough, but back then she'd only had eyes for Jeremiah. A year after she became pregnant with Casey, Cal had moved to Arizona and she hadn't seen or heard from him until her godmother's big Memorial Day party this past summer. When Ashley Fulmer through a party, everyone attended, giving Cal the perfect opportunity to reacclimate himself back into the community. Annie had definitely noticed him at the barbecue, the two dancing and chatting, erasing the passage of time between them as they began a new path forward together.

Candi pulled a sip from her coke, her cheeks hollowing. "I bet he could come up with an idea to help you earn some money with this woman. Cal is smart that way."

That's where Annie begged to differ. Yes, he was smart, but Cal had become friendly with Malcolm, a man equally invested in Nick's hotel development. If Cal let on to Malcolm or Nick that Annie was even considering a discussion with Ms. Devane, Annie had no doubt the men would be angry. Lacy had given Annie a blow by blow on the history between Nick and Jillian, how Harris Hotels and Eco-Domani were in constant competition and how six months ago Jillian Devane had paid a visit to Fran's Diner, putting Nick on notice she intended to build in Tennessee as well. If Annie worked with Ms. Devane in any way, it would be seen as crossing enemy lines, something you didn't do around here unless you packed two barrels and were prepared to fire them. "Why don't you ask him?" Candi asked.

"I think Lacy and Malcolm would have something to say about it," Annie replied. "Any involvement with this Devane woman will be seen as a betrayal."

"Well, Lacy and Malcolm don't have a say in what you do. They're not helping you make ends meet, are they?" Candi vehemently shook her head and said, "No, ma'am. It's your decision. Yours and Casey's, I mean."

Yes, Casey. Casey was the named owner, but Annie was the designated trustee. When Delaney had Felicity sign over half of the land, she'd stipulated Casey was not to receive control over the property until she turned thirty years of age, or she wouldn't receive the first acre. Because Casey was too young and not ready for that kind of responsibility. Because Casey had a history of instability.

But Annie was ready. Seemed responsibility was all she knew, like it was her whole life. Expelling a sigh, she smacked the business card onto the table. "I don't know what to do, Candi. I only know I wish it wasn't so damned hard."

Annie had finally won the battle—Ladd family recognition for her daughter and the procurement of her rightful inheritance—yet she had no way to keep it. Sure, Cal had helped her secure a loan to pay the back taxes but there would be a new tax bill this fall. In another month, she'd be facing the same dilemma all over again. Her eyes went quickly to the hills out the window. A panicky need to escape weaved through her soul. As it was, she was stretching her last dollar bill to pay the current loan for the taxes. How was she ever going to afford another payment?

Candi scooted close and wrapped an arm around Annie's shoulders. She hugged her close and Annie was grateful for the connection. It was warm, reassuring. Solid. "I know it's hard, honey, but you'll think of something. You always do," she added, eyes shining with encouragement. "You got that paternity test out of Jeremiah, didn't you?"

"I did."

"And the property out of Delaney."

"Yes."

"Well, you can get some money going, too." Candi hugged Annie to her side, a draft of her perfume rising between them. "I know you can."

Leave it to Candi to see the positive in her situation. It was her nature, always had been. Candi was the one who'd encouraged Annie in high school, convinced her to try out for the lead role in a school play, acted as cheerleader when Annie earned straight A's two semesters in a row, even encouraged her to chase after the boy she dreamed impossible to get. Her stomach tightened. Well, she couldn't hold *that* against her. Annie couldn't see past Jeremiah at the time and he was all she wanted. Now she wanted money. Income. As trustee, it was her job to not only pay the taxes but to ensure her daughter's future. She was entitled to a percentage of earnings for her time and trouble, but they were earnings Annie had to *earn* first. If she couldn't, all she'd be handing over to her thirty-year-old daughter would be a big fat tax bill.

"I'll talk to Cal," Annie said. "He's looking into some logging possibilities for me. We'll see what he's come up with."

"Logging? You mean to tell me you're going to cut down all the trees?"

Mildly amused by the look of horror pasted on Candi's face, Annie shook her head. "No, only a hundred acres or so. According to Cal, it might be all we need, until I can figure something else out, that is."

"Like how to rent the land to a hotel developer, same as Delaney?"

Annie suppressed a grin. Candi knew her better than anyone. Whether Lacy and Malcolm and Delaney and Nick cared or not, Annie was a survivor first, a group player second. She had to look out for Casey's future, same way Delaney had looked after Felicity's. Now in college, Felicity was set, her future carved in stone. *Gold* stone, Annie mused, a tinge of resentment curling her heart. Delaney included the section with the gold find in Felicity's half, enabling her daughter to not only earn income from Nick's hotel deal but from selling the gold discovered in a rock, deep in the forest.

Gold. On Ladd Springs. So far, the vein had yielded more than anyone expected and Nick and Delaney were taking full advantage. They were having a local jeweler design a pendant in the shape of a wishing well, a pendant they intended to sell in a hotel boutique store. It was supposed to represent the natural springs on the property, a symbol of eternal hope and spiritual fulfillment. To Annie it represented yet again how she and her daughter were left to fend for themselves.

Annie snatched the business card and glared at the telephone number. "I'm going to call her."

"You are?"

"Yes. There's no reason I shouldn't explore my options."

"That's right," Candi agreed, faithfully manning her imaginary pom-poms as she encouraged her friend. "No reason at all."

"Why can't I lease our property to Jillian? How would that hurt anything?"

"Exactly."

"I mean, if Nick and Malcolm are afraid of a little competition, how good can they be?"

"Now you're talking!" Candi bounced on the cushion beside her. "Why should they have all the profits from a hotel business and not you?"

While Annie couldn't quite share Candi's level of exuberance, a tinge of misgiving squiggling through her belly, she did share her viewpoint. Why shouldn't she be able to use her property any way she saw fit? Would they rather she destroy acres and acres of trees? After all, Nick's claim to fame was his sensitivity to the environment. Wouldn't that make him a hypocrite if he advised someone to log the land instead of build something in tune with Mother Nature?

Gaining steam, Annie decided it was the right thing to do. Casey was stuck in a dead-end job waiting tables at

Fran's Diner, and if Annie could give her daughter something better to look forward to, wasn't that what she should do? Her Aunt Fran was sweet to give Casey a job, but that didn't mean she had to keep it for the rest of her life.

"When are you going to call her?" Candi asked.

"Tomorrow." Annie twisted the card in hand. "I'm going to call her tomorrow."

Chapter Two

A prickle of concern irritated Calvin Foster's calm as he took in the woman before him. Annie was agitated. Pensive, impatient but more, she was cagey, her pretty blue eyes dodging him at every turn. In Cal's experience, the combination spelled trouble. When a woman withheld information, it was because she planned to use it against you, or planned to use it without you. Either way, it was a lesson he'd learned the hard way but learned it just the same. Cal rolled his shoulders to ease the tension from them. She had invited him over to discuss logging options for the property, but as they discussed the issue, it felt like she was stonewalling. Did she want his help or not?

"Are you alright, Annie?" he asked softly, knowing it was best not to push. Corner a woman and she's likely to strike with an aim to kill.

Sitting on the opposite end of the couch, Annie stiffened. "I'd be better if I had a surefire plan, if I was certain this logging could work."

She gave a quick shake to her glossy black hair, hair that fell straight and thick to her shoulders. Despite the late hour and a full day's work behind her, Annie's skin was ivory perfection against the black turtleneck she wore, her makeup masterfully applied, black eye-liner underscoring the allure of her big blue eyes. Visibly trim in snug-fitting jeans, Annie was the kind of woman you wouldn't miss walking down a sidewalk. She was a striking beauty, one he was coming to adore.

If only she'd let him help her. "You can be as certain as you're willing to be."

She paused, taken aback by the blunt comment. "This isn't easy for me, Cal."

"Never said it was. But you're fightin' harder than a cat pawin' molasses and I'm not sure why."

"Why?" She looked at him with a thinly veiled anger— or was it desperation? "How about I'm financially strapped? How about we're not even sure if we can find a forester inter- ested in logging the property? And if we do, Delaney will most certainly have something to say about it, probably fight me every *branch* of the way."

"Naw, she won't."

Annie stared at him, her big blue eyes dismissive. "You don't know Delaney anymore. She's not the same girl from high school. She's changed. Hardened."

"Now, Annie. She gave Casey half the property, didn't she? She can't be all bad."

Annie thrust her shoulders back. "Because I forced her hand."

"Annie." Cal eased forward but didn't seek her hand. "I've known Delaney a long time, and while it's true I've been away in Arizona the past fifteen-odd years, it doesn't mean I don't understand where she's coming from. She's a woman, a mother same as you, and she wants what's best for her daughter. I'm sure she'll be amenable to whatever we want to do. It's your land."

Annie glanced away and Cal chuckled. She was spirited but about as unsure of herself as a new born foal. He under- stood she was struggling financially which is why he offered to help her secure a loan to pay the property taxes. Money matters were easy for him. Back in Arizona, he'd made more money by investing in the stock market in two months than he'd made earning salary in a year's time from the retirement golfing community. It wasn't for everyone but for him, in- vesting was a simple matter of numbers—ratios, costs, earn- ings—plus a healthy dose of risk. Keeping Annie's confi- dence afloat going forward was proving to be the bigger chal- lenge.

But Cal Foster never walked away from a challenge. Challenges were what fired life into his blood, gave him a reason to wake up every morning and keep his eye on the prize. Currently, he was in a battle for the prize of his life and it had nothing to do with Annie. When Cal left Tennessee for Arizona, he had expanded more than his horizons. He met a woman, married and had a child—all of which he lost. Much like Annie, his struggle stemmed from poor decisions made before he realized the weight of those decisions. But he'd since learned choices had consequences. Hard consequences, lasting consequences. It wasn't until six months ago he understood fully what those entailed. Annie had a child with a man who wasn't her husband, a man probably not fit to be one, either. Cal had a child, but with the actions of one night, lost all ties to the girl. Regret weighed heavily on his heart.

Reaching for Annie's hand, Cal was thankful she didn't pull away. It seemed they were venturing onto some rocky ground and he had to be careful not to slip due to moving too fast. *Slow and easy wins the race*. That was his new motto. "Listen," Cal said, "a professional forester will take care of the land, not destroy it. He'll cut only what he needs, cut only from land you agree to log. Delaney won't be able to complain on that count, and depending on which section you choose, you stand to earn near a quarter of a million dollars."

The statement sucked the breath from her. "Quarter of a *million*?"

He squeezed her hand, her very warm and slender hand. He and Annie had been officially dating for the last couple of months and Cal was ready to take it a step further. Annie was rock solid. She was a good woman, a beautiful woman. If he could help Annie realize a substantial gain from her land, then by God he would. Hopefully, her future was his future. "Yes ma'am, quarter of a million, and I daresay that's enough to pay off your loan, cover the taxes for a few years to come and provide you and Casey with a comfortable lifestyle—until you decide what you really want to do."

Cal believed that's what was driving Annie's insecurities. She was floundering, floatin' like a duckling without its momma. It was a sentiment that Cal understood. He, too, was ready for change, a new road to travel. He'd come home to Tennessee for that very reason, and while he hadn't found it yet, it didn't mean he'd given up looking. Same went for Annie. Patience. That's all she needed.

She spewed a sigh. "A quarter of a million dollars... The things we could do with that money."

Struck by the sheer intensity of her gaze, Cal laughed. "You look like thoughts are ricocheting off the walls of your brain!" She flashed those gorgeous blue eyes of hers his way and he roped them in, best he could. "That's a compliment, darlin'." Chuckling to himself, Cal thought yes, Annie Owens definitely reminded him of his horse-training days. She was a feisty mare that needed coaxing by a cool head and a soft touch. Luckily, it was Cal's specialty.

"Is it really worth that much?" she asked.

Cal leaned near. "Depending on the grade of timber, your profit might even go higher. It all depends on which trees they cut and who they sell them to. You might even ask they set aside a few logs for you and Casey to build."

"Build?"

He smiled, darting a glance to her lips, her very lush lips. Lips that were full and glossed with a hint of pink, lips he could kiss right this minute. "You want to live on the property, don't you?" Cal assumed that's why Annie had fought so hard to acquire the title. Casey was a Ladd. She was part of the family. It made sense she'd want to live on the land of her ancestors, even if her kin weren't right friendly. It didn't matter. Family was family. Blood ran deep through the heart of the South. One only need ask his brothers how cantankerous relations could be, between stealin' kisses from the sweetest girls in school to bar room brawls with the toughest thugs in town, the Foster boys were known for their turbulent relations with one another and the community at large. Folks called it a "reputation." Cal and his brothers used to call it "plain fun." The boys had their disputes, but never once did they question their loyalty to family.

At Annie's reticence, Cal repeated, "Isn't that what you're after?"

She slumped back against the cushion and placed a palm to her forehead. "I don't know."

The tortured quality to her voice pulled at him. A mix of want and need tangled with a mess of doubt Cal didn't quite understand. "What's holding you back, Annie?"

From across the sofa, she looked at him, and that's when he caught it. A sliver of reluctance passed behind her eyes. She *was* holding back. There was more to her story than she was saying. Cal could recognize a holdout when he saw one. There was always a clue, a shift in the eyes, a slant in the gaze. A hiccup, a blink, but the guilt was there just the same. "Talk to me, Annie. Tell me what's going on."

As though balancing a fine line between truth and evasion, Annie hesitated. "Everything is happening so fast. Nick and Malcolm have been staking those orange flags everywhere, marking their territory like two dogs on a Saturday night. Did you know they've already drawn up plans for the hotel, restaurant—everything? According to Lacy, all they need now is approval from the county and they begin building. Building!"

Cal leaned back, extending an arm the length of the sofa. "Well, it's not their first rodeo. Why, I've seen entire communities pop up out of thin air in the desert and they were nothin' to scoff at. Mighty nice homes, too, so I know it can be done. All you need is money and experience."

"And they have both."

"They have both," Cal agreed. Was this the crux of her displeasure? Money? Delaney and Lacy had it and she didn't?

Well, he could tell her a thing or two about money. It didn't fix everything and he had an ex-wife and a police record to prove it. But if money is what Annie needed, then money is what he was going to see that she received. "Why don't you let me talk to Delaney and discuss matters right calmly? Then I'll call a forester friend of mine. He's been in the business twenty years and is the best of the best. Why, you give him the okay and you could have your money by Christmas time."

Annie's eyes widened. "That soon?"

Cal nodded.

"Wow." She allowed her gaze to drift. "I guess I have something to think about."

"Do you need to discuss it with Casey?" Cal wasn't exactly sure how the trustee agreement had been written. Did Annie have sole control over what she could do with the land or did she have to consult her daughter?

"I can't sell it without her approval, but I can decide what happens with it until she's of age to receive it in full."

Cal slapped hands to knees. "Alrighty, then. Sounds like we have a plan."

Annie slid him a sharp glance. "Thank you. Thank you for all your help with the property. I think I'd be lost on my own."

The abrupt change pleased Cal. While he liked Annie's strong and spirited side, he liked her sweet and soft side even better. "You don't have to thank me, Annie, I'm glad to help." At her quick smile, he relaxed back into the cushion and sidled up next to her, pulling her close. "Now how about you tell me what else is on your mind?"

A small smile crept onto her lips. "Am I that transparent?"

Cal grinned, relishing the ejection of tension from her deep blue eyes, he replied, "You are to me." Breathing in the scent of her, he picked up hints of a faded perfume. Leaning close, he brushed a sweep of silky hair behind an ear punctuated by a large silver hoop. He traced a finger around it and she sighed. Staring out into the sea of night, he wondered what was going through her mind. Cal interlaced his fingers through hers and her gaze mellowed, her pupils swallowed whole by the luminous glow of a nearby lamp.

"I want something to do, Cal. I want something exciting, challenging."

"More challenging than paintin' all those pretty nails?" he teased. Annie clamped her lips, but he gently shook her. "Aw, c'mon Annie. You know I'm just having fun. I think you're the best in the business, but I understand what you're saying. The same goes for me. I need a new direction. I've been helping my Daddy out at the ranch but all he keeps trying to do is lasso me into the bank. It's not what I want to do."

"Did you not like working in Arizona?"

"Arizona was real fine, but once you sold one house, you sold them all."

"I thought you managed the community."

"I did, eventually, but even then it was all the same. Selling, or managing the selling, all began to feel the same. It made me itch for something new." He paused, allowing a swell of regret to pass through him. He might have been bored with his work life, but not his personal. At home, he'd been happy. He loved his wife, loved his daughter. Unfortunately, it was they who got their fill of *him*. He tamped back a swell of regret. "I want to try my hand at something different. Ever since I gave up the drink, I've been driftin'."

"Is it hard for you to be back home?" she asked. "You know, with all the memories? Your brothers?"

Cal shook his head. "Not really. Not when you've changed your heart, it isn't. Now if I was still struggling with it, sure. But I'm not." He couldn't afford to struggle with the bottle. He had too much riding on his sobriety back in Arizona, and he was determined to make things right. Moving back to Tennessee was his chance to prove himself, prove he could remain sober, hold down a job, and be the man his daughter needed him to be.

"What do you think you want to do?" Annie asked.

"Not sure." And that was the hardest part of all. Cal had no burning desire to do anything. He loved working with horses, but he was getting too old to spend every day in dusty corrals and pens with wild stallions. He liked investing money. Found he had a knack for it, but he didn't want to invest other people's money, only his own. Cal didn't know what he wanted to do and that was his problem. A problem he needed to solve. Proving he could walk the straight and narrow meant getting his life back—the most important piece, anyway. His wife was through with him. She'd moved on and Cal didn't blame her. But his daughter was a different matter.

Emily needed him and he needed her.

"Seems we both have a lot to think about," Annie murmured.

Cal nodded. "Agreed." Why Annie had to withdraw her hand from his was perplexing. Did she want those thoughts of hers to include him?

Chapter Three

Annie walked her last client of the day to the receptionist's desk and caught a glimpse of a dark-haired woman walking in the front door. Long black hair fell in a straight, sleek line behind her back, her very narrow back. She was almost a stick of a figure, draped in gold jewelry and expensive leather jacket. As she neared, Annie noted her lips were glossed a tawny brown, a sheer tone that melted into her brown skin. But it was her eyes that leapt out at you. Cat eyes, turned up at the ends, or maybe it was the heavy black makeup that created the effect. Annie guessed her identity in a heartbeat. Jillian Devane. She had to hand it to Lacy. Her sister had described the woman perfectly. Wealthy, stylish, she looked right at home amidst the ultra-modern interior of the Trendz salon with its minimalist black and white design and cool blue ceramic lamps hanging overhead in the way of lighting.

Annie turned to her client. "Bobbi Jo will get you scheduled for next time, okay?" The woman smiled and the two hugged. "See you then."

Ms. Devane hovered near the desk, waiting her turn to speak with the receptionist. But there was no need. Annie extended a hand. "Ms. Devane?"

Jillian noted the gesture with a knowing smile, as though fully aware Annie had been forewarned of her intentions. "Ms. Owens," she purred in a heavy Spanish accent. Her voice was smooth and sultry, and rather deep for a woman. As they shook hands, Annie marveled at her slender grasp, fine-boned yet firm in its connection. Her skin was silky in texture, her nails professionally maintained. Annie knew from experience that an older woman didn't retain the supple skin tone of youth without professional care. Gesturing toward her nail chair, she said, "Thank you for coming."

"The pleasure is all mine, I assure you."

Annie didn't doubt a word. She could feel the woman's claws sinking into her in a most visceral way. Ms. Devane was here for the kill, there was no mistake. Second thoughts flooded Annie's gut. It was an attack she had invited with a single phone call, a willing phone call. "My friend told me you were asking about my daughter's half of the property."

"Yes," the owner of a hotel empire replied, sliding her gaze around them as though making sure the path was clear when she pounced, "I understand you are the one in charge of the property."

Annie cleared a rush of nerves from her throat. "I am." While she might be intimidated by this woman, she wasn't going to let on to the fact.

Jillian smiled and moved closer. "As you know, I am in the owner of Eco-Domani, the number one hotel spa company in the world where we pride ourselves on working in tune with nature. It is my business to build hotels—fantastic, beautiful hotels—that seamlessly blend with the land around them, allowing guests to lose themselves in the luxury of nature." She slowly circled Annie, taking note of her white leather nail chair and black ottoman, a line of shiny bottles filled with a broad spectrum of nail enamels that comprised Annie's nail station. "Your property is incredible in its beauty and location, and I should like to work with you on how to make it the number one destination in the world. People will come from all over the world to visit your mountains and woods, seeking to become at one with your land. By selling, you will become wealthy beyond your wildest dreams."

Ms. Devane dripped with extravagance when she spoke, pulling Annie in with her lavish description and promises, as she created a dreamy vision with her talk of lavish hotels and land conservation. It was easy to see how this woman could spin a person into her web, sucking them clean without spilling the first drop of blood. Annie shook off the elaborate images and asked, "Haven't you already purchased property for your hotel?"

Plunging into a shrewd smile, Ms. Devane's flinty eyes grew calculating. "So we don't play any games, okay?" She straightened her slim frame and stood eye-to-eye with Annie. "I will tell you that I am still looking, but I'm most interested in your property." She tipped her head and glanced askance. "I'm willing to pay you handsomely for it," she said, then dropped all pretense, pinning her with a hard gaze. "Am I to take this meeting as a *yes*?"

Stunned by how quickly the cat turned lion, Annie hesitated. She hadn't decided anything because she hadn't heard anything! Darting a glance to the drips of blue lighting overhead, she felt suddenly heated, despite the salon's contrived ambiance of calm. "What are you proposing?"

Jillian smiled. "What do you want?"

Annie had no idea. She didn't know what the property was worth, other than what the tax assessor said. But Cal had explained to her that the tax assessed value wasn't the market value, only the amount she was paying taxes on. If she were to sell, the amount would be much higher—which made no sense to her. How could there be more than one value for the same property?

Staring at Jillian Devane, Annie felt the hairs of doubt tickle her neck. She was out of her league, swimming upstream and losing her kick. "I haven't decided, yet," she said quickly, preserving an image of authority. She might not know the value of the land at the moment but she certainly wasn't going to let this woman make her look like a fool.

"I'm willing to offer you five hundred thousand dollars for the entire tract of land."

Annie gasped.

Jillian smiled, a gesture that never reached her eyes. "But of course," she rolled out, "you need time to consider your options."

Five hundred thousand dollars? The amount staggered Annie, ringing in her ears like a church bell on Sunday afternoon. *Five hundred thousand dollars*. All hope for sounding fancy and sophisticated shot clear out the door. "Yes," she stammered, her jelly-boned legs threatening to collapse beneath her. She balanced herself with a hand to her nail chair and said, "I have other things to think about. Can I call you tomorrow?"

"Yes. As a matter-of-fact I'm enjoying myself in your country town and will be here for a few short days. After that, I must close the deal on my *other* property," she said pointedly. "Once I do, I'm afraid there will be no more room for discussion with you."

Annie felt the punch. She'd been put on notice. Hurry up or Eco-Domani money goes elsewhere. "Yes," she said, fumbling for self-control, confidence, anything to shake the tremor in her voice! "I understand."

"I hope that you do." Jillian smiled richly. "I'd hate to see you miss out on the opportunity of a lifetime."

A cell phone rang and after a brief moment, Annie realized it was hers. Jillian watched with interest as she answered the call. "Hello?"

"Annie, do you know where Casey is? She hasn't shown up for work yet, and the dinner crowd is already shuffling in."

"I'm sorry, Aunt Fran." Fran Jones was Annie's aunt and the owner of Fran's Diner, a staple in town. She'd given Casey a job—one the girl obviously didn't value—and was now looking for her. Annie eyes dodged those of the appraising Ms. Devane, embarrassed by her daughter's lack of responsibility. "I'm sure she's on her way. Can you give her a few more minutes?"

"Well, she'd better get here quick. I'm short a hand tonight, because Jimmy called in sick."

Candi's nephew. He also worked at Fran's Diner and minus the two of them Annie knew the kind of pinch it would put her aunt in. The commotion of the kitchen in the background, the usual din of a busy restaurant, sounded as though the Friday night dinner rush was already in full swing. "I'll run by the apartment and see if she's home. Maybe she forgot her shift," Annie defended weakly.

"She better start remembering 'fore I fire that child!'"
Fran hollered into the phone.

"I understand," Annie replied, feeling a flush at her neck
and cheeks. She'd never been late for a single day of work in
her life. Not at Trendz and not at the salon before it. The fact
that Casey was skirting her responsibilities ground Annie's
last nerve into the pavement. Ending the call, she said to Ms.
Devane, "If you'll excuse me, I have to go."

The woman's face lit up with a smile. "Of course. I understand the stress of raising a child by yourself," she said
thickly, her accent mumbling through the last word.

Annie didn't think Jillian had children, let alone the first
clue about struggling. By the looks of the jewelry hanging
from her body and the money she was throwing around, it
was clear Ms. Devane had the resources to pay other people
to worry about her troubles. Suddenly irritated, Annie said,
"I'll call you tomorrow."

"Yes. Tomorrow."

Annie raced home as fast as she legally could, anger
building with every mile she drove. If Casey was at home, the
girl was going to *wish* she was at the diner—Annie was gonna string her up by her toes! She and Casey had been going
through a rough time, but to put Fran in a bind when Casey
knew she'd been nice enough to give her a job in the first
place?

It was completely inexcusable. Banging a fist to the
dashboard, Annie jabbed at the lighted arrow for the vehicle's
heat. She'd dashed out of the salon so quickly, there was no
time to warm up the car and it was cold! Cold as a cast iron
commode in the winter, she thought. Cold as Ms. Devane's
intentions as she tried to force Annie's back against the wall.
I'd hate to see you miss out on the opportunity of a lifetime.
Beneath her fancy sympathetic words lay a lizard tongue.
That woman was slick in her manipulation and Annie didn't
care for her one bit. But the money she was offering couldn't
be ignored. Half a million dollars? Did that woman know

what Annie and Casey could do with that kind of money? They could live comfortably, buy a decent car. Maybe with her share, Annie could afford the down payment for a salon. Candi had been dying to get her own place. They could be partners! Candi would take care of the hair, Annie would take care of the nails. Why, she could even afford to send Casey to college if the girl would screw her head on right and stop battling the world. Casey had her entire future to look forward but instead she was stuck in the past.

Because of Jeremiah.

Casey had been so angry to learn he was her father, she'd rejected him outright. The minute Annie revealed the news, Casey screamed and cried and pitched a fit—none of which Annie could blame her for. Shame skulked in, coursed through Annie's veins. She didn't much care for Jeremiah either, regretting she ever slept with the man in the first place, though she didn't regret having her daughter. Casey was the only bright spot from the affair. A wave of ambivalence washed through her. Just because they were having their difficulties at the moment didn't mean she didn't love the girl. She did. Casey was the most important person in Annie's world. She only wished they had an easier go of it, but Casey was troubled.

Annie's sister Lacy was fast becoming a crucial part of her life, too, but it was slower going. Getting over Lacy's betrayal with Jeremiah had been difficult. It wasn't until Annie let go of the hate, realizing her sister had been a mere child at the time, that she was able to begin the process of forgiveness. At the time Lacy ran away, she was younger than Casey. Headstrong and free-spirited, she had yearned to break free of her small town and see the world. Unfortunately, she thought Jeremiah was her escape route.

Lacy had been wrong. Like Annie, she had chosen the wrong man to hitch her wagon to and paid the consequences. When Annie learned the details of Lacy's life since leaving Tennessee, her heart split in two. Her sister might have made some poor decisions, but she didn't deserve to be abandoned by Jeremiah in a big city like Atlanta. Annie shuddered, and this time it wasn't from the chilly temperature. Lacy had it rough yet she bounced back and bore hardly a scar. A smile pulled at her mouth. In that regard, her sister was amazing.

Thoughts of forgiveness diluted Annie's anger. Expelling a sigh, she turned onto the road for her apartment complex. Casey was young and headstrong, too. Her rebellion stemmed from choices she didn't make, situations and circumstances beyond her control. Remorse twisted Annie's insides. Most of what Casey rebelled against wasn't her fault. It was her mother's.

They were facts Annie couldn't change. She could only move forward and do the best she could. Thinking back to her conversation with Jillian Devane, Annie wondered what the right thing to do would be in her current predicament. Cal said the logging could bring in a quarter of a million dollars. Ms. Devane offered double that amount. Excitement flitted across her breast. Would a sale on the open market bring even more?

She didn't know, but these were definitely things she needed to discuss with Casey. After all, it was *her* property. The decision rightfully belonged to Casey, though it was crazy how quick a mind could get infected when tempted with big dollar signs. Big dollar signs. Huge. Half a million dollars would change their lives. Pulling into her assigned parking space, Annie cut the engine and wrapped a thick scarf snug around her neck. Stuffing the rising tide of greed back into its corner, she tightened the belt around her coat, braced against the chilled damp mountain air and hurried up the stairs. Cold metal keys jangled in her hand as she tugged them from the door. Flipping on a light switch she called out, "Casey, I'm home!" Closing the door, Annie surveyed the contents of her apartment. Sofa, table, television, all were clear, the room silent. She walked farther into the living room, dumping her purse on the dining room table. "Casey?"

No answer.

Surprised, Annie walked down the hallway to her daughter's bedroom, an uneasiness setting in. Casey had attempted an overdose once before. Had she done so again? Her pulse jumped wildly out of control as Annie yanked open her daughter's bedroom door. "Casey?"

Annie's heart leapt into her throat. There was nothing. No Casey, no nothing. Had she gone to work? Had she gone out?

A dreadful thought seized her and Annie rushed to the bathroom, whipping open the door. Again, no Casey, no nothing. Annie focused on the vanity. No toothbrush. A looming sense of apprehension choking her, Annie marched back to the dining room and dug into her purse for her cell phone. She dialed Casey's number but there was no answer. Next, she called Fran.

"Fran's Diner."

"Fran, its Annie. Did Casey show up for work?"

"No, darlin' and I'm going crazy busy right now."

Fear fired hot in her chest. "Well, she isn't home, so I don't know if she forgot or what happened," she said, unable to erase the empty toothbrush holder from her mind.

"Tell her to call me first thing, will you? Right now I've got to go."

"Yes, sure. Will do," Annie replied, but Fran had already hung up the phone. Ending the call, her hand began to tremble. *Casey, where are you?*

Chapter Four

Annie stopped in at the diner first thing in the morning. She had called Casey ten times over the course of the night and the girl never answered, never returned her call. Worried, Annie calmed herself with the fact that Casey's toothbrush was missing, which meant there was no foul play involved. But it didn't mean foul play couldn't catch up to her. It was a crazy world out there. Any one of a number of things could happen to her. Her car could break down. She could run out of gas. She could get lost. Annie had no idea where Casey could have gone or why, but the scenarios for disaster grew by leaps and bounds in her imagination. When the thoughts became too much to bear, she called Candi and confided in her what happened. Candi called her nephew right away, but Jimmy didn't know anything. Not that Annie would expect him to, but he was the closest thing Casey had to a friend these days, and if she was going to run away, she might have told him.

Run away. It was beginning to be clear that's indeed what her daughter had done. Upon further investigation last night, Annie had discovered that Casey had packed a suitcase, cleared out her drawers and taken a few of her personal belongings. The framed portrait of her and her mother was not among them. That detail still hurt. The picture had been taken during happier times, a trip to the fresh water aquarium in Chattanooga two years ago. Casey had been thrilled with the wildlife, creatures she didn't know existed, many of which lived in the lakes and streams around their home. It had been a great day. Two years ago, mother and daughter had been happy and carefree.

Today looked a whole lot different. Bells clanged as Annie pushed through the front door of Fran's Diner. Seven-thirty a.m., but the diner was already serving a half-packed restaurant. Black and white checkered floors were spotless, red vinyl booths gleamed. Guilt threaded through her. Fran and the dinner crew must have stayed late to fill in for the two missing bodies last night. If she'd thought about it, Annie would have come and helped clean up after the dinner crowd herself, but truth be known, she'd been in no condition to go anywhere last night. Casey's disappearance was shredding her last nerve.

Venturing toward the back, Annie picked out Fran's red hair without effort. Tucked within the confines of a sheer hair net, the bright-colored hair dye echoed the booths, the stools, practically everything in the restaurant. But red was Fran and Fran was red—firecracker red, most days—in both style and temperament.

Fran sailed out of the kitchen, a tray loaded with orange juice and coffee in hand. "Well? What did the child have to say for herself?"

"Nothing," Annie replied. An uncomfortable feeling lodged tightly in the pit of her stomach.

Fran's penciled brow rose sharply. "Nothing?" Her gaze shot to the ceiling. "Well, butter my butt and call me a biscuit, that child has no sense of obligation," she said, breezing by Annie en route for her table destination. Annie smiled grimly and watched her aunt deliver the beverages, jot down an order and return with a severe look of displeasure etched across her usually cheerful brown eyes. "What's a matter with her, Annie? Doesn't she know I was relying on her?"

"Casey's gone, Fran."

Her expression fell. "Gone?"

Annie nodded and tears pushed behind her eyes, a rush of angst peppering her chest. "I think she ran away."

Concern swamped Fran's eyes with a doe-like distress. "Oh, darlin' *no*."

She nodded again, but this time there were no words. Standing near the breakfast counter, Annie slumped to a seat. Casey had run away. It was a smack in the face to her mother,

her aunt, and everything that spelled home. Casey wanted none of it. She had rejected those who cared about her most and did so without the first scribble of a note. Annie only wished she knew where Casey went. *Where did she have to go, anyway?*

"Oh, sugar." Fran eased heavily to a stool beside her, instantly ejecting the needs of her restaurant in favor of her family. "Are you sure?"

More sure than she cared to admit. Annie took a deep breath and calmed herself as best she could. "I found a suitcase missing, her drawers were empty, her car gone." The last observation hit home in Fran's gaze. She had purchased the used car for Casey to encourage her independence—not enable her escape.

Fran wiped a hand across her forehead, a common tension pulling between the women. Underlying the initial shock of a teenager's rebellion, both understood the consequences could have ramifications Casey might not have considered. "Have you called around? Are you certain?"

"I'm certain. But I don't know where to go from here. Where do I begin to search for a girl who's up and left without a note? I have nothing to go on." And it was killing her. Not only had her child left her, Annie didn't know of any friends to reach out to. Other than Jimmy, Annie came up empty. She felt helpless. A heap of failure.

Hot tears sprang to her eyes and rolled down her cheeks. Fran kicked into "fix-it" mode, rubbing a hand up and down Annie's back. "Don't you fret, Annie Grace. We'll find her. She couldn't have gone far in that tin can I bought her." But the wise crack fell flat. Annie knew Fran was just as worried as she beneath her façade of bravado. In reality, Fran didn't know any more than Annie did about how to find Casey, but she wouldn't let it show. She had a restaurant to run, customers waiting. It was the same determination she showed when her husband Deacon died. One day he was here, next day he was gone, third day Fran buried him and returned to work. That was her way. "Let me get you some coffee, sugar, and we'll put our minds to it. We'll get to the bottom of this black well, in no time." With that, Fran up and made a bee line for the kitchen leaving Annie to herself.

Not a good idea. Surrounded by townspeople she knew, who knew her, Annie felt isolated. Tears streaming down her face would beg questions, set fire to gossip. Annie wiped her cheeks and cleared her throat. She had to pull herself together. She had to think, reason. If she were Casey, "where would she go?"

That's as far as she made it until an hour later when her sister Lacy strolled into the restaurant in search of food. Four months pregnant, the woman had turned into an eating machine, though she didn't show the first pound. Of course she was wearing a coat, but the hot pink jacket was cinched snug, forming an hour glass to her round hips and thin legs, currently clad in black leggings and black boots. Despite the cold and her pregnancy, Lacy opted for a mini skirt. Add her stylish black-haired pixie-cut and artfully applied makeup and her sister could pass for a fashion model.

"Annie!" Lacy waved gaily and hurried over.

One look at the radiance in her sister's face and Annie couldn't help but smile. Her happiness was contagious, if fleetingly so. "Hi, Lacy."

Lacy bent down and pecked her cheek. "What are you doing up so early?" She swept down to the stool beside Annie, her blues eye bright, eyes that felt eerily similar to her own. The Owens girls had many differences but the resemblance in coloring was incredible—not only their fair skin and inky black hair, but their blue eyes, both color and shape. Once Annie allowed herself to be compared to her sister, she accepted the facts. A stranger would not mistake the relationship between the women. It was uncanny. "I thought Saturdays were your lazy days," she said, loosening her sash.

They usually were. "I'm not having a great day."

The comment caught Lacy like a hooked fish, her mouth agape. "Why? What's wrong?" And then scrutinizing Annie's face as though seeing her for the first time, Lacy asked, "Something's happened?"

"I think Casey has run away."

"Oh, no!" Lacy clapped a hand over her mouth.

Annie nodded and shoved the empty coffee cup aside, the mere sight of the stale brown liquid rubbing her stomach raw. "And I don't know what to do about it." It's why she'd been stapled to this stool since seven-thirty. She had no place to go. No idea where to begin. Jimmy didn't know anything. Fran didn't know anything. No one had a clue. "I'm worried about her."

"Well, of course you are!" Lacy exclaimed. Now that Lacy was with child, Annie had noticed a brand new layer of sensitivity to her sister. Before, Lacy didn't have the first inkling as to what Annie had been through on account of Casey. Now, she was beginning to understand or, at the very least, think about the subject. Lacy skimmed the restaurant, an uncomfortable air hovering about her. Her gaze returned to Annie, but she didn't say a word.

"Lacy?" She honed in on the new energy circling about her sister. "Do you know something?"

She made an evasive dodge before venturing hesitantly, "Have you called Troy?"

"*Troy*? Why would I call him?"

Lacy clamped her shiny pink lips closed.

"Lacy?" Annie studied her sister's features, zeroing in on her eyes. Well accustomed to Lacy's tendency to fib and cross her fingers, Annie would have none of it. "What do you know?"

Her sister slashed her gaze about the diner and asked, "Where's Aunt Frannie?"

"Don't 'Aunt Frannie' me—what's this about Troy? Is Casey with him? Do you know something?"

"I don't know," Lacy stumbled over what obviously was a "yes" response. "But I think they were seeing each other for a while and maybe he might know where she went."

Troy and Casey were seeing each other?

When did this happen? For how long? And how come she didn't know about it and Lacy did? A fresh pour of determination filled Annie's spine. "Spill it, Lacy. I want to know everything."

Lacy did as she was told and divulged everything she knew—from Felicity's revelation at the diner six months ago to Travis' information on his brother's whereabouts after he left town. Troy had moved to Murfreesboro. He had decided to quit college before he ever started and, instead, work with a horse trainer friend of his father's. Lacy wasn't sure, but according to Delaney who heard it from Felicity, Troy had been keeping in touch with Casey.

"If he convinced my daughter to leave home and move in with him, I'll ring his neck quicker than a Thanksgiving turkey."

Lacy blinked. "But Thanksgiving is weeks away, yet, Annie. You're not going to wait, are you?"

Annie growled under her breath. "It's not meant to be literal."

"Oh."

Annie felt a quick stab of regret. She didn't mean to come off so harsh. Lacy never finished high school and took *most* things literally. But that was her world. She lived in "literal" land and occasionally missed the subtle underlying meaning of things. It was neither here nor there. Annie had bigger fish to fry. "How can I get in touch with Troy?"

Lacy perked up at the opportunity to help. "I could call Delaney. I bet she could find out with one phone call."

Annie didn't care to involve Delaney Wilkins in her personal business. She'd already been poking around, wedging herself into Casey's life at the diner, trying to make friends. She claimed they were family and needed to start acting as such, which sounded good but Annie didn't trust Delaney. She'd been no friend of the Owens family in the past and they didn't need her friendship now. She was probably trying to keep a hand on the Ladd Springs property to ensure that Casey did her future bidding. Resentment curled Annie's toes.

She'd always been the controlling sort. But if Delaney was the only way to locate Casey, then so be it. "Can you do it? Will you call her right now?"

"Sure!" Joy glittered in Lacy's eyes. Pulling a cell phone from her purse, she dialed and waited. In seconds, she clipped, "Delaney, its Lacy. Can you call Felicity and get me Troy's phone number?" She paused, probably waiting through the predictable "what for" from a woman who didn't do anything without knowing all the details beforehand. "Casey has run away and I think she might be with Troy."

Lacy winked and gave Annie the thumbs up. Apparently Delaney didn't need any more convincing. Maybe Cal was right. *She's a mother, same as you.* It was the first time Annie had thought of Cal since discovering her child had run off, but now that she had, his image stuck. She would have to call him. He would want to know.

"Thanks, Delaney! Toodles!" Lacy set her phone on the counter and announced proudly, "She's going to call Felicity this instant."

Annie expelled her breath, the first release of pressure since the ordeal had started. "Thank you."

"No problem! And don't worry, Annie. I'm sure she's all right. She's just a girl trying to find her way."

Like you once tried, Annie mused. The similarity between Casey and Lacy drew a tight string around Annie's heart. Is this what their mother went through when Lacy ran off? Did she worry and fret and feel all was lost?

A sober reality dribbled in. Their mother couldn't have felt the way Annie was feeling. Annie was distraught, anxious. She was beside herself with worry. Not Momma. Her response had been to up and move. The memory gouged a fresh hole in Annie's heart. She simply accepted the fact that Lacy had run off and decided the girl could fend for herself. Came to the same conclusion with Annie. She was eighteen, of legal age, which meant she could take care of herself. A few days later, Momma up and left, abandoning the homestead right after Lacy.

Lacy's phone rang and she snatched it up. "Hey, Delaney." She nodded. "Okay, thanks." Pulling the phone from her ear, she peered at the tiny screen. "She's going to text me his contact info." *Bling.* "There it is!" She handed the phone over to Annie. "Do you want to call him?"

"Is there an address?"

Lacy pressed a button on her phone. "Yep, there sure is!"

Annie tensed. "I'd rather do it in person."

"Good idea," Lacy said. "That way they can't ignore you."

Lacy was right on the mark with that one. Casey had ignored her all night long. But phone calls were easy to mute. A live, hot-blooded mother with an aim to drag her daughter home was another story. While their Momma didn't chase after Lacy, Annie was darn well going to chase after Casey. Her daughter might not be happy to see her, but eventually she'd understand and be grateful for the fact. Abandonment was an emotion that never left a person. It branded the heart forever. Annie felt a rush of nerves. Casey was eighteen. Her life at home was no kite flight in the park. Would she come back with her?

Chapter Five

Cal watched as Annie placed her cosmetic bag over top of the clothes in an overnight bag. It felt odd, being in the personal space of her bedroom. He liked it though. It was a nice mix of feminine and sensible, nothing too frilly or expensive, nothing silly and unnecessary. Clean, organized …it smelled of her perfume. He stole a fleeting glance at her open bathroom door, the shower stall partially visible. To date, they hadn't crossed the line into intimacy, but desire was always with him. Particularly in the privacy of her bedroom.

But at the moment, Annie had more urgent matters on her mind and he was going to respect them—though it wasn't sufficient enough to prevent him from reacting to her female presence. Dressed in jeans and ivory cable sweater, Annie didn't look a day over twenty-five. Her figure was trim and fit, her face a beautiful combination of porcelain beauty lined with pure country determination. She stopped her hands mid-motion and closed the lid of her overnight bag. "You don't have to go with me, Cal."

"What if I want to, Annie? You might need help convincing Casey to come home. Let me give that to you."

"I appreciate the offer, Cal, but I don't think there's anything you can do. This is between me and Casey and it could get ugly."

Cal chuckled. "Oh, believe me, darlin'. I've seen ugly before and it doesn't scare me."

"Not with a rebellious teenage daughter. They're a whole different kind of ugly," she said, adding a smile to lighten the brunt force of her rejection.

While he didn't think Annie meant to be patronizing, that's how her smile felt to him. She was pushing him away because she believed he didn't understand the crisis at hand.

She wrote him off as an unmarried man with no experience. However, Cal was a whole lot more familiar with "ugly" than Annie could possibly know, much to his shame. But she didn't know about his "ugly" because he hadn't yet revealed it to her. But one day, one day he'd share it all. It was inevitable. She'd have to know his scars if he expected to have a future with her. Doing so when she was knee deep in hers wasn't going to happen. He was here as support, and that's all Annie would hear from him for the foreseeable future.

Cal strolled over to her and stood by as she zipped her case closed. He reached down and took it from her hands. "I'll take that," he said, firming his grip on the handle in case she resisted.

"I can carry my bag, Cal."

"I know you can, but I'd feel better if I carried it for you." Annie surrendered with a thank-you and walked out to the living room to retrieve her purse. Cal followed, turning out the light behind him, a last tamp to his desire. "Have you considered it may get hostile?"

"Hostile?"

"Yes, hostile. Casey is a runaway. They're not known for their amenable attitudes."

"Believe me, that I understand. But I don't think it will get any more hostile than harsh words." She paused, the calculations whirring behind her eyes. "Do you?"

He shrugged. "It might. From what Lacy said, it sounds like the boy has a chip on his shoulder." A chip the size of Texas, to hear Macolm tell it. Troy had a twin brother, an identical twin in looks but nothing else. Travis Parker was the twin who won the girl, made the grades, pleased his parents by going to college, criticizing Troy at every turn. Add the fact that Troy had allowed his libido to get the better of him, sleeping with Jeremiah Ladd's girlfriend and the whole town had come down on him pretty hard, Casey included.

According to Malcolm, Troy Parker was a bull in a china shop where every customer wore bright red clothing. He rammed full speed ahead, took heads off when they poked into his business... Cal understood a young man prone to temper. He'd spent his childhood living with three of them. Beau, Clint and Jack never met a brawl they didn't like, biting back harder than necessary and in most cases drawing first blood. Like Troy, seemed the fight was bred into them. "Things could escalate."

"Escalate? What are you saying, Cal? That I should fear for my safety?"

"Now don't go puttin' words into my mouth. But it's like I told you before, you're entering an unfriendly situation at a disadvantage. Troy will be on his turf and Casey will be covered under his umbrella. If they want to fight you on this, what are your alternatives?"

"My alternative is to say, no. Casey is coming home with me, and that's the end of it."

"Now I don't know about you, but demanding others do it my way by the force of a bat never did work too well. I say you try a softer appeal. This has to be about *her*, not you."

Annie eyed him with a wariness that looked to be born from epiphany. Was she catching on? Did she realize he might know what he was talking about?

Cal sure hoped so. It would save her pounds of heartache down the road.

Annie slumped and dropped to the arm of her sofa. "This *is* about her."

"I know it is, "Cal said, setting her overnight bag on the side table. "And you know it is. But I think Casey is going to need some convincing. Some convincing that might take time."

"What do you mean, time?"

"What I mean is..." Cal lowered to the cushion beside her, but not too close. He didn't want her to think he was taking advantage of the situation. He and Annie had been inching closer over the last several weeks, and if she needed time to let him in, he was going to give it to her. No longer a man of push and shove, Cal had learned a tender touch was a tougher approach, but one with the biggest payoff. "Casey might hear what you have to say, but she might not act immediately. She might have to let it sit and stew for a while before it makes good sense."

Black lashes shuttered as Annie looked away. "You're saying I might have to leave her there...with Troy."

Cal hated that Annie's voice was strained. She sounded broken, beat, and it was the last thing he wanted for her. Annie was a strong woman with personal courage and determination. A woman who went after what she wanted, even when she feared it might not go her way. But this time she had everything riding on the outcome. It was an investment he understood all too well. When the one person in the world with the power to crush drops the hammer, life can feel like it ain't worth living. "I'm suggesting patience might be the best route. Give Casey the room to make her own decision. Let her know you're there for her, but be clear it's her decision from there."

"What if she decides not to come home?"

Cal hated to say it but she needed to hear it. "Then you have to accept that."

Tears swam into her eyes and she turned from him. Cal gently took her chin in his hand and drew her back to face him. His instinct was to brush her tears free, kiss her pain away, make love to her until she understood she was not alone in this world but he couldn't do any of it. Annie wasn't ready. Like her daughter Casey, Annie needed time.

"Maybe you *should* come with me." She smiled through bleary eyes. "If I break down like this, she surely won't respect me enough to come home."

"That's where you're wrong. Casey will love you every step of the way." Annie laughed, the sound of sweet heaven to his ears.

"How did you become so wise?"

"The hard way, darlin'. I turned wise the hard way."

Cal drove Annie to Murfreesboro, the near two hour drive a comfortable visit between friends, though privately,

Annie was beginning to view Cal as much more than a friend. When he cupped her chin today, she nearly wrapped her arms around him and hugged him tight. Her feelings went beyond friendship. Stabs of longing moved deep inside her, stirring urges she hadn't felt in a very long time. Cal was there for her. He didn't take no for an answer. He stayed, he persisted. He let her know in no uncertain terms that she mattered. That he cared.

A tingle of delight scurried through her. Dressed in a hunter green flannel button-down and jeans, Cal looked good, the colors blending with his hazel brown eyes. Fine brown hair fell in soft layers, his summer tan long since faded. Woodsy, masculine, unlike the more rugged ways of his brothers, Cal struck her as a more subdued cowboy, a country gentleman. Fed up with the cocky, boisterous types of men floating through the town's streets and bars, Annie preferred Cal's laid-back style. It was quiet, respectful, yet every ounce as strong. And for her, a very special feeling to be valued by such a man. After Jeremiah, there had been a few nice men, but eventually the relationships soured. Men seemed more interested in themselves than her and her young daughter. She had a busy life, a commitment to Casey. Somehow, men seemed to be squeezed out of the equation. Annie glanced to her side, Cal's hand steady on the wheel. But not him. He stayed. He knew today could get ugly yet here he was, driving her there himself. Was he a masochist?

No. She suppressed a faint chuckle. Cal was no masochist or weirdo. He was good old-fashioned manliness.

A few miles before they reached the town of Murfreesboro, Cal turned at a sign reading Creek's Bend Ranch and followed a long winding dirt road through a sprawling estate. Oiled-brown board fencing outlined the property, cutting well-manicured pastures and marking horse runs. In the distance sat a length of stables, painted barn red and trimmed in white. They were impressive in size and Annie imagined capable of housing at least two dozen stalls. With gentle rolling hills, expansive fields of green against a backdrop of fall-drenched mountains, the ranch looked like it was peeled clear off a brochure boasting the finest in Tennessee living. "Wow, this is some kind of beautiful."

"Sure is," Cal acknowledged. "Dwarfs our ranch back home."

"But your place is gorgeous, Cal." He smiled, as though her comment was no more than an attempt to elevate the stature of his family's ranch. She placed a hand to his forearm. "I'm serious. Your place is beautiful. I've always admired it."

"Have you?"

She smiled, a shade timidly. "I have."

"When's the last time you went riding, Annie?"

"Oh, gosh..." She exhaled heavily, releasing him. "It's been forever since I've been on a horse."

"Would you like to go riding sometime? My Daddy has a stable full of horses that would love the pleasure of your company."

Annie grinned at his obvious ploy, yet she found she liked the idea. It had been years since she'd been riding. She loved being on horseback, and a trail ride with Cal held an added appeal. It would be romantic riding around with him, the two of them alone in the woods. Annie trimmed her thoughts, thrusting her gaze out the window as a rush of desire flipped her belly. It would be lovely. Absolutely lovely. "Yes, I think that would be a good idea."

Cal reached over and patted her hand. "I'll set it up."

Nodding, and very aware Cal left his hand over hers, she stared out through the windshield. Hopefully Casey would be back home, allowing her to relax enough to enjoy the ride.

Cal parked outside the paddocks and opened the door for her. "You'll be doing all the talking. If you want me to step in, just give me a nod, and I'll do what I can to help."

"Thank you, Cal. For everything."

"You know it's my pleasure, Annie." He pecked her cheek with a kiss, then steered her toward the building. Together, they sought the main entrance, a door labeled, "Office."

Angst exploded in her chest and her heart fluttered, but Annie was determined to get her daughter and see her home. Since it was close to noon, she hoped the staff wasn't out to lunch. Biding her time in a strange ranch would only ramp up her nerves. Cal opened the metal door and she entered, finding the interior larger than she expected. Quite spacious and clean, it was infused with the familiar scent of leather, hay and horses. Tack adorned the walls along with a miscellany of memorabilia and ribbons, a few photos. Cal had told her the ranch specialized in breeding, but it appeared they also did quite well showing their horses, too.

A stout man sat behind a wooden desk, his head balding, his plaid shirt groaning at the seams. He smiled as they walked in, the folds of his friendly eyes crinkling beneath his glasses. "Can I help you?"

"We're looking for Troy Parker."

He nodded. "Is he expecting you?"

"No," she stumbled over the reply and silently cursed her ineptness. She needed to be calm and firm. Normal. Her only chance to see that Casey listened to reason.

"No problem." He rolled back in his chair. "I'll go fetch him for you."

But that wouldn't be necessary. In through the rear exit door walked the young man himself. Wearing a black cowboy hat, with his brown hair poking out a bit in front, Troy slowed when he saw who she was. His dark brown eyes turned black, suspicion mingling with concern. He flashed to his boss who grinned. "Well speak of the devil. These folks are here to see you, Troy."

"Yes sir," he replied perfunctorily. As he took note of Cal, curiosity seemed to underscore his concern. Removing his hat, he said, "Hello, Ms. Owens."

"Troy."

Cal walked over and extended a hand. "Cal Foster. I'm a family friend." Warily, Troy shook it.

"Can we speak to you in private?" Annie asked.

Troy checked with the man, who apparently was a boss of some sort. The older man nodded. "Take all the time you need." Then to Annie and Cal, he added, "Troy is one of our best hands. We're real proud of him around here."

Annie smiled. She wasn't interested in his accolades. She was here for her daughter.

Troy slipped on his hat and walked out the front door. Strolling to a spot several yards away, he stopped, shooting a glance around the property. "What can I do for you?"

"We're here to retrieve Casey."

"I ain't her keeper," Troy replied, his annoyance mildly concealed.

"Is she with you?"

Troy glanced askance. "No."

"Is she here?"

"Not *here*, no ma'am."

Growing aggravated with his evasive replies, Annie straightened, intending to make herself perfectly clear. "Is she here in Murfreesboro? I need to know, Troy. She's run away and I need to know that at least she's safe."

Troy looked away. "She's safe."

Annie heaved a sigh of relief. "Thank you."

For a moment no one said a word. Cal hovered by her side, Troy peered at her from the shadows of his hat, probably wondering what she was going to do about her grown child who had left her, run off because she wanted to be with *him*. She could feel the adversarial tone in his stance, the edge to his attitude.

Troy was on Casey's side. He wanted her here.

The crisp air seared a chill into her cheeks. A few puffy white clouds floated overhead. A single cowboy led a horse from behind a nearby paddock. Slow, easy, their pace was unhurried. Annie's patience hung from a thread. "I want her to come home, Troy."

"She's an adult. You may want to check with her."

"But you have influence with her."

He glared at her, as though to underscore the fact that Annie did not. Losing the steam of her conviction, Annie turned to Cal. He looked at her with the question in his eyes. *Do you want me to step in?*

She shook her head. This was her battle. Returning to face Troy, she asked, "Will you have her call me? I need to speak with her."

"Casey has a mind of her own," he replied, as if Annie didn't know her own child. "If she wants to talk to you, she'll call."

Rattled by his stubborn refusal, she glanced around the ranch, grappling for alternatives. The compact blue car barreling toward them, spitting a wake of dust, stopped her heart. *Casey.*

She whipped back to Troy. "Why didn't you tell me she was coming here?"

In a horribly inadequate manner, he merely shrugged. *He knew she was on her way?* Annie turned her back on him and waited as Casey parked. Circling the vehicle, the girl froze. Even from this distance Annie could see the influx of shock and anger. A dry wedge lodged in Annie's throat. Had she expected Casey to be happy to see her?

Casey stormed over. After a cursory glance toward Troy, she demanded, "What are you doing here?"

"I've come to take you home."

"I'm not going home."

"Casey—"

"This is my home now," she said, but that didn't prevent her from checking with Troy. He nodded. "So you can turn around and go back where you came from."

Annie marveled at how Casey marched over and took up residence by Troy's side. He wrapped an arm around her shoulders, an arm she was clearly comfortable with having. The two stood in solidarity.

When did this happen? How long had they been together?

"Casey..." Annie paused, reason warring with instinct. "I think we can discuss this like two rational adults."

"There's nothing to discuss. If I had wanted you to know where I was, I would have left a note. I would have answered one of your zillion calls. I didn't." Disgust wrinkled her features. "Can't you take a hint?"

She didn't want to take a hint—she wanted her daughter home! Annie desperately tried to sidestep the quicksand burying her feet. "I don't understand you. I've been fighting for your rights, paying money to keep Ladd Springs so your future is set and this is how you repay me?"

"You're not doing any of that because of me. You're doing it for you."

"How can you say that?"

"Your name is on the deed, too."

"As trustee!" she cried, realizing at once her daughter had no idea what that meant, how it played into her life. *Shoot!* Annie had only learned when Delaney made the designation and explained it to her.

"It's crap and you know it," Casey spat.

"Casey Melody!"

She flicked a glance toward Cal and said, "I'm not going, so why don't you two get back in your truck and go home."

Annie felt Cal's hand circle around her arm, the sweater no barrier against the heat of his palm. He gently tightened his hold, but Annie refused to budge. "I don't understand, Casey. What brought this on? Why are you behaving this way? You ran out on your Aunt Fran, you worried me to death..."

Casey swung her weight to one booted heel, the one closest to Troy, and countered, "I doubt it. Nothing is about me. It's never been about me." The accusation cut deep. "I don't give a crap about Ladd Springs or the man you slept with me to create me." Casey twisted her face. "How could you ever have been with someone like him?"

Chapter Six

It was a question Annie had asked herself many times. *How could she have been with a man like Jeremiah Ladd? What had possessed her?*

Was it his looks? Was that it? Had she been so shallow as a teenager that all she wanted were looks in a man and she'd give herself willingly to him? It made Annie sick. Same as the look in her daughter's eyes, it made Annie sick to think she had wanted a man like Jeremiah, then chased him for two decades to prove *he* was the father of her child. What she should have done was leave well enough alone. Tell Casey she was adopted and make up a "father" story. Anything but the truth.

Rising from her car, Annie reached for her coat but abandoned the effort. It was a thirty second walk into the diner from here. She could make it in her sweater dress and leggings. She tossed the door closed and headed toward the retro-styled building. Fran hadn't changed a thing since her husband Deacon had passed, including the bleached out exterior blue paint. The red neon lights spelling out *Fran's Diner* were straight out of the fifties, a tired exterior that Annie thought her aunt should update. Surely she had the money to refurbish it. At least, re-paint the darn place. It made it look old, rundown. But renovating a restaurant wasn't her problem, Annie mused, swinging open its glass entrance door. Casey was. Time to tell Fran her employee wasn't coming back.

Lingering in the diner entryway, Annie felt a pinch of yearning. She was supposed to be meeting Cal for lunch today but in no mood to discuss logging matters or rehash the scene with Casey and Troy, she'd cancelled. She'd been in no mood yesterday, either, wanting nothing more than to get home, curl up into a ball and die. She'd settled for crawling into bed, but it hadn't done any good. Standing alone now, engulfed by the scent of fried chicken and oven-baked buttermilk biscuits, a hint of Fran's Sunday Roast Beef floating into the mix, Annie regretted the need to cancel on Cal. It sent the wrong signals. He'd only been trying to help.

But there was no help for Annie. Casey and Troy pervaded her dreams, the two of them taunting her, laughing, saying horrible things behind her back. How could Casey be with that boy after he paraded around town with her father's girlfriend? Did she have no sense of decency, no shame? The whole town knew about Troy and Loretta Flynn, Lacy's friend, the stripper from Atlanta. Annie knew it was true. Lacy said so herself.

How was it possible?

The world felt like it was upside down. Sitting in church this morning had helped a little, but it didn't erase her problems. Her daughter hated her. She couldn't afford the property taxes. Her life was a mess.

"Ms. Owens."

The serpent-smooth voice curled around Annie like a steel rope. She looked behind her, startled to see Jillian Devane three feet away. Dressed entirely in black, the woman iced her with an accusatory gaze. "You said you were going to call me."

Annie had completely forgotten. "Yes, well," she replied, no energy to lie or play coy, "I had more important things on my mind."

Jillian smiled through the insult. "Do you have time now?"

Annie looked at her blankly. Now? Here? She ran a quick inventory of the witnesses privy to this interaction. No Nick, no Delaney, no Lacy, no Cal. No one in her inner circle—though any number of people could spread the word that would eventually make it to their ears. Good thing she wasn't meeting Cal for lunch. Annie honed in on Jillian. She'd have a heck of a time explaining this one, yet ventured nonetheless, "I have a second."

"Thank you. Care to join me?" Jillian gave her a wry smile and strolled over to a booth by the front window. Annie spotted a glass of water and half-eaten plate of sliced red tomatoes and realized Jillian was in the middle of lunch.

Annie groaned inwardly. Nothing like broadcasting their meeting to everyone inside and out! But she slid onto the bench seat across from Jillian and prepared herself for the conversation. She'd had no time to think about the offer, no time to discuss the details of a logging contract with Cal. She'd been consumed with Casey's whereabouts. Cal said Delaney was fine with the logging deal, but other than details, prices, Annie had nothing solid to compare numbers. Cal mentioned a quarter of a million dollars. Could it be more? Less?

"My offer for five hundred thousand is a very good price for your property," Jillian began. "It's more than generous and you'd be wise to take it."

"Yes," Annie agreed blindly, sorting through the possibilities as she spoke. It sounded like a lot of money to her but what did she know? She was no expert in the field.

"I can pay you in cash."

Cash? Annie pushed back in her seat, her mind whirring at high speed. What was she going to do with half a million dollars in cash?

"I'll want time to complete a survey," Jillian continued, "but I don't expect that to take more than a week or two. Upon closing, I'll wire the money to the bank of your choice."

Annie only half-listened as Jillian Devane reeled off business details of buying the land, preparing for closing, her mind busily trying to digest the money aspect. What would Gerald Foster do when she strolled up to a teller's window with a check for five hundred thousand dollars? He'd probably keel over on the spot. Annie Owens was not a woman of means. Her bank account rarely held five hundred dollars let alone five hundred *thousand*. Her gaze shot to the front entrance. A group from church entered the diner, bells sounding as an elderly man held the door a bit unsteadily, chatting with another man as the women passed through. Aunt Fran waved to the women, calling them to a large table in the back.

Things were happening too fast. There were so many questions she didn't know where to begin. Annie's throat closed. If only she could discuss it with Cal. He knew real estate. He could help her wade through the details of a big sale like this. Nick had handled the initial transfer, but would not help her sell to this woman. In fact, Nick was more likely to do everything in his power to *stop* her.

Hypnotic golden-brown eyes drew Annie in, reducing the restaurant to the two of them. "Well?"

Annie wanted to confer with Cal, but couldn't mention the first word. He wanted to log the property. He wanted her to build a home on it. "I have to think about it."

Jillian's lips pulled into a thin line. "Yes, that's what you said Friday. But Ms. Owens, there's something you have to understand. Real estate is a very fluid market. When my investors hear the word 'wait' they do the exact opposite and move on to the next deal. As you know..." Long finely manicured nails painted blood-red tapped on the rim of her glass. "I'm looking at another property north of yours. Do you want me to buy that one instead? They're calling me this afternoon for my decision."

Pressure built in Annie's chest. It was the property Lacy had originally mentioned. Jillian Devane was here to ruin Nick. Time ticked away in her skull. Black eyes speared her to the seatback. Five hundred thousand dollars were slipping through her fingers. "I don't know."

Jillian frowned. "Shall I take that as a no?"

"I'm going through some personal issues at the moment, and they've distracted me from the details of this deal," Annie replied, intuitively knowing she was divulging too much but ill-prepared to play hard ball. This woman didn't need to know her business. She didn't need to know what she was considering, or why. Annie couldn't help it if this wasn't her realm of expertise. Expertise, *hell.* Mega real estate deals were like talking a foreign language!

Five hundred thousand dollars was a lot of money. Twice what Cal was talking and Annie didn't want to walk away from a potential sale. She wanted to think about it. She needed to research, consult with an attorney. Time. It was logical. It was reasonable. No one could fault her for taking the time to consider her options. But if this woman wanted to buy another property, there was nothing stopping her. "Is there any way you can give me a few days?"

A glimmer of victory lit up her cat eyes. "If you assure me there is a possibility we have a deal, then yes, I think I can convince my *impatient* investors to wait a few days," she said, suddenly inflecting a tone of camaraderie with Annie.

"Thank you." Annie exhaled against a knot forming in her chest. Selling hundreds of acres of wilderness in Tennessee couldn't be an easy prospect. It wasn't like there were people lined up to buy a piece of land that size, let alone lined up with that kind of money. As it was, most people around here could hardly afford a fifty thousand dollar mortgage. Five hundred thousand dollars for nothing but rocks and trees was for developers or the super-rich. *And the taxes*? Annie didn't even want to think about the tax bill that would arrive in the mail next month.

Nerves skirted through her pulse as she glimpsed Malcolm and Lacy strolling past the front window. Annie leapt up from the table, catching her thigh on a corner. Biting back a moan, she said, "I'll call you when I have an answer, but right now—I have a lunch date." All she needed was her sister and husband to walk in and see the two of them together and Annie would have to explain why she was cavorting with the enemy!

Jillian replied genially in her extravagant accent, "Of course."

Good Heavens, the woman even *sounded* rich, Annie thought, and hurried to the lunch counter. Five hundred thousand dollars cash. Annie clutched the worn Formica edge, still trying to wrap her brain around that angle. What did one do with five hundred thousand dollars cash? Open a bank account? Investment account?

Checking for signs of Fran, Annie wondered if her aunt had witnessed her meeting with Jillian Devane. Fran kept an eye on everything and everyone. Didn't seem possible she could have missed Annie's meeting with Jillian, but she seemed consumed with her growing lunch crowd, chattering away with the large party from church.

Bells jangled again and Annie turned in time to see Malcolm and Lacy stroll in. They caught sight of her instantly. Lacy waved. Annie waved back, darting a glance toward Jillian who was looking at Malcolm and Lacy. Annie gulped. *Would she say anything?*

Nearing, Lacy smiled, her lips colored a bright pink, her dress a thin fuchsia woolen material. She wore black leather knee-high boots, sleek and expensive. "Hi, Annie!"

Behind her Malcolm sported black slacks, gray cardigan and a white turtleneck. Annie was still getting used to his shock of white hair. Cut in fine layers against his tanned skin, it gave him a "celebrity" look. Together, the couple appeared as if they had just strolled off the pages of a glamour magazine. Two pairs of brilliant blue eyes zeroed in on her, trapping Annie in place. If Jillian wanted to sashay over here and tell the two of them what they'd been discussing, Annie had no power to stop her.

"Are you here for supper?" Lacy inquired.

"No, I er—of course," Annie said quickly, realizing her error. "Why else would I be here?"

"Oh, good." Lacy glanced around them. "Where's Cal?"

Annie released her breath. "I don't know. Haven't talked to him today."

Lacy appeared confused. "Well, he'll be joining you, right?"

Annie shook her head. It wasn't a good time. Too much going on.

"How's the logging deal coming along?" Malcolm asked. "Cal told Delaney you were considering logging the property as a way to earn some income." Hanging a hand from Lacy's shoulder, he nodded his approval. "I think it's a great idea."

Surprised by his easy acceptance, Annie hemmed, "Well, I haven't made any decisions yet." Walling her peripheral vision against seeking out Jillian, she said, "I'm not sure how we can manage to log without a road in, with no way to get the wood and all."

"Cal told me his forester friend was taking care of it. All you need is a permit and that shouldn't take but a few weeks or so."

Once again, Annie felt things were moving too quickly. The logging deal would be ready before she could decide whether or not to sell. She had no idea if Jillian's offer was the right amount without checking the market. And she still had yet to talk with Casey, discuss their options. Logging would provide them with money and allow them to keep the land, but with the land came expenses, taxes. Jillian's offer would allow her and Casey the freedom to walk away with a lump sum. It was tempting. "Yes, well, Cal is an optimist."

Malcolm returned a thoughtful gaze. "And you're not?"

"Of course she is," Lacy quipped. "And Annie knows value when she sees it. She knows it's a lot of money."

"Value," Annie repeated. "Yes." Value. Money. *Cash*— and lots of it, possibly more than five hundred thousand dollars. Resisting the urge to look over her shoulder at Jillian, Annie spotted Aunt Fran as she emerged from the kitchen.

"Hey, sugar!" Fran wiped her hands on a red waist apron, her standard uniform attire along with her starched white dress, and made a bee line for the three of them. "I thought that was ya'll I saw out here." She brushed wayward red curls beneath her hair net, aqua-blue eye shadow jumping out against a line of heavy black lashes.

A rush of nerves unraveled Annie's calm. "We're here for lunch," she blurted.

Ignoring the obvious, Fran asked, "Did you find Casey? I've been worried sick as a coon huntin' at noon."

Malcolm and Lacy remained mute, assuming they knew the answer.

"I did." Annie cleared her throat. "She's in Murfreesboro. With Troy."

"Troy Parker?"

Annie nodded. "Seems the two are an item." She glanced at Lacy, reminded of another young girl who thought she wanted to escape on the heels of a boy. "Casey thinks she wants to be with him for a while."

As though Fran understood completely, she ceased further scrutiny. Rolling her lips together, she shared a glance with Lacy and said, "Give her time. She'll be back."

"The chicken smells awful good, Aunt Frannie."

Fran accepted Lacy's invitation onto easier terrain with only a slight pause. "Now you know I don't make anything but the best." Glancing between them she asked, "Three orders?"

Malcolm looked to Annie for confirmation. "Actually, I just realized I told Candi I'd be by her place after church," she lied. Resisting the urge to look over her shoulder, she couldn't very well afford to stick around and have Jillian make an approach!

"You want a couple orders to go?"

"No, thanks." At the disappointment staring back at her, Annie added, "I don't want you to go to any trouble."

"Now, sugar you know it's no trouble at all."

Annie managed a small smile. "Two chicken dinners to go would be great, Aunt Fran. Thank you."

The light returned to her expression. "Four fried chicken dinners, double the biscuits!" she called out gaily and whisked back to the kitchen service window. Calling the order back, Fran turned on her white-soled heel and retrieved a host of glasses. Setting them on a tray, she filled them with ice, grabbed a pitcher of tea and delivered the goods in seconds. "Now c'mon ya'll, sit." She poured four glasses full. "Just holler if you want more."

Malcolm grinned. Guiding Lacy to a seat on a cushioned stool, he said, "You spoil me, Fran."

She winked. "It's my specialty."

Annie lowered next to her, trailing Fran's backside down the counter and around the corner and into the kitchen. The woman didn't sit still for half a second. Was it possible she missed Annie and Jillian altogether?

"Is there something else concerning you, Annie?" Malcolm glanced to Lacy. "Other than access and trees, I mean?"

It wasn't a judgmental question, rather easy and considerate. Like Lacy, Malcolm Ward was eager to help. Not a trait she expected in a man from Los Angeles, a city renowned for its glitter and fast living, but she appreciated it all the same. "Oh, I don't know," she replied. "Sounds like a lot of red tape to me."

Malcolm smiled knowingly. "Shouldn't be too bad. Nick and I have found the county to be very accommodating and have developed a great working relationship with the guys in the office. If it will help, I'd be happy to submit a permit to the Department of Transportation on your behalf. It might help smooth the process for you."

"Oh, Malcolm, would you?" Lacy peered up at him in naked awe. "That would save Annie so much time, wouldn't it?"

"I think so." With a quick wink to his wife, he said, "I'll call first thing in the morning and see what their time frame is running."

Government. Bureaucracy. Time. More decisions, more waiting. If she wasn't being pressed for a decision, she was waiting for one. "Is there a possibility I couldn't get a permit?"

Malcolm punched a straw open and stuck it in a glass for Lacy. Handing it over, he repeated the process for himself. "No, you'll get it. As legal owner, you have a right to access your property. It usually takes a month or so, but I think we can manage it in a couple of weeks. You can probably get the forester to cut you a driveway and take the cost out of the proceeds."

Money. Loss of proceeds. It also meant she'd have to decide about Ms. Devane's offer without a solid idea of how much money she'd receive from a forester to compare. And how was she going to ask anyone about the true value of her property without raising the quilt on her dealings with Jillian Devane?

Hank Dakota was her lawyer. A native to the area, he helped her prove paternity, helped her close the initial real estate deal with Nick and Delaney. Hank was a fixture in this town, entrenched as she and while attorney-client privilege was the law, Annie didn't trust the information to stay sealed behind closed doors. People talked. They slipped. It happened. Everyone knew what everyone else was doing and if she was seen talking with Hank, someone was bound to make the connection. At least ask questions.

Questions she couldn't afford to answer. Not until she had all the facts, a decision made. Popping a straw through its paper, Annie drew a sip of sweet tea. Cold and sugary, the beverage was a welcome relief to her parched throat. Maybe she could find what she needed on the internet. Maybe she didn't have to ask anyone for help.

Malcolm raised his glass, the liquid a light brown as it mixed with ice and didn't mention another word. He probably assumed she was running through the information in her mind, glad to have him guiding her along. Suddenly the cash offer looming in the forefront of Annie's brain made her feel like a heel. Here Malcolm and Cal and Lacy were working on her behalf while she was working against them. If she sold the property, all their time and effort would be for nothing. But she had to do what was best for her daughter, didn't she? Isn't that what being trustee was all about?

Ten minutes later Annie walked out of the diner with a warm paper bag in hand. The scent of fried chicken and biscuits pulled hunger pains from her stomach. *Forgot she had to stop by Candi's after church.* What kind of weak excuse was that? Was Candi even home? Toting a bag full of food with no place to go, Annie thought maybe she *should* go to Candi's place. She could use the company and the ready ear.

Chapter Seven

Cal walked into Fran's Diner, not surprised the place was cackling like a hen house at feeding time. He dodged aside as a toddler bumped into his legs. "Sorry!" came the automatic response from a young mother, a woman who didn't appear old enough to have a child let alone one she had to chase down and corral in a crowd. Cal waved it off with a smile. But that was Fran's. Folks of all ages frequented the restaurant, from his Daddy's generation right down to the students that made Fran's Diner part of their after-school schedule. Most of today's crowd was dressed in their Sunday best, relaxing over good old-fashioned country cooking with friends and family after a morning of church services.

Cal inhaled the scent of roasting meat and fried food, the heavenly blend of baked goods saturating the air. For him this was milk to a baby. There was no better meal than a southern one, even if it did come from a restaurant. Too bad he was dining solo today. He was pumped with news for Annie. His forester friend said cutting a road would be no problem at all and shouldn't add more than a months' time to the job, maybe less. Already familiar with the land, he was willing to pay Annie up front, too. She couldn't argue with those terms, Cal mused.

Spotting Malcolm and Lacy at the counter, he paused. Malcolm waved him over. Inwardly, Cal smiled. Maybe he wouldn't be eating alone after all. "Afternoon," he said as he joined them.

"Good afternoon," Malcolm replied.

"Hi, Cal!" Lacy chirped and looked around him as though searching for his lunch date. "Did you see Annie?"

Cal frowned, noting the two plates of half-eaten fried chicken, biscuits and okra. "No. Was she here?"

"She just left." Lacy delivered the news as if he'd been ditched, adding cheerfully, "You can join us, if you'd like."

"Well, don't mind if I do." Cal slid onto a stool next to Lacy, marveling how similar in appearance she was to Annie. Jet black hair, fair complexion and those notably blue eyes, the sisters could almost be twins. Next to Malcolm's white hair and tanned skin, his eyes a pale blue, Cal thought the two looked good together. He'd come to like Malcolm, getting to know him over the last several months. He was decent, smart, and definitely sweet on Lacy.

She smiled. "Fran will be out in a second."

Noting she was hitched so close to Malcolm's side it was a wonder if the man would be able to eat, Cal surveyed the restaurant. Cooks in white dashed from a smoking grill to the service window, sliding plates, pulling tickets in rhythmic precision complete with shouts of, "Order up!"

"Fran really packs 'em in, doesn't she?"

"That she does," Malcolm agreed.

"Oh, poo." Lacy waved him off. "That's nothing new. Aunt Frannie's has always been the only place to eat in town, you know that."

"You won't hear any complaints from me." Cal loved southern cooking, and next to his momma, there was no one better than Fran, particularly when it came to her peach pie. He'd never admit as much aloud but sure as he was sitting here, Fran's was the best, three counties wide. Settling on to a thick-cushioned seat, he asked, "How's the baby?"

Lacy's face lit up brighter than the hot pink of her jacket and she tapped his arm. "Good, and you're sweet to ask." She paused with an odd look in her eyes, appearing suddenly confused. "When is Annie gonna get it through her brain that you'd make the perfect husband?"

Malcolm twisted toward her. "Don't you think you should let your sister decide that?"

Lacy pouted. "Not when she's being so mulish. Why look at him." She gestured toward Cal. "He's a fine man and been so patient with her. If I were you, Cal, I'd demand she officially be your girlfriend or tell her you're gonna leave her flat!"

"You think threatening will help?" Malcolm asked.

Lacy scowled. "It might."

Cal laughed and leaned forward on his elbows. "Thanks for the suggestion, Lacy, but I think I'll hang in there a little while longer. Your sister has a lot on her mind these days." Grabbing her iced tea, Lacy sipped, eyes alert but apparently content to have said her piece.

Fran whisked out from the kitchen, delivering a bowl of steaming peanuts. "A little something to start you off with, Cal."

He breathed in the distinct scent of warm, salt-boiled peanuts and drawled, "Well, thank you, Fran. That's mighty nice of you."

She winked. "You know I take special care of my favorites."

Lacy scrunched her nose at the bowl. "Why are you always eating those things?"

"Habit." Ever since he quit drinking, Cal found that tossing back a pile of boiled peanuts replaced his urge to pick up a drink, especially when he was around his brothers. The nuts were satisfying in their own right, especially when boiled by a woman with experience. Placing his nose over the bowl, he inhaled. And Fran was certainly a woman with experience. It was her addition of ham hock that sealed it for him. In Arizona no one knew what a boiled peanut was, let alone a ham hock. Recalling the first time he'd asked after them, Cal chuckled. *Boiled what? Why would anyone do that to a peanut?* He split one open, heedless to the hot juices dripping down his fingers and thought, because they're tasty. "You oughta try one, Lacy."

"They're too mushy."

Fran planted a hand to her hip and said, "Now don't you go disparagin' my cooking, young lady. To each his own, you hear me?"

Lacy flipped her face up to Fran and frowned. "Sorry."

Fran took Cal's order, departing as quick as she'd come, promising him a cup of peanuts to go. It was a gesture he appreciated. Living at home for the time being, his momma wasn't one for boiling peanuts. Didn't like the stink in her kitchen. As a boy, his daddy boiled peanuts out by the stables in a huge steel pot, simmering them for hours and adding his secret spices. When he was satisfied they were ready, he'd load the boys up with cups full and send them on their way. Those were good times, good memories. "So," he turned to Malcolm, popping open a second peanut, "you must be excited about the prospect of becoming a new father."

He raised a brow. "Excited, nervous, scared out of my mind—all of the above."

Cal chuckled and downed the warm, soft nut. He remembered the swell of emotion well. The day he learned Caroline was with child was the first day in his life where he seriously took stock of his manhood. Was he ready? Prepared for the change that would come with the new arrival? Could he take care of an infant, a tiny person completely dependent upon him for his or her every need?

It was a tall order and one he had to get used to, but he'd done it. When Emily was born, his heart burst with feelings and sensations he'd never before experienced. She'd been beautiful, the most beautiful baby on the maternity floor. Regret drenched his memories. If only he could hit a reset button and start over. He wouldn't make a mess of things the second time around.

"There's nothing to be afraid of," Lacy said. "Women have been having babies since the beginning of time."

"Yes," Malcolm agreed, a glint of humor in his blue eyes, eyes a shade lighter than Lacy's but every bit as sharp.

"Have you decided on a name?"

Lacy beamed, her eyes deepened. "Emma Jane."

"Emma Jane is a beautiful name," Cal said wistfully, the similarities hitting home. Lacy was happy as a woman in love should be and looking forward to the birth of her child. It was the way life was supposed to work.

"Thank you," she intoned, as though he'd given his personal approval

"Are you sure it's going to be a girl, then?"

"Yes. A psychic told me."

Malcolm smiled over Lacy's head. "My fault. When we were in California to meet my parents, she spotted a sign advertising psychics and made me pull over. Marched right inside and demanded to know about her pregnancy." Sliding a hand down her back, he continued, "She was only eight weeks at the time, but the psychic assured her it was a girl, a little baby girl who was going to grow up just like her mother."

"Well, she *will,*" Lacy insisted.

Malcolm held his hands in the air. "It's been a girl ever since. She named it on the way home, in fact. Emma Jane was something we both agreed on."

"Will you be upset if it turns out to be a boy?" Cal asked.

"It won't," Lacy snapped and plucked a biscuit from the edge of her plate.

Malcolm grinned. "I think it's going to be a girl but it's only a guess. Lacy refuses to get an ultrasound to check."

"That's cheating," Lacy said. "Besides, I already know *she's* a girl."

Cal laughed, hiding a deep sorrow that penetrated his soul. What he'd give to be with his own daughter. He'd move mountains—was trying to do so with his return home to Tennessee—only he wouldn't see the results for some time. Although he'd been sober now for ten months and three days, his daughter Emily couldn't stand to be in the same room with him. One terrible mistake and she had closed her heart, ripping him from her life forever. "I hope it is," Cal said quietly and reached for another peanut. *Girls are gifts from heaven.*

"Speaking about a lot on her mind these days," Malcolm said, "I told Annie I'd be happy to help her along with those permits she needs. Nick and I have established a nice rapport with the guys in the county office, and since we're already familiar with the paperwork, I think we could manage a permit in a couple of weeks, maybe less."

Cal turned on his stool. "That would be great. I know she'd appreciate it."

"Consider it done."

"How's the progress of the hotel construction coming along?"

"Right on schedule. Groundwork for the hotel has been pretty well wrapped up and we're moving on to the building and hiring stage and—"

"Already?" Lacy interrupted, a fork full of golden-fried okra suspended before her mouth. "But you haven't built the first building. How are you going to hire people with nowhere for them to go?"

He smiled indulgently. "I said we're moving on to the hiring stage. We have to prepare, don't we?" Malcolm shifted his focus to Cal. "We want to have our doors open by Memorial Day of next year."

Cal let out a low whistle and tossed an empty peanut shell into his bowl. "That's pretty aggressive."

Malcolm nodded. "Nick is organizing our construction crew now. Soon as we're ready, we'll ship our people in and get started."

Cal cocked his head. "Still, seven months is pretty tight."

Malcolm laughed, a confident man dealing in child's play. "That's what sets Harris Hotels apart. We get in, we get open. Our guys are the best in the business. We've got half a dozen crews that come in. One attacks the hotel, another will take on the stables. A specialized crew out of California will handle our landscape, another the interiors, and the restaurant will be taken care of by an amazing woman out of San Francisco."

Lacy's attention perked at the mention of "woman." "What woman?"

Leaning toward her, he said, "An old, wrinkled woman who looks like a man."

Realizing the tease, she smirked. "Very funny."

Malcolm kissed her nose. "Nobody you have to worry about, my dear."

Blue eyes glittering with distrust, Lacy pointed to the front door. "Unlike that woman."

"What's she doing here?" Malcolm asked, appearing genuinely surprised.

Cal turned his head to see a dark-haired woman standing by the hostess stand in line to pay her bill. She was staring at them. She looked completely out of place in a slinky gold blouse and metallic jacket, her hips wrapped in some kind of spandex skirt with boots that soared clear up to her thighs. Her very thin thighs. "You know her?" he asked.

Lacy nodded vigorously, swallowing. "Malcolm does. Her name is Jillian Devane and she used to date Nick. Now she's trying to build a hotel nearby and put them out of business."

"She's a hotel developer Nick and I met during a build in South America. She and Nick hit it off but when it was time to move on, let's just say Jillian wasn't quite ready to let go."

"Ah..." The woman was a vixen if Cal had ever seen one. Taking a second glance, he noted she was waving to their table, but rather than approach, turned on her heel to leave the diner. "Guess we don't have what she's looking for," he commented, picking up another peanut.

Lacy gasped. Malcolm commented, "Don't look now, but we might be in for a cat fight."

Cal looked between them. "Huh?"

With a hand to her mouth, Lacy pointed wordlessly.

Delaney Wilkins had entered and now faced off with Jillian Devane, who towered over her in four-inch heels. Cal could feel the tension from here. Oblivious diners crowded around the duo. Jillian's shiny black hair fell straight as a board against her metallic gold jacket and brown skin. Delaney's pale blonde hair flowed well past her shoulders, blending in with her creamy-white sweater. Jillian wore a full face of makeup while Delaney had barely a touch. A striking pair, they were like night and day. "The two don't care for one another, I assume?" Cal asked.

"Delaney should scratch her eyes out," Lacy hissed. "That woman has no business here and the sooner she leaves, the better."

Delaney tried to walk past Jillian, but the woman stopped her. They exchanged words. Delaney reached up and fiddled with a necklace, or something at her neck. Cal couldn't quite make it out from his vantage point. Jillian smiled, but it wasn't a friendly smile. Delaney's reaction was unmistakable. She was not happy. Whether Jillian didn't catch on to the anger or was intentionally trying to provoke her, Cal didn't know but watched with wary interest as she leaned forward and said something to Delaney. Whatever it was, Cal mused, it hit the mark. Delaney appeared stunned, then shoved a finger into Jillian's face. The woman smiled, turned, and made her exit.

"Good job, Delaney," Lacy said, trailing her figure to a back table in the corner where she joined an elderly woman already seated. Cal didn't recognize the woman and chucked the peanut into his mouth. "Jillian is not welcome here," Lacy went on. "She needs to pack her bags this instant and *scat*."

"It's a free country, sweetheart," Malcolm replied, unaffected by the scene. "She's free to come and go as she pleases."

"But she's here to destroy you! You said so yourself."

Malcolm hugged Lacy close. "I'll keep an eye on her, okay?"

Lacy huffed, but Cal liked that Malcolm wasn't worried about the woman. It was a sign of confidence. He knew his business and wasn't concerned about a little competition. Cal had come to like Malcolm. Although Malcolm was a city boy from Los Angeles, Lacy was weaving the country into him one day at a time. Smart, friendly, the man had an easy way about him and fit right in. Unlike the developer Cal worked for in Arizona, Malcolm was in tune with those around him. He didn't seem like a one-way road kind of man but a two-way fellow filled with detours and yield signs. Living with Lacy probably made it a must!

Speaking of business, Cal had been tossing about an idea he wanted to run by Malcolm. While it wasn't his place to tell a man how to run his business, there was no reason he couldn't offer a friendly suggestion. "I've been thinking about the hotel," he said, swallowing, not sure how Malcolm would receive the idea but compelled to try. "Have you given any thought to providing history tours for your guests? I mean, I don't want to overstep my boundaries, but if you're interested in being in tune with the community, the land, I think folks would get a kick out of hearing about the history of these parts. They might find it intriguin' to know that Tennessee is the Turtle Capital of the World."

A wry smile pulled at Malcolm's mouth. "Really?"

"Sure is. We're called that because of the many species of turtles that inhabit our great state. Literally thousands of turtles live in Reelfoot Lake, including varieties like stinkpots, mud, sliders and map turtles." Malcolm laughed while Lacy shot a bored look to the ceiling. "Reelfoot Lake itself is a wonder, too," Cal continued, thoroughly in his element. He loved history and his home state was full of it. "Did you know it was created by the largest earthquake in American history?"

Malcolm sat back. "You don't say?"

"Yes sir. Occurred in the winter of 1812 up in the northwestern part of our state."

Malcolm laughed. "Sounds like a great idea. I think guests will love it, and I know just the man to handle the job. What do you say you take on the position of General Manager and organize the entire experience?"

Malcolm could have run over him with a dump truck, his shock would have been the same. Cal gaped at him. "Me?"

"Yes. You have experience working in a real estate community. You know people. You have experience. I made a phone call to your old boss, frankly, a man who couldn't say enough nice things about you."

"You called my boss?" Cal asked, alarm mingling with surprise.

"You don't mind, do you? I check out all my new hires before I put them in the running. Though I'll warn you, you're top of my list."

Lacy smiled at Cal, as though reaffirming how great she thought he was, too.

Cal's gut tightened. *If only they knew*. One night in Arizona had changed his life, changed his relationship with his wife, his daughter Emily. Worse than the suffering he'd caused at home, he'd cut a hole in the life of a stranger—a gaping hole which couldn't be repaired. One night, one bad decision, monumental consequences. Consequences he lived with every day. He was only surprised Peter had spoken so highly of him. On second thought, Cal asked, "Who did you speak with?"

"A guy named Peter Malone."

So it had been Peter. Cal turned the information over in his mind. The last day he saw Peter had not been a pretty one. Peter was angry, disappointed. He felt like Cal had let him down.

He had. More than quitting without notice, Cal had been a constant thorn for Peter. Between the drinking and the hangovers and the accident that made front page news, Peter had been hounded by Cal's mishaps. He never missed a day of work because of his drinking, but he sure had been asked to leave for a few. *One more fight and you're fired*. Short and sweet. Cal understood. A loose cannon was unpredictable and unpredictability was bad for business. It was bad for marriage, too. Alcohol had made a mess of his life, a mess of others, so he set the bottle down ten months ago and walked away. Clean cut, no second thoughts, he never looked back.

What had Peter been thinking? He didn't know Malcolm was a friend. Cal narrowed his gaze on the man sitting across from him. What had Malcolm said during the phone call that made Peter so amenable? Why would he stick up for him after their falling out?

Allowing the questions to course through him, Cal eased free of the burden. No matter. He was grateful for the small miracle and would take a break wherever he could get one. His drinking days were over. No going back. Some days it amazed him. Other days he understood completely. When you had something to fight for as important as he did, the bottle didn't stand a chance. Longing pricked at his heart. He missed his daughter. Leaving Emily had been like leaving a piece of his heart. She was the reason Malcolm's job offer meant so much to him.

Clearing his voice, Cal reined in his thoughts and said, "Well, it's nice to hear." Adding privately, a man never wanted his past employer to be left with a bad taste in his mouth, and Peter Malone's should be spittin' mud to this day.

"I don't think you have to worry. The man said you were great with the residents, reliable on the job and smart. Odd," Malcolm paused, "but he underscored your potential almost as much as he commended your past. While you don't have direct GM experience, he didn't have any qualms recommending you if I was willing to train you. Which I am." Glancing sideways to Lacy, he continued, "As you know, I'm setting down roots here, but in the future, Lacy and I will be traveling quite a bit and I'll need to know I have a good man holding down the fort while I'm away." Malcolm smiled, and Cal almost felt guilty at the outpouring of trust in the man's pale blue eyes. "I think that man is you."

Cal couldn't believe his good fortune. He and Malcolm had established an easy rapport over the last several months, spending more and more time together on account of Annie and Lacy, but he never expected a job offer. The position of General Manager for an exclusive boutique hotel sounded incredibly appealing. He'd be interacting with international guests, intriguing people from all over the world... Cal had done his share of managing, making him feel secure on that count. The scale of operations they were talking was hundreds of employees versus thousands, people from this area, people he understood. The South. In Arizona folks didn't understand the Southerner in him. They heard his accent and immediately thought redneck, hillbilly, neither of which he was. He was a southern gentleman, an educated man who was raised in the hills of Tennessee but understood the finer points of life. Cal considered himself a simple man, but a man of civility. "It sounds like a great offer," he replied.

"So you're interested?"

"'Course I am. It's a heck of an opportunity for a small town guy like me."

"There's nothing small town about you, Cal," Lacy interjected. "You've spent the last fifteen years in the big city, haven't you?"

"Same as you, but it doesn't look like it's changed you any." Lacy frowned and he chuckled. "That's a good thing, darlin'."

She rebounded instantly and batted her lashes. "I'm a country girl at heart, you know. That's why I came back home. There's no place like Tennessee and I'll never leave it again,"—she reached for Malcolm—"except to travel the world with you, of course."

Malcolm laughed softly.

"Tennessee is the best place on earth," Cal declared and meant it with every fiber of his being. Arizona was a beautiful state, extremely diverse and filled with natural wonders, like the jaw-dropping vista of red rocks and canyons in Sedona and the nearby Grand Canyon, but Arizona wasn't home. He'd tried to make it his home, but when his marriage fell apart he realized it wasn't meant to be, though it would always be a part of him. The most important person in his world was there waiting for him.

Only she didn't know it, yet.

Chapter Eight

Cal arrived at Annie's apartment at eight o'clock, a mix of excitement and trepidation roiling in his gut. The position of General Manager for Serenity Springs was a big deal. The more he thought about it, the bigger and better it seemed to him. Not only did it sound exciting and challenging, it would give him a chance to start fresh in his hometown, near the woman who was becoming to mean a lot to him.

Becoming, hell. He was in love with Annie Owens and it was high time she knew about it. A flurry of nerves skated through his pulse. Cal had been in love with her for most of the summer, only Annie didn't know it, yet. Not officially. But he needed to be sure of his direction before he took the next step. It was a big one—a step that might sink his boots, preventing him from taking another. Annie didn't know about his daughter, Emily, about her issues with him. Annie didn't know about the accident that changed his life forever. Cal felt the usual discharge of adrenaline whenever he thought about it, the consequences it carried, the lives he ruined. Annie couldn't know, because he'd kept it to himself. It was a part of his past no one needed to know. They only needed to know about his future.

The way Cal saw it, his life was about where he was going, not where he'd been. It was about moving on and making things right. He needed to prove to Emily he was the man she wanted him to be. *Needed* him to be. But if Annie were to travel that road forward with him, she'd have to know everything about the mess of road he'd left behind.

Cal rapped briskly on the door. With the job as General Manager, he could rebuild his reputation in Tennessee. It could be a door to opportunity and travel. Before moving to Arizona, he'd dreamed of traveling the country, exploring wide open spaces and big cities. When he met Caroline, the two traveled around the state, made a brief trip to Colorado, Nevada, but that was the extent of it. As a member of the Harris Hotels management team, Cal could visit their other properties, stay in the finest hotels around the world and call it a business trip. He grinned to himself. Maybe he could help open a hotel abroad, rise up in the chain of command at Harris Hotels and really make his mark.

Staring at the white metal door, he thought, with a solid woman by his side, he could rebuild his trustworthiness, return to Arizona and reclaim his position as father, a man worthy of his daughter's respect. The door opened in a rush, sweeping a new round of nerves through his system. "Hey, Annie."

"Hi, Cal." She smiled, her blue eyes easy and welcoming as she stepped aside. "C'mon in."

Cal strode in shaking the clamp of cold he hadn't realized was gripping him. "I think it's getting colder by the second out there!"

She laughed lightly. "I know. It's almost like Mother Nature has it out for us this season."

"She can be a feisty one." Cal pecked Annie's cheek, wondering how best to open up the subject of the rest of his life. Following Annie over to the sofa, he watched as she settled in on one end while he lowered to the other. Skimming over her royal blue turtleneck dress, black leggings and black fashion boots, he thought it was her best color. "You look mighty pretty today."

Annie looked down as though she'd forgotten what she'd put on this morning and replied, "Thank you."

Cal smiled. "Do you feel better today?" Upset over Casey running off with Troy, she'd been avoiding his calls. He understood her concern, but thought it might be a bit overstretched. The kids were adults. They'd be fine, once they worked out which path to take, which hills to conquer.

"I'm okay," she replied, her tone non-committal.

"How was work today?"

"Good. Busy," she added, but evaded his direct gaze. "I had three new clients and I don't know how I'm going to fit them in long-term."

"Oh, I know you'll manage." Not only was Annie great with nails, but he found her to be well-organized and on top of the business side of her profession. "Where there's a will, there's a way. Besides, you can't be upset over being in demand."

"Work can be a mixed blessing, can't it?"

"It sure can," he said, "and speaking of work, there's something I wanted to talk to you about."

Her brow furrowed. "What's on your mind?"

Adjusting his body to face her more fully, Cal cleared his throat. "Well, I received a job offer this week and I wanted to run it by you."

She clasped her hands. "Oh, Cal—that's wonderful!" At her joy, relief rushed through him. "You've been looking for a while, it must be a great one to have caught your attention."

"I think it is."

At his hesitation, Annie prodded, "Well? What's making you so excited? Tell me!"

"Malcolm offered me the job as General Manager of the new hotel."

The elation slipped from her eyes. "Malcolm?"

Cal nodded. "He's working on staffing the hotel and offered me the job. What do you think?" His heart pitched at the displeasure swamping her gaze. To her credit, Annie tried to cover it with a smile, but it wasn't near bright enough to conceal her true emotions.

"Why, it sounds like a *great* offer," she said, "but I thought Malcolm was going to manage the hotel himself. That's what Lacy told me."

"In the beginning, yes, but after that his plans will take him away to scout new locations for future hotels. He aims to set roots here, on account of Lacy and the baby, but they won't be here all the time." Cal inhaled deeply and explained,

"That's where I come in. I'll be acting manager on site, in partnership with Malcolm."

"I didn't realize you had hotel management experience."

"I don't," he said, tamping back an influx of disappointment. "I have management experience with a residential community, but Malcolm seems to think I can use it to manage the hotel." Blue eyes gaped at him in obvious doubt, but she didn't say the words. Cal shifted his weight, drawing his knee away from Annie. "Malcolm called my old boss who reinforced the notion."

"Wow," she mumbled. "That's wonderful for you."

Cal detected no "us" in her reply. His pulse skipped as he asked, "Is it a problem, Annie?"

"No, why would you ask?"

"You don't seem real excited about the idea of me working over there."

"Well..." She stumbled in her reply, clearly caught off guard by his blunt statement. "You know I'm not on great terms with Delaney. I love Malcolm and think he's great. You'd be working with him, mostly, right?"

"Nick and Delaney will both be a part of the equation. There's no getting around it." Cal needed to be direct and firm. He needed to be upfront and honest. It was time to lay his cards out. "I need this job. A position like this can go a long way to making me whole again."

"What do you mean, whole again? There's nothing wrong with you, Cal." He didn't respond and she continued, "And you don't need Delaney's hotel to prove it, either. Why, you were a success in Arizona and you'll be a success anywhere you go. Are there no other hotels in the area where you might like to work?"

He liked the staunch support he heard, but Annie didn't have all the facts. "Not like Serenity Springs." While Annie sounded supportive, she didn't appear to be on board with his working with Nick and Delaney. If she wasn't on board, he had to reassess his entire position. "They're an international chain. The guests will be a caliber above the other hotels in the area. The amenities, the spa." He paused. "Why, you might even be able to get a job working in the spa doing nails. I'll bet the pay will be better than what you're earning at Trendz," Cal said, mentally withdrawing his initial plan of divulging his past while sharing the news of his job offer.

Folding hands in her lap, Annie dropped her gaze.

"Would you be upset if I accepted it?" Cal asked, coaxing her to reengage with him.

Annie looked up and the determination he saw staring back at him startled him. "No." She shook her black shiny hair and Cal thought she was about to cry. "I'm upset over Casey is all. I think it's a fine opportunity for you."

But not for her. Annie didn't want anything to do with Delaney, and that included dating a man who worked her property. Cal didn't think marriage would change her mind on that count.

"I feel unsettled," Annie went on, "like I'm at a crossroads in my life. Like I've been struggling for so long yet I haven't made any progress."

"Aw, Annie," he said, scooting closer to her. Reaching for her hands, he pulled one free. It was warm and soft and delicate and made him yearn to hold her, to shield her from life's rocky road and reassure her she could make it. All she needed was to hold on tight to the grit and determination he knew she possessed. "You've made great progress. Look at the clientele list you've built, your schedule so busy a new gal can't hardly get in." She smiled and the gesture was like sunshine to his soul. "You should be proud of your accomplishments."

"I am," she returned faintly. "I just want better for Casey." For herself, too, he heard, but didn't comment. Like him, Annie had to the right to speak her mind on her own terms. "I don't want her to think that a job at the diner is all there is to her life. I want her to dream big, let her imagination take her places. She's smart, Cal. She can accomplish so much if only she'd put her mind to it. Instead, she's chasing a boy who will only end up hurting her." Tears pushed into

Annie's eyes and ripped at his heart. "I'm thinking of moving, Cal. Maybe Chattanooga, Knoxville. I think the change will do Casey good."

The rips turned to shreds. The sofa lengthened between them. Annie was planning her life around Casey—the girl who'd run away from her mother to chase a boy to Murfreesboro. Did Annie not understand that her daughter was making her own choices? Different choices? Glancing down at their enfolded hands, Cal wondered what was really driving Annie's desire to move. He didn't believe it was all about Casey. He believed Annie wanted a change for herself, too. She wanted to broaden her horizons, same as he'd done. Caressing her hand, admiring her finely done burgundy-colored nails, Cal realized it was a move that might not include him. Chattanooga was only an hour away, Knoxville a good bit farther. Accepting Malcolm's offer would mean a long-distance relationship for the two of them. Cal lifted his head to face her.

Marriage would be out of the question.

As Annie stared at him expectantly, Cal felt a torrent of emotion flow between them. They were on the verge of something big, yet seemed to be adding miles to the bridge instead of closing the distance. Cal wanted this job with Serenity Springs but he could tell Annie wasn't thrilled to have him take it. She was talking change but in the form of a move. It was a desire he understood. He'd felt it once himself. But his travels had returned him home, bruised and battered and somewhat worse for the wear. Except for his daughter. While Annie might not make the disastrous mistakes he had, she was heading for unchartered territory, blazing new trails through a wilderness unknown. Picking up stakes was risky, and without money behind her a move would be tough. With no contacts, no support network, living away from home would prove even harder.

Cal didn't want to reveal his disappointment. He wanted to be seen as her ally, her support, even if it meant helping her to move away from him. "Have you decided on the logging, then? A move will cost money and the income you receive would sure help pay for it."

Annie hesitated, then dodged his direct gaze. "I haven't made any final decisions. Not on the logging or the move." Looking back to him, she withdrew her hand. "What are your feelings, Cal? Are you set on this job with Nick and Malcolm?"

His mood plummeted at her sudden retreat. She was asking if had he committed to the position or was there room for her, as in, *He can't have them both*. "I'd like to take it but I haven't signed on the dotted line." Cal wanted to ask, *Had she*? Annie said she hadn't made a final decision, but did she mean it?

As though sensing his question, Annie avoided him. For a long moment, she remained still. Quiet. Cal ached to know what was going on behind those beautiful blue eyes of hers. He longed to know if she'd ever considered a life with him as man and wife the way he hungered for one with her. But Cal couldn't take the first step without revealing the truth about Emily. Shame slithered him. About himself, not Emily. The truth about *him* and what *he'd* done. One horrible decision that had set his life on a crash course. A soft sigh escaped him. "I guess we have a lot to think about."

Angst peeled back the layers of indecision in her blue eyes. "I guess..."

Cal's gut winced. Was there any possibility they could move forward together?

Chapter Nine

Annie sucked in her breath at the sight of Jillian Devane waltzing into the Trendz salon.

"Ouch!" an elderly woman cried.

"Oh, my gosh—I'm sorry!" Annie apologized to her client quickly, unaware she'd been pinching the woman's fingers. Jillian's eyes curled around Annie like a snake as she hung by the receptionist's desk. Lips glossed in a shimmery maroon, eyes concealed behind oversized sunglasses, Jillian was wrapped in a black fur coat, her head covered by a matching fur hat. She was completely out of place in the rural salon. Ms. Devane should be walking a red carpet, boarding a private jet or dining in a five-star restaurant in some exotic locale.

What was she doing here? Didn't Annie tell her she needed time, that she'd call her when she was ready?

Sliding the glasses from her face, Jillian tucked them into a deep pocket. Next, she tugged the leather gloves from her slender hands, her nail-enamel a blood red against her bronzed skin.

Annie tried to ignore her. Drawing a nail brush laden with mauve lacquer down her client's nail bed, she forced herself to concentrate on the task at hand. She was working. Jillian could wait. Annie swept another length of color down the nail bed, nicking the woman's skin. She cursed under her breath. Abruptly releasing the woman's finger, she dunked the brush back into its bottle. "Will you excuse me for a moment?" She was only halfway through the manicure, but she couldn't sit here while that Devane woman stared at her. She'd ruin her client's manicure and have to start all over!

Her elderly client huffed, but allowed her to go without verbal objection. She would not make a scene. It simply wasn't done. Annie hurried over to Jillian. "Ms. Devane."

"Ms. Owens."

"What are you doing here?" She darted a glance toward the receptionist. A young brunette who had been with Trendz for two years, Bobbi Jo dropped her green-eyed gaze to her appointment book, pretending to skim down the schedule. She might be young but she was smart. "I thought I said I'd call you when I decided."

"Unfortunately one of my investors is placing pressure on me to move forward with the purchase of the other property. I'm here to give you one last chance. Have you made a decision?"

No. Yes. The amount of money continued to swell in Annie's mind even as she and Cal worked on the logging deal. Malcolm said he'd help which would definitely make things easier, but still... Jillian Devane's offer was straightforward and simple. Cash. A niggle of excitement shot through Annie. Maybe she should sidestep the whole logging headache and let *this* woman deal with roads and permits. She and Casey would have their money and Jillian could fiddle with the county government. "I have," Annie replied as coolly as she could, "but I'm unable to discuss it at the moment." She gestured over her shoulder to the woman sitting not so patiently in her nail chair. She also needed to get final approval from her daughter—Casey, the girl who'd run away. "Perhaps we could discuss it at another time?"

Jillian's eyes flashed but her face remained calm. "Perhaps you have not heard me. I am in need of making a decision. I have offered you five hundred thousand dollars for your interest in the property. Your daughter's interest," she clarified, a tad insultingly. "Either she is interested in selling or she is not."

Annie stepped back, glanced around the salon. Did Jillian have to say it so loud, right here in the center of her workplace? As expected, stylists were staring, dividing their attention between heads of hair beneath their hands and the scene unfolding in the foyer. Annie wished they could be having this discussion elsewhere, but Ms. Devane seemed intent on having it now. "Do you plan on building a hotel there?" Annie asked, taking a few more steps toward the front door, putting them as far out of earshot as possible.

"That is the plan."

Standing beneath a tangle of blue lighting fashioned into an abstract chandelier, Annie crossed her arms. "Don't you think it's a little close to the one Harris Hotels is building?"

"I do not worry about Harris Hotels," she purred, though Annie sensed that wasn't entirely true. Especially after the earful she received from Lacy on the subject.

"You know they've already started construction. Their hotel will be open well ahead of yours."

"That does not concern me." Golden eyes turned predatory, discarding any and all attempt at polite conversation. "Nor should it concern you." She retrieved a slim gold purse from a coat pocket, opened it and withdrew a check-book. She removed a pen looped to its side and held it ready. "Five hundred thousand?"

Annie balked. "You're going to write me a check?"

"Yes."

"For five hundred thousand dollars?"

Jillian nodded.

Annie couldn't believe it. Just like that, Jillian Devane scribbled out a check for five hundred thousand dollars. She handed it to Annie. Staring at the freshly inked handwriting, Annie reached for it, a mild tremble to her hand. On one slip of paper she held half a million dollars. Blow dryers whirred behind her, competing with idle small talk. Annie wrangled her attention to the check in hand. If Jillian was willing to pay this much for the land, Annie could only imagine what building a hotel would cost. The roads, the driveways, the permits... When would she start? Would it really interfere with Nick and Malcolm's hotel? Would she steal their guests? And Cal's job? Guilt seeped into her bones. He wanted that job.

He wanted to work for Harris Hotels. Doubt sank around her like a blanket of Smoky Mountain fog. Annie wasn't kidding herself. Selling could end any hope for a future with Cal.

"Ms. Owens?"

Annie hesitated. Ms. Devane was offering a lot of money, but the land might be worth more. She hadn't looked into it yet, not with everything going on. There hadn't been time! What she did know, was Trendz was not the place to negotiate. High money deals were not something one did standing around a salon. And Casey. Legally, it was her land. She should have input into this decision.

What would she think? Would she be okay with selling? Casey didn't care for Jeremiah, she'd made as much crystal clear. Sharing in the legacy of Ladd Springs would not be an important factor to her. Annie dropped her gaze to the check. But money would.

"Can I assume we have a deal?"

"What about a contract?" Annie realized in the spur of the moment. They should have something in writing, shouldn't they?

Jillian smiled thinly. "I only do business with people I trust."

Trust? She didn't even know her!

This was pressure, pure and simple. Jillian Devane was trying to force her into a deal, but Annie would not allow it. She might not know real estate like Ms. Devane, but she knew a sledgehammer when she felt one. Fighting a fresh rise of nerves, Annie responded in the most business-like tone she could muster, "I need to discuss final details with my daughter." She thrust the check toward Ms. Devane. "As you mentioned, it's her name on the deed. I'm only the trustee."

The vigor went out of Jillian's expression, reminding Annie of a cheetah who'd just lost its prey. "Yes, your daughter. However, as trustee, it should be your decision to sell or not."

Annie straightened, growing more comfortable in her role as savvy businesswoman in charge of hundreds of thousands in wealth. Pushing the check into Jillian's hands, she said, "I will consult with my daughter this evening so we may confer with our lawyer and finalize details," she declared with dignity, impressed how the brilliance of "conferring with her lawyer" struck from out of nowhere. What a great excuse—and a legitimate one at that! Dashing a glance toward the receptionist, Annie realized it was the truth. She *would* have to talk with her lawyer. Without a real estate agent, he'd be the one to transfer title.

Jillian reclaimed the check and slowly returned it to her purse. Snapping the clutch closed, she slipped it into a pocket. "You have my number. I'll be waiting for your reply tomorrow."

Annie stood firm, but even in boots she was several inches shy of Jillian's height, a height enhanced by black stiletto heels. "Thank you. Unfortunately with the holidays upon us, it might not be until the following week."

"Of course." Jillian dismissed her with a pert smile, clearly aware it was nothing more than another excuse. Annie held her breath and watched Jillian's fluid leggy stride sway beneath the length of fur as she pushed out through the front door. Lacy was right. Jillian Devane looked like she belonged on a runway in Paris and not in the hills of Tennessee.

Returning to her client, thoughts divided between work and Jillian, Cal and Casey, Annie sat rigid in her chair and reached for an unpainted fingernail.

"Are you okay to continue?" her client asked.

"Yes, Mrs. Weatherford, I'm fine." Annie reached for her hand again but the woman pulled back. "You don't look fine. What kind of business do you have with a foreigner like that, anyway?"

Startled by the blunt question, Annie wanted to belt back, "None of your business," but refused to be rude. "Mrs. Weatherford, what business I might or might not have with that woman is not important at the moment. Your manicure is." Annie touched upon her finger. "Now, please. If I may continue?"

Mrs. Weatherford sniffed. "Well, I *never*. Who walks away from her job without explanation?" She whipped a glance around their immediate vicinity. Annie thought she was actually going to get up and leave but managed to hold her tongue. Strap it to her cheek was more like it. God knows she didn't need to alienate Mrs. Weatherford, one of the busier gossipers in town. She was likely to *make up* things to say about Annie and the strange woman in town! Calming the spatter of nerves in her chest, Annie replied, "She's new to the area and looking to have her nails done. I was only trying to accommodate her."

Sufficiently mollified, Mrs. Weatherford didn't say another word about it and Annie could only hope it stayed that way. She had enough trouble keeping her lies under wrap as she was beginning to feel like Lacy and her crossed fingers and non-fibs!

The door to Trendz swung open again and Annie's heart caught. Lacy breezed in and made a beeline straight for her nail chair. Annie's pulse hammered between her ears. Had she seen Jillian Devane leave the salon?

"Hi, Annie."

"Hi, Lacy." Annie thrust an unwelcome edge into her voice, informing Lacy that she was busy working and couldn't talk.

Without missing a beat, Lacy asked, "Did I just see Jillian Devane leave here?"

Annie groaned inwardly. Her sister never had been very good at taking hints. Pretending not to hear her, Annie asked, "Are you here to get your hair done?"

"No. I came to see if you wanted to go maternity shopping with me." Lacy acknowledged Annie's client with a smile and announced, "I'm four months pregnant."

Mrs. Weatherford smiled. "Congratulations, dear!" Eyeing Lacy's stomach under the black fitted silk sweater, she complimented, "And you're not even showing the slightest lump."

"Not yet," Lacy beamed with a light pat to her belly, "but she's in there."

"You already know it's a she?"

"I do. I spoke with a psychic and she said I was going to have a baby girl," Lacy informed her proudly.

"A psychic?" Mrs. Weatherford's enthusiasm took a nose dive as she pretended to take Lacy seriously. "Really?"

Annie rolled her eyes and swiped nail polish over the woman's nails as fast as she could, catching a strong whiff of polish as she dunked and painted, dunked and painted.

"Yes," Lacy replied unequivocally, then returned her sights to Annie. "I don't know why that Devane woman is still poking her nose around here. You'd best steer clear of her. I told you, Malcolm says she's up to no good."

Annie was tired of hearing about Malcolm and Nick's fears when it came to Jillian Devane. "He has nothing to worry about. His hotel has already been started. Why should it matter if another one goes up?"

"Matter?" Lacy gasped, spanking Mrs. Weatherford with an indignant glance. "Because she's out to sabotage them, that's why!"

Annie grunted. She did not want to be having this discussion, especially in front of a client. "I think you're blowing it out of proportion."

"I am not," Lacy nipped back. "She'd tried to ruin Nick and Malcolm before, and she's trying to do it again."

"They look like they're doing fine to me."

"Only because Malcolm is a genius."

Annie could see holes burning through Mrs. Weatherford's otherwise detached demeanor. If she was trying to act like she wasn't listening, she was doing a horrible job.

Lacy perched a hand on her hip. "Now listen, what I came here for was to ask you if you want to go with me to buy some baby clothes. I was thinking maybe this Saturday we could drive to Chattanooga."

"Fine," Annie replied. Anything to move Lacy away from the ears of Mrs. Weatherford—even if it meant shopping over Thanksgiving weekend, the busiest time of the year!

"Perfect. How about we go after breakfast?"

Lacy and Malcolm had breakfast at Fran's every Saturday morning. Like clockwork, they arrived at nine and left at ten. "I'll meet you there."

"Yay!" Lacy squealed. "Toodles!"

"Toodles," Annie muttered under her breath and watched her sister scamper out of the salon, praying she kept quiet about the Jillian Devane sighting.

Chapter Ten

As Annie turned into her apartment complex, the futility of her situation swallowed her whole. It wasn't fair that Delaney's life was turning out so perfectly. Her daughter Felicity was in college, her tuition bills paid in full, her love life complete as she dated Travis Parker—the good son. Annie's daughter opted for the drop-out, the one Parker child who refused to attend college. Then there was Delaney's love life. It was as picture-perfect as her daughter's, her wagon hitched securely to the wealthy Nick Harris. Not only would Delaney run the stables for the hotel, she'd build a home on the property, a magnificent retreat for herself and Nick. According to Lacy, they were working with one of the architects for Harris Hotels and creating a real masterpiece of a log cabin, including cathedral ceilings, massive exposed beams and huge antler chandeliers. Lacy said they were building a personal spa, too, complete with sauna and hot tub.

Annie considered the aging two-story apartment building in which she lived, and her spirits sank even further. She couldn't afford a home, modest or otherwise. Supporting two on her nail income over the years made it tough to save up for a down payment let alone keep up with mortgage payments, taxes and insurance. The little money she had managed to accumulate went to pay the hospital bill for Casey's overdose. It was a bill she paid gladly, grateful to have her daughter alive, but still. Her finances had since careened into a ditch.

Parking, she dropped her head back against the headrest. Life stunk. Stunk like road kill. Cutting the engine, Annie stared at her building, feeling no desire to go inside. It was empty. An empty apartment in a barren, rundown complex. Staring into her rearview mirror, she pondered the night ahead. Friday night would find her home alone. Cal had called every day this week, but she'd blown him off. She wasn't in the mood. She wasn't in the mood for anything. The blue car parked in the row of spaces behind hers drew her attention. She sharpened her focus. *Casey?*

Annie bolted upright in her seat and pushed open her door. Leaping from her vehicle, she ran across the parking lot to be sure. Scrutinizing the license plate, the numbers confirmed it. She whipped her head toward her building. Her pulse kicked. *Casey was home?* Grabbing her purse, Annie ran up the stairs and jabbed her keys into the door, opening it with a shove. "Casey?" she called out, heart pounding as she stumbled inside. "Casey, are you here?"

The light slanting out from beneath her daughter's bedroom door opened the flood gates of hope. *Casey was home.* Annie hurried down the hallway and rapped on the door. "Casey."

Within seconds, the door opened and she found herself staring into the sullen-faced expression of her only child. Black hair fell limp around her face, blue eyes were devoid of cheer as Casey hung a hand from the door jamb. "What?"

"What are you doing here? I mean, you're welcome to be here," Annie added quickly, a rush of nerves flitting through her chest, "but why? What happened?" Panic sliced her heart. "Are you okay?"

"I'm fine."

"Then what?"

"Troy got fired."

Annie's pleasure skidded off the road. "Fired? What happened?"

Casey walked past her mother and into the living room. Annie followed, a million thoughts zipping through her mind—the reason Troy could have been fired, the consequences... Casey plopped herself onto the sofa and crossed her arms over her chest. "He showed up for work late and they fired him."

"For being late?" Annie asked. "He was late one time and they fired him?"

"Yep."

Annie stared at the back of Casey's black head of hair. Something wasn't right. The man she met in the office spoke very highly of Troy. Being late once didn't warrant a firing. Something else had to have been at play. But unwilling to start a fight, Annie focused on her daughter. She rounded the sofa and sat next to Casey. "So you came home." Casey glared at her as though she were an idiot. *She was here, wasn't she*? Annie took a deep breath and exhaled slowly, controlling her reaction. She was here. Casey was home. "Do you plan to call Fran and ask about your job? I know she could use the help."

"I don't want to work at a diner." Casey picked up the television remote and pointed it at the television.

"Well, I realize it's not what you want to do forever, but until you figure out what you do want to do, it'll pay the bills."

"What bills? I have Ladd Springs, remember? I should be *getting* money, not paying it."

Irritated she had to compete with the television volume, Annie said, "Casey, earning money from the property will take time. It's like we discussed before, Felicity's deal has been in the works for months. Cal and I are working on a plan that will bring in quite a bit of money. Or possibly we could sell," she broached warily. "Sell the land outright and collect a lump sum. Either way, there would be enough money for you to go to college, start a savings account."

"I don't want to go to college."

"Why not?"

"Because I hate school."

"Oh, well, sure, high school is boring but college is different. You get to pick which classes you want, take only those subjects that interest you." Annie didn't know any of this from personal experience. She was only going off what she'd heard at the salon over the years. Most stories about college were positive, people claiming it was the best time in their lives. Why would Casey want to pass up the opportunity? Going to college completely paid for seemed like an easy yes. Didn't get any easier than if it slid off a greasy griddle. Why fight it? "Why don't we look into it a bit before we decide? You might find that you'll change your mind."

"Doubt it."

Annie suppressed the urge to fuss at Casey for her horrible attitude. She was being downright ornery when all her mother was trying to do was make a plan. There was no reason they couldn't discuss the issue of college, but for the moment Annie thought it best to let it go. She wasn't dying on that hill tonight. "Are you hungry?"

"No."

"Are you sure? We could go to Fran's for a cheeseburger."

"No thanks."

Expelling her breath in a ragged stream, Annie cut her losses and accepted that her daughter had no interest in bonding. Shouldn't be a surprise. Casey hadn't been interested before she left, why would she care to now? Didn't mean Annie had to give up, merely change tactics. Picking a fuzz of lint from her skirt, she broached, "Did Troy come back with you?"

Casey looked at her. "Is it a problem if he did?"

"No. It's just a question."

"Yes."

"Did he go home?"

"Yes."

Yes, no, yes, no—Annie was getting nowhere. Probing Casey for details was going to reveal nothing more than the fact that she was home, which Annie could see with her own two eyes. Casey pushed up from the couch and headed for her bedroom. Once again, she closed herself off from the world.

Annie stared at the television screen, a rapid-fire commercial squawking a hundred miles an hour about cleaning supplies. Grabbing the remote, she muted the noise. Tomorrow she'd stop by the diner and tell Fran Casey was home. While she said she didn't want to work at the diner, she might change her mind—provided Fran was willing to take her back. Frustration soured in her belly. Where had she gone wrong with Casey? It couldn't be by her example. She'd worked at Trendz for almost ten years, and another salon for eight years before that. Never had she shown up late, or missed a day, unless it was utterly impossible for her to get there. Some days it meant slinging a baby bag over her shoulder and traipsing in with a baby on her hip. Other days it meant calling on Candi for a favor. Babysitters called in sick, child care centers were expensive... Annie managed the best she could and while there had been difficult days, she saw to each and every one of her responsibilities without fail. Why did Casey take to hers so carelessly?

First thing in the morning, Annie headed to Fran's Diner. The heat in her car was on the blink and she'd been frozen the entire ten minute drive. It was even colder outside, the wind biting against her skin. Thankfully she'd thought to wear a hat, leaving her face the only part uncovered. Hustling toward the old retro-styled building, she tucked gloved hands beneath her arms and hastened her step. As she reached the door, it swung open as Cal Foster held it for her. "Well, isn't it my lucky day. The sunshine just walked in."

Annie grinned despite herself and ducked her head as she passed him. "Hi, Cal."

"Aren't you a sight for my pair of lonesome eyes?"

Enveloped by the warm interior of Fran's Diner, the air laced with the aroma of baking biscuits and fried bacon, Annie frowned. "I'm sorry I haven't called you, but I've been so busy I haven't had the first chance." Removing her gloves, she stuck one in each coat pocket.

"You don't need to make excuses for me, darlin'. I understand."

She smiled, genuinely happy to see him. Shaking her hair, she removed her coat with Cal's assistance, then loosened her knit scarf. Suddenly she was famished. "Have you eaten breakfast?" she asked him.

"Waitin' on you."

It was a pathetic lie, but one she jumped on. "Care to join me?"

Gentle hazel brown eyes cradled her within a gaze accentuated by the soft camel flannel of his shirt. Coupled with jeans and boots, Cal was pure country, pure gentleman. "Couldn't think of a better way to start my day."

Fran breezed. "Good morning, sugar!" She kissed Annie's cheek and asked, "You two need a table?"

"Please."

"I happen to have the best one in the house available." She waved them to follow her past the rounded glass pie case and into the back corner by a window. It was private yet offered a nice view of the sunny outdoors. A woman waved to her and from a distant table, a client from the salon. Annie acknowledged her as Fran dashed off to the kitchen promising, "Coffee and juice, comin' right up!"

Taking her seat, Annie peered out the window at vacant lot behind the diner littered with leaves, the trees swaying in the wind. It was supposed to warm up considerably, reaching a high of seventy-five. Perfect fall weather, if you asked her, even more perfect after a good night's sleep. Annie had slept clear through to morning, knowing her daughter was home. Seeing Cal only added to her pleasure. "Guess who came back home last night."

"Casey?"

She nodded, warmed by the satisfaction swirling in his eyes. Sweet eyes, gentle eyes, Cal was a man who understood things, could connect emotionally with a woman where so many men could not. Annie found it a very appealing trait in a man. She had no use for bold and blustery. She wanted a man with a good head on his shoulders and a sympathetic ear. "I'm real happy she's home. She wasn't very friendly last night, but I'm sure she'll get over it."

"Give her time. She's probably smarting from the sting of failure. Girl runs away from home, the last thing she wants to do is return with her tail between her legs. I'd give her space. She knows where to find you."

Again it occurred to Annie that Cal was wise beyond his experience. It was almost as if he understood what she was going through from personal experience. But as far as she knew, he didn't have children. An ex-wife, but no kids. And considering all the time they'd been spending together, she should know. "I think you're right. Unfortunately, Troy's home, too."

Cal cocked his head. "What about his job?"

"He was fired for being late."

"Being late? How late we talkin'? Did he not show up?"

Annie shrugged, the savory scent of eggs and bacon filling her nose as a waitress delivered plates the table beside them. Her stomach growled with envy as she took in the sight of food, complete with a side of steaming grits and plump biscuits. She pulled her attention away. "I don't know. Like I said, Casey wasn't in a talkative mood. All I managed to get from her was that he was fired for being late."

"Hmm."

"Didn't sound right to me, either."

A waitress appeared tableside. "Can I get you some coffee, juice?"

"I think Fran has got us covered," Cal replied.

"Okay." The young brunette practically bubbled with enthusiasm. Pencil and notepad drawn and ready she asked. "Do you know what you'd like for breakfast?"

"I'll have two eggs, sunny side up with a stack of pancakes, bacon and a side of grits."

Annie added, "I'll have an order of scrambled eggs and grits."

Fran swept in behind the girl, sliding cups and saucers onto the table with a smile. "You two have everything you need?"

"We do."

Satisfied, Fran and the waitress trotted off.

Cal pursed his lips. "So they're both back..."

"They are."

"Well, maybe I can help Troy." Cal eyed her cautiously. "If it's okay with you, that is."

"Help him how?"

"He works with horses and the man at the ranch said he was a real fine boy..." Cal paused, as though churning something through his brain. "I might be able to get him a position working my Daddy's ranch—until he can figure out his next step, of course."

Annie reached across the table. "Cal, you don't have to do that."

"I want to."

A slow smile creeping onto his lips, he took her hand and held it. About to protest further, she thought better about it. Cal was a good man. A kind man. But he was also smart. He knew Troy's situation. If he felt it was a good match, who was she to disagree? "Thank you, Cal." Three words she was beginning to say an awfully lot to this man. "That's nice of you to offer."

"Consider it done." With a light squeeze, he released her hand and said, "Now on to a more positive note. I talked with the County Manager and he told me the permit would be no trouble. Two weeks at most."

"Really?"

Cal set elbows to the table, crossing his arms. "So things are looking up."

Annie felt it was true. Casey was home, the permit would be no trouble—if she decided to go with logging—though she hadn't made a decision. The subject of selling was something she had yet to discuss with Casey. Jillian had given her time, but she wouldn't wait forever.

Cal quieted, and she sensed he had something on his mind. "Cal?"

"Yes?"

"You look as though you have something important on your mind. Care to share?" she asked with an encouraging smile. Annie wanted him to share. She wanted him to feel comfortable enough with her to share whatever was on his mind. If she was being totally honest, she wanted a lot more than that. A zip of desire scurried through her. Peering at his clean-shaven skin, his soft brown hair, she wondered what it would be like to be with him. His appeal was easy and natural. Even his cologne was subtle. She savored a private smile. But then again, everything about Cal was subtle and mellow. Easy.

Yes, she decided. That's what he was. Cal was easygoing and comfortable. The twinge low in her belly warned her she thought he was all that and more, but it wasn't her place to make the first move. It was the man's.

A smile worked its way onto his lips and his gaze softened. "Well, since you asked, our discussion has been weighing on my mind."

"Our discussion?" And it hit her. His job offer. Annie's heart fell. *How could she have forgotten*?

Cal slid the napkin-rolled silverware aside. "Have you given it any more thought?"

Which part, she wanted to ask—your new job or me moving?

"Annie?"

Bothered by the sudden plunge in his mood, she felt bad. Annie didn't want to be the sour milk in his cereal. She wanted to be happy for him. It was clear he wanted the position as General Manager. But she and Delaney didn't get along. If she and Cal ever did become serious, it could put a damper on their relations. A confusing predicament. Muddled. Delaney was leasing the land to Harris Hotels. She was practically married to the owner of the company, Nick Harris. Working for Delaney was the last thing Annie wanted to do. While Cal didn't seem to mind the connection, she did. "I think the job is a great opportunity for you, Cal," Annie said, injecting as much cheer into her voice as she could. "I'm just not sure where I fit in."

"I'd like you to fit in with *me*." At her confusion, he laughed, a flush tingeing his cheeks. "You know what I mean."

Annie tensed. Drawing her coffee near, she was hit by the moist, sharp scent. "As in me work for the hotel, too?" she asked, swept up in visions of Delaney marching around, barking orders.

Cal grew serious. "Is it only me, Annie?"

"Only you what?"

"I thought we had something growing between us but you seem to be avoiding it."

"I'm not." She gulped. "We do." Heart suddenly racing, she nodded. "We do."

"But it can't include Serenity Springs," he concluded dully.

"I didn't say that," she objected quickly, then dropped her gaze to the cup and saucer in hand. She encircled it with her fingers, the white porcelain cup hot to the touch. Kinda like the hot rise at her neck.

"Okay, but are you *feeling* it?"

Annie didn't know. She didn't know what she was feeling other than she liked Cal. She liked him a lot and had been pondering a life with him. She knew he was interested but things were complicated. She had a past. She had issues. Cal didn't understand what it was like to struggle. He'd grown up with money and land, prestige and position. The Fosters were a staple in the community, one tied to Delaney by their son Jack's marriage, their granddaughter Felicity. Cal and Delaney were family. Annie didn't feel it was fair to allow her relationship with Delaney to stand in the way, but honestly, that's what if felt like at the moment.

Slowly, Annie lifted her head up and met his expectant gaze. Somehow, Delaney Wilkins had once again managed to insert herself into Annie's business. Sort of. "It's complicated, Cal. I have a history with Delaney, a history that isn't wonderful."

"This isn't about Delaney. It's about you and me."

"Cal."

"Annie."

The busy restaurant melted away. The clamor of cooks in the kitchen, the rush of servers moving in and around tables, nothing existed but her and Cal and the mountain of emotion between them. He was asking her a question. He was asking if a future together was out of the question if he accepted Malcolm's job offer. "I don't want to stand in your way of a great opportunity, Cal, but it's like I said, I've been needing a change and well..."

"You don't want to limit yourself to Ladd Springs."

When Cal said it, it made her sound like a bad person. Shallow. Almost as if she was dumping him for greener pastures. "I don't want to limit myself at all."

"I see."

Annie shot a hand across the table but Cal didn't yield. "But that doesn't mean I don't want to be with you, I *do*."

"Do you want me to move with you?"

The seat bench dropped out from beneath her. "What?"

"I would. If you want me to..."

"Cal."

"Annie."

She was stunned. She didn't know what to say. Cal would forgo a fantastic job offer to be with her? Nerves sputtered and popped. It was the last thing she expected. It was more than she expected. Thoughts of the two of them together in a very serious way flooded her mind, her heart. She and Cal, *together*. But they'd never said the words, the kind of words that would warrant such a sacrifice. Annie pressed trembling fingers to the table.

"Let's say we start with something more simple," he suggested, easing her building angst. "I'd like you and Casey to join my family for Thanksgiving."

"Thanksgiving dinner?"

"I think it's time the family got to know you better." He smiled. "We start around one, if that suits you."

Amazed by Cal's seamless switch from offering to move with her to the Foster family dinner, Annie's mind was spinning. Was this a trial run for the two of them as a serious couple? Annie already knew the Fosters. His family was well-known throughout the community, the boys ranging in age from hers to several years older. She'd known them all her life, but going to their home with Cal for a holiday meal was something different. It was significant. Serious.

Annie glanced about the restaurant, the normality of hometown gossip against a backdrop of clinking utensils and suddenly felt foolish. Almost forty years old and she was *nervous* about going to a grown man's home for supper. It was ridiculous! Insanity, though a fresh swarm of nerves pushing through her stomach and chest served to undercut the notion. "Sure," she replied, mentally scrambling through her schedule and wondering if Casey would prove resistant.

"My folks will be pleased. They've been hearing an awful lot about you."

Which meant Cal was talking an awful lot about her. Anticipation zipped her spine tight as a rod. "Yes, well..." she stammered, "that's nice of you to say."

"There's a whole lot more I'd like to say." He glanced around the diner. "But this isn't the place."

Chapter Eleven

Arms perched along the four-board fencing of his family's ranch, Cal spit a peanut shell into a Solo cup as he watched Troy Parker work a horse. The midday sun soaked the landscape around them in warmth, fending off the worst of the chill. His cowboy hat kept the glare from his vision. Hills rose on all sides of his family's property, the colors of fall vibrant, invigorating to his spirit. Fall had always been Cal's favorite time of year because it signaled a time to slow down and cozy up. Thoughts of Annie came to mind, the two of them nestled around a fireplace, snuggling close. These days, thoughts of Annie permeated him, acting as a constant reminder of all he lost in Arizona and everything he wanted to regain in Tennessee.

Drawn back to Troy who stood in the middle of the round pen, a coiled rope in his hand, Cal watched with interest as the boy kept pace with the horse, forcing the animal to run the perimeter. Dressed in a black T-shirt and jeans, he and the mahogany-colored horse stood out against the white four-board fencing. The boy's attention never left the animal as he walked a tight circle in the center, the animal in constant motion along the fence. Troy was pushing him, creating a sense of leadership between horse and human. Troy spoke the entire time, making an occasional clicking sound from his mouth. With one ear locked down, Cal could tell the animal was listening to Troy's every word, waiting for his next command. Troy made a quick-charge step, then backed off. The horse reacted, slowing his pace. Cal smiled when Troy increased his pace in the center of the pen, noting the horse did likewise. Another quick step and Troy stopped. The horse stopped, shaking its head with a loud neigh. When Troy didn't move, the horse approached him warily, tentatively, walking all the way to Troy, who reached out and stroked his snout. "Atta boy," he said calmly, patting the animal's side. "Good job." The horse licked his lips, a sure sign he understood.

Cal was impressed. This horse had come to the Fosters from another ranch to be re-trained and sold. The animal used to be a show jumper but about a year ago went sour. The horse had no more interest in being ridden, in fact, he'd bucked a rider off, causing his owner to take him out of commission. At the moment Troy was evaluating the animal's personality, assessing how much work would be needed to get the horse back into shape. Cal believed the animal simply needed someone to trust, and from his vantage point Troy was the right man for the job. "He's a smart one," Cal called out.

Troy glanced over and nodded. "Sure is," he replied, then began the process again.

"Cal!"

At the frantic call, Cal pushed from the fence and started jogging in the direction of the voice. Coming from the stables, it belonged to a senior stable hand known around the ranch as "Old Joe." "What's going on?" Cal shouted.

"Ginger is having a baby!"

He tipped his hat back. "She's foaling?"

"Right this minute!" The elder man eagerly waved him over. "Come see."

Without thinking, Cal turned and called out to Troy. "Troy, come see! One of the mares is foaling!" Watching a foal come into the world was one of the most beautiful sights to behold. His daddy used to include the boys in every birth, teaching them the ways of the ranch, and it seemed natural to include Troy.

Troy hesitated, his expression gripped by the confusion of an employee who'd just been asked to perform a duty outside his job description. "*C'mon*, son. We drop everything around here for a new baby!"

Erupting into a wide grin, Troy gave the animal a vigorous stroke, then adjusted his hat and ran over. Cal clapped him on the back. "Have you ever seen a foal being born?"

"Yes sir. My daddy had Travis and me practice whenever possible."

"He's a good man, your father. It's one of the most incredible events I've ever witnessed." Cal managed every foaling but missed the birth of his own daughter. A fact that ate at him to this day. "Let's go."

"Yes, sir," Troy replied gladly and followed Cal back to the stables.

A walnut brown mare paced the center corridor, taking her time as she walked back and forth, swishing her bundled tail side to side. Cal could see the first bubble of white placenta poking free from her rear. He tossed his peanut cup into a barrel-styled garbage can and looked to Old Joe.

"Her water broke and she's squirting milk," Old Joe informed Cal and Troy as they approached.

"She's ready," Cal agreed. As they neared, he could hear the mare's mild grunts. The rise of hay was strong against his nostrils, along with the scent of leather and horse. "C'mon, Ginger. Slow and easy wins the race."

"She's a beauty," Troy said, admiration shining in his eyes.

"One of our finest Arabians," Cal replied.

"We have Quarter Horses," Troy said, then pointed to her tail bound by hot pink tape. "We wrap the tails before birth, too."

"It's a practice we began years ago. Once we began breeding for other folks, my daddy insisted."

"The pink is a nice touch," Troy smirked.

Cal winked. "That's my momma's input. No mare should be foaling in anything but pink. Not on her ranch."

Troy chuckled and watched with Cal as the Foster's senior stable hand guided Ginger into an open, spacious pen. The horse went without protest. Circling, she dropped gently to her side. Panting, she undulated, then rolled onto her back, kicking her legs up and out like a dog scratching its back. She thrashed her head back and forth across the hay-covered floor, trying to work her baby free. Powerful rear muscles contracted, relaxed, and a milky sac emerged. A slender hoof was visible through the sheer pliable membrane. "Lookee there!" exclaimed the stable hand. "She's a coming through!"

Excitement swept through Cal as he watched the placenta spit out in fits of air and liquid. The mare continued to grunt as the three men stood idle. In awe, really. The birth of a foal was an incredibly normal act of nature, yet it never ceased to amaze him, affecting him in a way words could not describe. He imagined the same would have been true had he been there for Emily's birth instead of passed out at home.

Pushing up to her feet, the mare paced again, this time with two hooves sticking out from her backside. Cal figured she must be in serious discomfort. Troy must have been thinking the same thing, whispering encouragement to the mare as she walked and pushed. "C'mon, girl. That's it. You're doing fine, really fine."

Cal smiled. Men were usually out of their element when it came to things like birth, but not Troy. He was up close and personal and seemed thoroughly intrigued. He was a horseman, Cal mused. It was in his blood.

Back down the mare went, rolling and moaning. "She's trying to get it into position," Old Joe observed.

Cal had seen this before. Some births came quicker than others, and a mare would do what she could to help her baby along. Sometimes a man could lend a helping hand by pulling on the hooves, but that was the last thing he wanted to do. Cal preferred to let nature take its course.

"She looks like she's struggling," Troy noted, vigilance entering his gaze.

"This here's her first," Old Joe told him.

Troy nodded, but remained intent on the mare and her progress.

It looked to Cal like Troy was analyzing the situation, summing up what needed to be done and when. So far, Cal liked what he saw in the young man.

Old Joe pointed to the emerging foal. "She's a good size."

Buttocks contracting, Ginger's enormous belly rose and fell with each effort. Her tail twitched and she moaned louder. Troy didn't say anything, only watched as the sac tore open revealing a slick black hoof. Resting, the mare paused her efforts. Concern rippled across Troy's features.

"Should I give her a hand?" Old Joe asked.

Cal stood by, waiting for the horse's lead. "Give her a minute." He looked to Troy. "What do you think?"

Without looking away from the horse, he nodded. "I'd give her a minute."

Satisfied they were of like mind, the men watched the animal lying on her side, veins bulging on the underside of her belly. She grunted, pushed, paused, pushed and paused. Fluid gushed out over the hay covered floor. Sticks of hay adhered to the creamy sac. When nothing significant changed, Cal gave the go ahead. "Give her a hand."

When Joe went to grab the legs, the mare snorted, made an evasive roll and pinned her ears flat as she raised her head to look at him. "Whoa," he mumbled and released.

Momma didn't want help.

Troy glanced at Cal's stable hand, then to Cal. Pushing again, the mare made an inch or two more progress, but the foal slipped back inside. It appeared the baby was stuck. The mare fought to expel it, thrusting and pushing, but came up short. She dropped her head to the ground, groaning. Troy edged his way closer and encouraged softly, "That's it, momma. You can do it." The mare eyed him warily. "This ain't nothin' but a stroll through the park for you. You've got it," he said, darting a glance toward her rear, checking for progress.

"Careful, son," Old Joe warned. "She's already proven she doesn't want any help and we don't want to upset her.

Troy nodded that he heard, but never removed his eyes from the mare.

Cal held up a hand to Old Joe, noting with keen interest that the mare didn't fight Troy's close proximity. She was aware of him but didn't signal she wanted him gone. As Troy continued to whisper reassuring words to the horse, Cal kept tabs on the foal. If it remained stuck for too long, they were going to have to step in.

"C'mon, baby, you can do it. Keep pushing," Troy continued. Heaving her belly, the mare seemed to respond. Panting and grunting she pushed, rocking back and forth as she tried to ease her baby out. Troy stood and moved to her rear, speaking to her the entire time. "That's it, momma, we're almost there."

The stable hand looked to Cal in alarm. Cal shook his head. *Let him be.*

Troy grabbed the foal's hooves and tugged, his movements strong and smooth. The mare swiftly raised her head, ears twitching. She was alert, Cal thought, but calm. *Steady as she goes.* Troy pulled harder and the horse assisted, pushing in sync with him. "That's it, momma. You got this."

Cal could see the foal's snout through the veneer of birth sac, a white star marked the inky black between the eyes. Moving closer, he could clearly see the nostrils but no discernible movement. As the foal slid halfway out, Troy began ripping away the sac. The foal was gasping which concerned Cal.

Moving to one knee, Troy held the foal as the mare spit the remaining body out in one big swoosh of sac and fluid. Within Troy's grasp the foal blinked. Remaining on her side, momma was exhausted, her stomach hollowed from giving birth. Seconds passed and the foal continued to gasp. Cal rushed to Troy's side. "She isn't breathing."

Troy whipped off his T-shirt and vigorously dried the baby's head and neck, wiping fluid from the nose. The foal continued its gasp-like breathing and Troy extended its neck, lengthening it along the ground. He quickly examined the nose, then plugging the downward nostril, Troy drove his head to the foal's snout, beginning inhalations into the upper nostril.

"Grab the tube!" Cal commanded Joe as he watched Troy blowing breaths into the foal's nose. Glancing sideways as breathed, Troy was watching for the same thing Cal was—the rise and fall of the foal's chest.

The stable hand returned with an intubation tube and a stethoscope. Without being instructed, he thrust the stethoscope to Cal. Thirty seconds later, Troy lifted away from the foal. Inserting the ear tips, Cal placed a metal chest piece on the foal's upper body and listened for heartbeats. Troy stood on his knees and Cal instinctively knew the boy was ready to perform chest compressions if need be. Cal shook his head. He counted the heart rate to be fifty-five. Sitting back on his heels, Cal watched and waited and checked again. Pulse was steadily increasing and strengthening. Sixty-eight. Cal exhaled a sigh of relief. "Good work."

The stable was quiet, the scent of birth and sweat saturating the air within the small confines of the stall. The mare was alert, partially sitting up on folded legs. As momma began to move, the men stepped out of her way, giving her unfettered access to her baby. The slender foal scooted near its mother, stretching its hay-clad legs as it nuzzled against her body. Momma licked her baby, grunting protectively. For the next several minutes, the men shared stories of foaling. Troy explained how he learned about CPR when he was fifteen. One of their mares went through the very same thing, delivering a whopping ninety-eight pound foal.

Cal laughed, relieved the crisis had passed. "This one here has got to rival that."

"I'd say she looks about a hundred pounds," Troy agreed.

"She's definitely a big one," Old Joe said. "And black as night. Careful, Troy, or this little filly might mistake you for her daddy!"

Cal reached down and lifted a hind leg. "She's a *he*," he announced.

Troy laughed. Cal detected a band loosening around the boy's heart. Knots of tension released from his features and he was glad for it. The boy had done an outstanding job.

At a nudge from the mare, the foal began the awkward process of wrangling its legs to a standing position. Each inch appeared to tax the young horse, gangly limbs struggling for balance. Wobbling, he fell flat. But the spirited foal didn't give up. Without delay, he tried again, held steady, then took his first step.

"Woo-hoo!" Joe called out. "We have a race horse on our hands!"

"And a fighter," Troy added.

"Delaney's hands," Cal corrected.

"Delaney?" Troy questioned in surprise.

"This one's already been promised to Delaney Wilkins."

Troy gaped at him. "Miss Delaney bought a horse?"

The mare rose to her feet and the foal instinctively headed for her teats. Another miracle of nature, Cal mused. Old Joe went about the business of caring for the umbilical cord, seeing that mother and baby were taken care of, a sight that pulled a smile from him. "This one and several others. Actually, she and Nick."

Realization loosened the hold on Troy's bewilderment. "For the new hotel."

"For the new hotel," Cal verified. "This one here's named Vegas."

"Vegas," Troy repeated, trying it on for size.

"Mr. Harris and Mr. Ward like to gamble," Cal told him, imagining everyone had their vice. But vices were fine, so long as a man didn't take them too far, losing control of himself in the process. Lassoing his thoughts around Troy, Cal wondered if Troy was continuing his hankering for alcohol. Annie had relayed the boy's history, a tidbit about her daughter Casey, included. She was concerned about the girl dating Troy and Cal understood why. Mixing alcohol and drugs was dangerous enough without the added pressure of emotional instability. *Had Troy quit on account of his girlfriend?*

Cal hoped so. Gerald Foster's four boys had blazed a bourbon-soaked swath through two counties and ten years, dropping the old man's tolerance to zero. If Troy was caught drinking, he'd be shown the door. Fixing a hand to Troy's shoulder, Cal asked, "What do you say you and Casey join Annie and me for Thanksgiving here on the ranch?"

Troy looked up at him, shock skirting through his gaze. "Sir?"

"Annie is joining my family for Thanksgiving next week. I'd like it if you and Casey would come, too."

Troy pushed his hat back and replied, "Well, my folks are expecting me home, but I can look into it."

Cal nodded. "Please do. I understand if you can't, but if you decide otherwise, you're welcome here. Festivities begin at one. We'll set two extra places for you, just in case."

Pleasure eased past the surprise in his dark eyes. "Yes sir, thank you. That would be great."

Chapter Twelve

Casey set glass and straw on the lunch counter before an old man, then retreated through a kitchen service door. The main lunch crowd was gone by now, giving her breathing room. The air in the kitchen was dense with oil which clung to her skin, permeating her pores. Nearby, two cooks talked idly as they watched four meat patties sizzling on a metal grill slab. Neither bothered to make eye contact with her, knowing she wasn't interested in chit-chat. Casey only cared to talk to Jimmy Sweeney and he was off today. Or Troy. A rise of desire flushed through her breast. But he was working for the Fosters now—because of her mother's boyfriend. Since the ranch was located a half-hour away, Troy didn't have time to come visit during her lunch break. She'd have to wait until after five to see him, speak with him. The time away was killing her, but when Fran had forgiven her, offer to take her back on staff, Casey had no choice. She didn't want to come back, but she needed a job, money. If not the diner, where else would she go, what could she do? Wash hair at the salon where her mother worked? Sweep the floors?

No, thanks. All the jobs stunk. All of them. She only wanted to be with Troy.

Then out of the blue her mother suggested college. While the idea of more school was not appealing, when her mom said she'd pay for her living expenses, Casey had almost said yes. If only to get out of this town and on her own, she'd go to college. Though Casey still couldn't believe she was going to get that much money from logging the property. Money she wasn't allowed to touch until she was thirty. Resentment poured into her.

Grabbing a plate of French fries, Casey pushed, backside first, against the door and delivered the food, serving up the perfunctory smile required by Fran. Whatever. College might be cool except then she'd have to leave Troy and that wasn't gonna happen. She loved Troy. He was the only one who cared about her, believed in her. Without Troy she was nothing.

Delaney Wilkins entered the diner and Casey tensed. Her long blonde hair was pulled back into a ponytail, her jeans and cropped denim jacket faded and worn. Now that she had money, why didn't she buy new clothes? Casey would. She'd buy a whole new wardrobe! Spotting her, Delaney headed over and Casey braced for impact.

Delaney strolled up to the counter. "Casey."

"Miss Delaney," she acknowledged, but didn't want to appear welcoming. She doubted Delaney approved of her relationship with Troy. Probably wished both boys were still chasing after Felicity. With a shoulder to Delaney, Casey checked on a couple seated at the end of the counter. When she asked if they needed anything, they barely acknowledged her. She glared down at them. Rude. People were rude.

"Glad to see you back on the job," Delaney said when she headed back her way.

"Can't say the same."

Delaney smiled. "Not your dream job, I understand. But sometimes we have to pay the bills first, seek our pleasure second."

"I guess." Casey sought a wet rag and wiped at the counter.

"Is Troy back, too?" Casey nodded. "That's great." Delaney lowered to a seat. "I hear he's working over at the Foster ranch."

Remaining intent on her busy work, Casey kept her response to a minimum. "He is."

"I've heard great things about him."

Emotion stormed to the surface. "Troy knows his horses."

"That's what I understand."

If Delaney was going to ask why he got fired from the other ranch, Casey wasn't going to tell her. It was none of her business and she'd only think less of him. And the firing wasn't even his fault. It was hers. Stuffing the damp cloth beneath the counter, Casey could feel Delaney staring, feel the questions and judgments swirling in her brain.

"Troy's a good guy," Delaney said, hooking Casey's gaze securely to her own. "He's smart, too. He'll find his way. You will, too," Delaney added.

Casey stilled. Did Delaney know *everything* about their lives?

"If you ever need anything, I want you to know you can call me."

"Why?"

"I care about you. We're family."

Casey ground her teeth. Family. Because of that man, Jeremiah Ladd.

"I'm not going to pretend it's the best situation, Casey. I won't lie to you. Your mother and I have our issues. But our problems shouldn't interfere with your well-being. You're a Ladd and I'm a Ladd. We need to start acting like it."

"How come you put my mom in charge of the property then?"

"Because you're still young."

"So is Felicity," Casey asserted. "But you didn't put yourself in charge of her half."

"I am. I'm in charge until she's old enough to take control on her own."

"That's not what my mom says."

"It's not written that way, like it is in yours. Ernie signed the estate over to her specifically, but it works the same way. I'm in control and she understands why."

Casey glanced away.

For a moment neither said a word, content to allow the din of conversation to fill the void. A cook called up an order, customers talked quietly amongst themselves. Casey wished she were anywhere but here. The diner felt like a prison. A red and white smiley-faced prison. Five days a week she worked here. Five days of mind-numbing boredom, complete with nosy neighbors and well-meaning family.

"What are your plans, Casey? Do you have any?"

"Plans?"

Delaney nodded. "Do you plan to go to college? I understand your mother is making arrangements to have a section of the property logged. With the money you'll receive, you could go to college."

"She mentioned it." Delaney looked relieved to hear it. "But I said no."

"No?"

"No. For now. Maybe later. Depends."

"On Troy?" she asked knowingly.

She nodded and Delaney remained silent. Did she not approve of her choices? Was she judging her right now?

Casey didn't care. It was her life. She was an adult. She could do as she pleased, whether Delaney or her mother approved or not. "I haven't decided what I'm doing yet."

"I see."

"Can I ask you something?" The question burst from Casey's lips before she had a mind to think better of it.

Delaney folded her hands atop the counter. "Sure, anything."

"Did your boyfriend have anything to do with beating up Jeremiah?"

Delaney's expression reflected the hit but she didn't move a muscle. "No. Why would you ask?"

"My mom thinks they might have followed Jeremiah, had him beat up to get him to leave town."

Delaney straightened on the stool. "She's wrong. They didn't need to beat him up to get him to leave town. They had information on him that they knew would ultimately land him in jail."

"He's in jail?"

"Didn't you know?"

Casey felt a rise of warmth around her neck and cheeks.
"No."

"I'm sorry. I thought your mother told you." Delaney
shook her head as though it were one more thing her mother
did wrong. "He was arrested for money he owed to a casino
out in Vegas."

Casey rolled her eyes to the ceiling. "What a loser," she
said, embarrassed yet again by the fact that he was her father.
What else weren't they telling her?

"Casey, Jeremiah's choices are no reflection on you. No
one thinks less of you because of him. You're eighteen and
your own woman." Delaney searched her gaze, an awkward
intimacy sneaking into their conversation. "Who you are from
here on out depends on *you*. No one else."

Tears pressed behind Casey's eyes. "Not in this town."
She crossed her arms tightly over her chest. "I might be a
Ladd but I'm Jeremiah's Ladd and people talk."

"They're not saying anything important."

"Hello, Delaney."

Delaney's smile evaporated and Casey was shocked to
see a brown-skinned Spanish-looking woman standing there.
She hadn't noticed her walk up. "So nice to see you again,"
the stranger said, sliding a huge pair of sunglasses onto her
head.

Delaney rose from her stool, squaring her shoulders with
the stranger. "What are you doing here?" she responded curt-
ly, and Casey sensed a cat fight coming on.

"It's a pleasure seeing you, too, Ms. Wilkins," the woman returned smoothly, mesmerizing Casey with her heavy
accent and overdone makeup. Her golden brown eyes were
lined thickly in black, her lashes brushed heavily with mascara, her cheeks bronzed a shimmery peach. Dressed in a
black fur coat and fitted black dress, she was thin as a stick.

"You have no business here," Delaney told her. "Your
property is an hour north."

"Ah, but that's where you're wrong. We're going to be
neighbors." She flicked a haughty gaze to Casey. "I'm pur-

chasing a beautiful tract of land that will suit my needs perfectly, allowing Nick and I to remain close," she emphasized, as though the words had double meaning.

"Neighbor? Who's selling?"

The dark woman smiled, wicked pleasure licking at her eyes. "You know I cannot reveal any details that might jeopardize my deal. Trust me that it is very near to you and we will be seeing quite a lot more of one another."

Delaney scowled. Troy breezed into the diner and Casey's heart skipped a beat. "Troy's here," she said for no reason, unsettled by the tension between the women. Delaney and the foreign woman both turned. Troy picked up on the showdown from across the diner and hurried his step. Where Casey was relieved, Delaney seemed unhappy to see him.

Handsome in his black T-shirt and jean jacket, his longish bangs combed to the side, Troy sized up the situation in two seconds. "Everything okay here?"

"It's fine, Troy."

Jealousy flared in Casey's chest as the woman ogled Troy. He looked at her and Casey's pulse bolted. "Hey, Troy," she said, shaken by the hammering of her heart.

"Hi, Casey." He smiled in that sweet way of his, drawing the attention of the stranger.

Lightly touching a gold pendant at her neck, Delaney said to the woman, "I think you should be going."

Ignoring the statement, Jillian took note of Delaney's hand gesture. "Is it real?"

"About as real as your face," Troy snapped.

Delaney placed a quick hand to his arm. "Troy, *don't*."

Troy reeled in confusion. "What? I can't stand by and let her talk to you like that—it ain't right."

Seemingly amused by the exchange, the woman smirked. "What do you know? A real live country bumpkin."

Like a hawk on a snake, Casey's great aunt appeared out of nowhere. Fran stared down the brown-skinned woman. "Is there something I can help you with, ma'am?"

"No, thank you. I believe I've everything I need." She tapped Troy with a lustful glance then said to Delaney, "I'll be seeing you again."

The four of them watched as the woman left the diner without another word.

"Sugar, you wanna tell me who that was?"

"A developer interested in ruining Nick," Delaney replied in what Casey found to be a shell-shocked tone.

"A developer?" Fran rolled her eyes. "If you ask me, she looks more like a harlot than a developer."

Casey's thoughts exactly.

"It's a long story," Delaney replied dully, then turned to Troy. "I appreciate what you did, but that woman is not worth the trouble."

"Dad gum, Miss Delaney, it wouldn't a been no trouble at all tossing that woman out of here after the way she was talkin'."

"Trust me. She's better left alone." Delaney glanced between them and walked away.

Casey thought Delaney looked like she was dumbstruck or something. She paused by the front door as if she didn't know where she was going. Was that woman after her boyfriend, Nick Harris? If so, Casey could see why she would have been unhappy to see her.

Troy settled onto a stool in front of Casey and Fran asked him, "Coke?"

"Sounds good," Troy said, eagerness erasing his earlier displeasure.

Fran ran off to the kitchen leaving the two of them alone. "What's up? You seem happy all of a sudden. And why are you here early?"

"Guess what happened at work today?"

Fear ripped through her. "What?"

"Dad gum, Casey. Wipe that look off your face—it ain't nothin' bad."

The clamp around her heart loosened. "What happened?"

"I helped deliver a foal!"

"You did?"

Troy nodded, joy pouring from his warm brown eyes. "Sure did. Saved his life, too."

Casey had never seen him so happy before. Every inch of his face was smiling. "How?"

"Gave him mouth-to-mouth."

She screwed her face. "Ew."

"Aw, it wasn't that bad." Troy laughed and proceeded to relay the story about what happened, how he helped, how Mr. Foster was real impressed with his performance. "It felt good, helping that foal. Really good."

It felt good seeing Troy so gratified. Made Casey want to have the same feeling about something she did, though it certainly wouldn't include mouth-to-mouth on a stinky horse. Casey glanced around the diner full of customers, most of whom she knew, many friends of her aunt, her mom. She didn't want to spend her life waiting tables, stuck in a town where things never changed. It was the same people, same food, day in and day out. She wanted something more exciting, something she could look forward to, be proud of. Like Troy. He was doing what he loved. What did she love?

"Listen, I wanted to ask if you could come to my parents' house for Thanksgiving."

Affection swelled. Troy wanted her to be part of his family dinner. "Sure. I don't think my mom will care."

"She's going to the Foster's place."

"She is?"

"Yep. Mr. Cal told me himself. Invited you and me, too, but my folks want me home."

And Troy wanted her with him. Unlike her mother. She hadn't mentioned the first word about a Thanksgiving invite from the Fosters. "I'll go." *And to hell with what my mother wants.*

Chapter Thirteen

Driving the half hour to Cal's family home, Misty Mountain Ranch, Annie wondered about her future. With Cal, without Cal, with Casey, without her. *I'm going to Troy's house for Thanksgiving.* Last minute, Casey had informed Annie that she wouldn't be joining her for Thanksgiving with the Fosters. She was going to her boyfriend's holiday meal. It seemed Casey was wrapping her whole life around Troy. Troy moved to Murfreesboro, Casey followed him. Troy spent the holidays with his family, Casey joined him. If Troy jumped off a bridge, would Casey take the leap, too?

Annie shuddered to think about it. Casey was young and impressionable and directionless. Feelings Annie understood. She had once been obsessed with Jeremiah Ladd. Whether he was good for her or not, she had wanted him and nothing but him. But at least she had a job. At least she had the sense not to chase him to Atlanta. But that was a long time ago. She was different. Cal was different. Cal was a good man, a steady man. The kind of man you could rely on to be there. He'd proven as much since he'd been back in town. Every time she needed him, from financing the taxes, logging the property to collecting her daughter from Murfreesboro, he was there. Funny how different he was from the old days. Back in high school Cal had almost been as wild as his three brothers, Jack, Beau and Clint.

Anticipation shimmied through her veins. Beau and Clint would undoubtedly be there today. What would they think about her and Cal? Would they accept her into the family? They'd never been over-friendly to her in high school. Would they be any different as grown men with families of their own? Cal had changed. Had they?

Annie took the turn onto the Foster property with a slight measure of ambivalence. Making her way through the rolling hills of Misty Mountain Ranch—acres upon acres lined with traditional white fencing, grass as green as spring against a palette of fall, horses grazing, their gentle swish of tails—she was nervous. The day felt formal, like she was officially meeting the family. Which was strange. She'd known the Fosters for as long as she could remember. But today felt different. New. Nerve-wracking!

Pulling up to a two-story brick home, an impressive estate with chimneys on either end, smoke curling up into a gray sky, Annie inhaled deeply, struggling against the wild thump of her pulse. It was huge, bigger than any home she'd ever been in before. From the front second-floor ceiling, an enormous black lantern hung above massive double wood doors. An open patio wrapped around the house, lined with rockers and bordered by a hedge of azalea. It was clean, pristine, the epitome of southern charm. Annie tensed as Cal rose from a rocker. He'd been waiting for her. He'd offered to pick her up, but expecting to drive Casey, Annie thought it better to drive herself. Now, with no Casey in tow, Annie blew out her breath. Would he be upset?

Rounding the hood of her car, Cal opened her door. As he helped her from her seat, the scent of wood smoke greeted her. A smell that smacked of fall, cooler weather and leaves changing. Autumn was her favorite time of year.

"My, but don't you look beautiful." Cal said easily. "That's a mighty pretty color on you."

"Thank you." The emerald green cashmere sweater was one of her favorites. Paired with an ankle length black skirt and boots, she deemed it simple, yet elegant. From her neck dropped a double-strand of faux gray pearls. Hopefully she'd blend in with the wealthy Fosters. Victoria Foster was a socialite type of woman. No doubt she'd be dressed to the hilt.

Cal leaned over and pecked her cheek. The touch felt electric to her skin. "No Casey?"

Annie shook her head, a shade embarrassed. Rubbing the spot on her cheek, she felt the sensation of his lips linger against her skin. "I'm sorry. She decided to go to Troy's, last minute."

"I invited him to supper, but his family has first dibs." Cal nodded. "I understand."

Cal invited Troy? Was he *trying* to put the two kids together?

Escorting her to the front doors, he went on, "Troy is a nice boy. Excellent with the horses."

"He is?" Annie didn't know much about Troy other than what Casey told her, which couldn't be trusted. She thought everything he did was perfection. Annie's heart pinched. Because she was in love. Troy could sink like a rock in a stream, yet she'd continue to swear he walked on water.

"Troy helped me deliver a foal this week. Poor animal came out of its momma in distress, but he handled it like a pro. Even took to giving it mouth-to-mouth without being asked."

Annie balked. "Troy gave a horse mouth-to-mouth?" The idea of her lips anywhere near a horse's mouth sounded utterly disgusting.

Cal grinned. "That he did." He dropped his gaze to Annie's lips. Sliding a hand over her shoulder, he cupped her neck. "Sort of like this," he murmured, then leaned down and kissed her. The slight brush of his mouth over hers sent hot tingles across her breasts. His touch was so tender, so delicate—so unexpected—it stole her breath away.

"Cal," she gasped, involuntarily scanning their immediate vicinity for onlookers.

"Sorry," he replied sheepishly. "Couldn't resist." Then he proceeded to relay the entire event of Troy's mouth-to-mouth as though nothing ever happened. Annie could hardly concentrate, her mind instantly divided between Cal, his kiss, and the elegant foyer of his family home. It was two-stories high, dominated by a huge diamond glass chandelier. A mix of wrought iron, animal horns and glass, the piece was a gorgeous, glittery spectacle of light and design.

Venturing farther inside, she was warmed by the sight of a huge fire dancing beneath a wood beam mantle, a thick log that ran ten feet long, adorned with family photos. Oriental rugs were sprawled across gleaming wood floors, sofas were supple brown leather, seams secured by rounded metal bolts. Lamps were shapely and unique. Fat, interior wood posts reached from floor to ceiling, supporting equally large beams overhead, their wood surfaces sanded to a polished shine. The Foster home was pure mountain luxury. Allowing her gaze to drift and settle, Annie imagined it must have cost a fortune to build and decorate.

"My mother is waiting to say hello," Cal said, nudging Annie back into the moment. Annie nodded and followed him over to where his family was gathered near the fireplace. Gerald and his two sons stood by the hearth, two ladies were seated nearby. Through the plate glass window, Annie could see one wife out back watching the children run around the yard, well clear of the pool. Beyond them were pasture and hills, the Appalachian Mountains miles off in the distance.

Cal's mother rose when she saw them coming.

With a gentle hand to Annie's lower back, Cal said, "Mom, you remember Annie Owens?"

"Of course I do," she returned, her voice bright and cheerful, though Annie couldn't imagine she remembered her. Not only had twenty years gone by, but they couldn't have met more than once and in passing, at best. No matter. Annie greeted her just the same. "It's so good to see you again, Mrs. Foster." The women shook hands. As expected, the elder woman was well-dressed in wool slacks, a long-sleeved cream satin blouse with a colorful silk scarf loosely wrapped around her shoulders. The shades of brown and apricot were pleasing against her fair complexion and wheat blonde hair. Annie dropped a fleeting gaze to her hand. Of course her manicure was flawless, setting off a huge diamond ring.

"Cal has been telling us all about you, what you've been up to over the years." Annie kept her smile firmly in place, musing, *there's a fun-filled ten minutes*. "And I've heard you are simply the most amazing nail tech in all of Tennessee, I absolutely must stop by and have you take a look at mine."

Annie's smile grew. Whether or not she believed Mrs. Foster was irrelevant. She prided herself on her ability with nails and it was always nice to hear good things about her results, even if they were nothing more than good manners speaking. "Thank you, Mrs. Foster. I'd be delighted to have you, any time."

Looking on, Cal said, "Her daughter Casey wasn't able to make it. She went with Troy to his family get-together."

Mrs. Foster nodded as though it was nothing less than she expected. Gerald Foster ambled over and smiled. The man was larger than life with his full head of brown hair and robust build. Dashing in his plaid flannel shirt and indigo blue jeans, he exuded country and confidence. "Nice to see you again, Annie."

"Same to you," she replied. The last time they'd met was during her loan application. With Cal's assistance, the entire process had only taken thirty minutes, with Gerald talking about horses and training the entire time.

"I hear you may be looking to sell your share of Ladd Springs?" The floor dropped out from under her. Cal looked to her, a distinct suspicion clouding his eyes. "Hank Dakota called me and said you might need to open a trust account. Course I told him it'd be no problem, we'd take right good care of you."

Avoiding the brunt of his father's surprise, Cal asked, "You're thinking of selling?" It was clear the senior Foster believed Cal was already privy to the news.

"No," she stammered, placing a hand to her throat. "Not really. I was only discussing potential plans with Mr. Dakota, and how any future sale would be handled on behalf of Casey." Which her lawyer apparently felt entitled to go blab all over town!

"Huh." Gerald mulled the situation over a minute, the atmosphere growing heavy. "Well, if you ever do decide to sell, I'd sure like a crack at it. Ladd Springs is a beautiful piece of land and I'd sure like to own a piece of it myself."

Annie privately scoffed. Gerald Foster had no need for more land, beautiful or otherwise. He wanted Ladd Springs because it had belonged to Susannah Ladd Wilkins. Everyone knew he'd been sweet on her in the day, but she turned him down for Harry Wilkins, a hayseed of a man without a penny to his name. It ranked as the top unrequited love story of their day and had grown to near legacy status in their small town. According to Aunt Fran, Gerald and Susannah were meant for each other, but Ernie Ladd hated the man and set out to bust them apart from day one. Harry Wilkins stepped into the picture and Susannah's heart was stolen right quick, the two marrying soon after. No one knew what really broke them apart, but that didn't stop the rumors from churning up muddy waters. Some even speculated that Delaney belonged to Gerald Foster. How was that for a backward romance? Annie savored a private chuckle. It would mean Delaney married her half-brother!

Cal grasped her lightly by the elbow. "Don't mind Daddy. He's always looking for a land steal."

Gerald laughed. "Not all of us can make our money on the stock market, son."

Which is how Cal supported himself. After leaving a steady income in Arizona, Cal claimed to have earned enough money investing in the stock market that he didn't have to rush out and find work. She sighed. Must be nice.

"If you all will excuse us," Cal said. "I'd like to show Annie around."

"Be my guest," Gerald said heartily.

After making brief introductions to the remainder of his family, Cal led Annie through a commercial-grade kitchen where a stainless steel refrigerator rivaled the size of Fran's fridge at the diner. Shiny stone counters were long and wide, mahogany cabinets decoratively carved and embossed. Moving out of earshot of the living room, Cal stopped and turned. "Are you thinking of selling the property, Annie?"

Gentle brown eyes held no pretense, no pleasantry. They were open and direct. Cal was asking her an honest question. A question he was surprised to be asking. "I don't know," she hemmed.

"Did you discuss the matter with Mr. Dakota?"

In the privacy of his office where matters were supposed to be *confidential*, yes. "I asked after the value of the land. If we're going to log, I'll need to know, won't I?"

Cal's gaze sharpened to a razor-thin line between belief and suspicion. "Not particularly."

"If we log a hundred acres, how much will it cost to build a house?" Cal had been the one to suggest she set roots and build a home for Casey, giving her daughter the stability she needed. "Will two-hundred fifty thousand be enough?"

"Depends on what kind of house you aim to build."

Cal was being cagey. He was testing her. "I want to know all my options," Annie declared, growing indignant beneath the glare of his spotlight. "It's my job as trustee to discuss the options and do what's best for Casey, isn't it?"

He nodded. "It is."

"And that's what I intend to do." Sensing his withdrawal, Annie tried to affirm his efforts on her behalf were not wasted. "It's all I was doing at the lawyer's office, Cal. I'm still interested in logging, but I need to know what it costs and what do I do with the money when they pay me?"

"I can help you with that, Annie," he said, and she felt something inside him close. Cal wasn't sure of her. He harbored doubt where she was concerned and it killed her. His withdrawal of trust hurt more than she expected.

"I know, Cal, and I appreciate it, you know I do. This is new territory for me, is all, and I want to be sure, make responsible decisions for Casey."

This pulled a smile into his mix of strain and ambiguity. "You're doing the right thing."

Relief fluttered beneath her breast. "Now, will you show me around? I'd love to see the house."

Cal extended an elbow. "By all means."

After a half-hour tour, Annie and Cal descended the spiral staircase, wooden steps that twirled beneath another magnificent country-styled chandelier. She felt like royalty sweeping down on the arm of her prince. Annie's emotions flipped between envy and awe, admiration and possibility. The upstairs of the Foster's home boasted more of the same impressive construction and décor and made Annie wonder at the type of home five hundred thousand dollars could build. Surely something as nice as the Foster estate. It should be enough to build a home and pay for college. On second thought, Annie deemed, gliding her hand down the smooth beveled edge of the railing, maybe she should ask Jillian Devane to pay more. The real estate listings she'd found online had suggested as much, hadn't they? Several were listed for well over a million.

A twinge of excitement skirted through her. She'd double-check tonight. "Oh!" Annie cried out breathlessly, bumping into Cal as he froze mid-step on the staircase.

Cal was stone still. Annie's heart caught at the sight of his brother standing a few feet from the base of stairs. Jack Foster, in the flesh.

Staring up at them, Jack took in Annie by Cal's side, noted their hands entwined between them. A glimmer of realization lit up his dark gaze—his lined, tanned, handsome gaze. Much darker than Cal, Jack looked weathered, rugged. Dressed for the occasion in black slacks and striped button-down, his trim figure suggested he'd kept in shape over the years. "Hi, Cal."

"Jack." Cal remained in place, but only momentarily, as if thinking better of it. Guiding Annie down the last few steps, he asked, "What brings you in town?"

A sardonic gleam entered his eyes. "It's Thanksgiving, brother."

"It is," Cal said, as though the revelation were insignificant. Glancing toward the living room, Cal eyed his brother Jack with a healthy dose of suspicion. "Does Daddy know you're here?"

Jack laughed, unaffected. "Actually, I only just arrived. Decided to surprise them with a visit from their baby boy."

Cal nodded. Was Jack's presence unwelcome? Annie wondered.

"So how've you been?" Jack brushed Annie with a fleeting gaze. "Since the accident and all."

Cal stiffened. "Fine."

Accident? Annie looked to Cal, then Jack. What accident?

Jack smiled, a dark pleasure swirling in his expression as he took in Annie. "That's good to hear." Hesitating briefly, he took a step toward the main living area where the family could be heard gathered. Conversation was muted, but amicable, joyous. Somehow, Annie thought all that was about to change.

Cal watched his brother enter through a wide, wood-framed opening. His demeanor felt ten shades cooler. "Cal?" she asked. "What accident was he referring to?" Jack made it sound serious, though Cal hadn't mentioned the first word to her in six months. Had he been hurt? Was he okay?

Annie's heart skipped a beat as he turned to her. Deep in Cal's eyes sat a secret, buried beneath layers of defense and privacy—layers Jack had ripped away. She could see it clear as if it were posted on a roadside billboard. She swallowed, and reached for the strand of pearls at her neck. It was unsettling to see Cal unnerved.

"It's nothing," he replied quietly. Without another word Cal led her into the living room, a room sucked clean of merriment.

Chapter Fourteen

Returning home, Annie found Casey on the couch. There was no light in the apartment, save for the illumination of the television screen. Wandering inside farther, she was surprised Casey wasn't with Troy. Flicking on an overhead light, Annie asked after her Thanksgiving meal. "How did it go with the Parkers?"

"Horrible."

Annie stopped. "Horrible? Why? What happened?"

"Felicity was there."

"So. She's with Travis. What would it matter?" Annie pulled the purse from her shoulder and set it on the dining room table.

"She kept asking a bunch of questions about Troy's ranch plans, his future, if he was going to reconsider his decision on college."

Annie came around and dropped to a seat next to her daughter. Brushing long bangs behind an ear, she asked, "And that bothered you?"

Casey stared at the television. "She doesn't have any business with Troy. It shouldn't matter to her what he's doing."

"Well," Annie broached gently, fully understanding that her daughter felt on the outs. "They're friends. Makes sense she'd be interested in what he's doing." Casey wasn't completely comfortable with the family of the boy whom she was dating. Annie had felt the same way during her meal with the Fosters. Jack's surprise arrival didn't help, nor did his mysterious comment about an accident or Cal's vague response. It left her unsettled, on edge, as though she didn't belong on the inside.

Casey grunted. "She doesn't like me."

"That's not true. Felicity likes you, just fine."

"No she doesn't." Casey turned her head. "She doesn't approve of Troy dating me, either."

"Why would you say that?"

"Weren't you listening? She kept trying to get him to go back to school."

Annie set hands to her thighs. "Which has nothing to do with you."

Casey looked at her mother as if she were an idiot. "Yes it does. It would take Troy away from me."

Annie stilled. "I think you might be over-analyzing it. Felicity believes college is the best route. She's there, Travis is there. She thinks Troy should be, too." And you, Annie added silently. Casey should be in college, too, not wasting her life chasing a boy. "It only makes sense that she'd try to sell you and Troy on it."

"Well, he doesn't want to go. He wants to stay here and work with horses. He wants to stay with me."

Annie smiled. "Cal had some really nice things to say about Troy."

A thunderbolt of surprise struck the tension from Casey's expression. "He did?"

Annie nodded. She reached out and stroked Casey's hair, taking comfort in the fact that her daughter didn't resist. Hope blossomed in her chest. Maybe this was an opportunity to repair the rift, close the space between them. "He sure did. Said Troy helped him deliver a foal the other day and perhaps saved the baby's life."

"Oh, yeah. Troy told me."

"Saved the animal's life, according to Cal," she said, "Though I don't know about that whole mouth-to-mouth thing!" She screwed her face. "But I'm glad he's okay with it. Annie yearned for the candid look in Casey's eyes to continue. Her daughter was a child again, a baby who still believed in the possibility of happily-ever-after. She was a girl, a young woman. She had hope in her eyes and joy in her smile.

Absorbing the revelation, Casey nodded. "He's really good. I told you, didn't I? Troy is really good with horses. He doesn't need college."

Annie's heart swelled and she dropped her hand. Casey was pure devotion. She was solid, supportive. "With you in his corner, Troy can conquer the world."

When her daughter opened into a full-fledged smile, Annie took the opportunity to broach the subject of Ladd Springs. "Have you thought any more about what we discussed regarding the property?"

"You mean selling it?" Annie nodded, her breathing suddenly shallow. Casey shrugged. "I don't care, really. I'm not going to see any of the money until I'm thirty, anyway."

"As trustee, I can spend some of it on you before then."

"To go to college."

"To go to college, to buy a car..." she added, reminding her daughter that she wasn't trying to force the issue, only offering it as an option—one of many. "We could buy a house."

Casey looked at her and Annie realized at once that her daughter wasn't considering a move-in with *her*. She was anticipating a move-in with Troy. Annie's heart fell. Of course she was. Who wanted to live with their mother for the rest of their life?

"House, car, there are all kinds of things you can do with the money," she said. Like start a business. Candi had been bugging Annie to go into a salon together. Maybe Casey could do something along the same lines, but what? What did she want to do? "If you could spend the money on anything, job-oriented, I mean, what would you spend it on?"

"What do you mean?"

"I mean," Annie said, formulating her thoughts as she spoke them, "say you could start a business. What kind of business would it be?"

Casey shrugged, but her features softened in contemplation. "I don't know. I've never thought about it."

Eighteen and Casey had never thought about what she wanted to do. Felicity knew she wanted a career as a flutist. Travis knew he wanted to be a lawyer. Troy knew he wanted to work with horses. But Casey? She knew nothing of the kind. Annie ran a hand down her daughter's back. "You should think about it."

"Think about what kind of business I want to start?"

"Think about what you want to do with the rest of your life." It was something Annie needed to start thinking more about herself, as well.

The next day, Annie met Cal, Malcolm and Lacy for lunch. Thanksgiving was over but the salon was closed, leaving her with a long weekend. Cal planned to take her riding this afternoon, but Lacy insisted they have lunch. She and Malcolm wanted to share some good news.

"Thanks, Fran," Annie said as her aunt finished a pour of coffee.

Fran winked. "You bet."

Annie looked to Lacy and asked, "Okay, what's the big news."

Lacy looked to Malcolm and he nodded. Turning back to face Annie, Lacy announced, "We want you to do the nails for Serenity Springs. You're the best in the business and Serenity Springs is going to be the best spa in all of Tennessee! It makes sense to put you together, don't you think?"

They were offering her a job? She glanced sideways to Cal who smiled. *Of course.* He would love nothing better than to see her work for Serenity Springs. He wanted the job as General Manager. Seems natural he'd want her there, too. Hadn't he already posed the idea himself? An odd thought struck. Would that make him her boss?

"You'll make good money," Lacy said, "probably three times what you're making now."

Three times the money? Trendz was the top-paying salon in town, but Serenity Springs would be big time, attracting wealthy people from all over the world. Maybe Nick and

Malcolm would pay her more, but she'd been at Trendz for a long time. What would they do without her? "But I already have a job..."

"You'll quit!" Lacy exclaimed. "They can find another girl to do nails." Her sister's blue eyes rounded as they grew serious. "Besides, we need you, Annie. The spa has to employ the best of the best and the whole town knows you're it when it comes to nails."

Malcolm's blue eyes equaled the enthusiasm of his wife's.

While Annie didn't know about all that, she had to admit three times the money sounded appealing. A swell of excitement moved through her. Three times the money would go a long way to buying a house. She wouldn't need Casey to live with her. She'd be able to do it on her own. With a brief glance to Cal, she asked, "When are you opening?"

"Not until May," Lacy said, dominating the conversation. Malcolm sat mute by her side, seemingly content to let his wife handle the hiring details. "You'll quit in a couple of months and then come work for us."

Us. The word hit Annie like a dump truck. *Us.* She'd be working for not only Delaney but Lacy, Malcolm Cal—everyone! Without looking to her side, Annie thought, Cal would be the General Manager alongside Malcolm, Delaney and Lacy would be wives to the owners...

The initial excitement drained from her. "I'll have to think about it."

"Well, don't take too long. We'll need you to design the layout of the nail stations. Set it up anyway you please," Lacy said gleefully. "You decide how it looks and who we hire. You'll be the boss."

Annie pulled her warm cup of coffee near. *After you and Delaney, Malcolm and Cal.*

"Think of the exotic people you'll get to meet," Lacy prattled on. "They'll come from all over the world and they're used to tipping a lot. Why, when we went to Vegas, you should have seen the money those people were throwing around!"

Malcolm placed a hand to Lacy's forearm. "I think Annie gets the picture. Why don't you let her mull it over for a while? She's invested a lot of years in her current job. She might not want to leave Trendz and the people there."

Lacy looked crestfallen. Glancing from Malcolm to Annie, she asked, "You want to do it, don't you, Annie?"

"Sounds like a great opportunity," she said, "but Malcolm's right. I need to think about it and how it will affect Trendz."

Cal agreed, though she detected disappointment in his tone. "Loyalty is a mighty fine trait in an employee. I, for one, admire you for taking your time."

Time. Time to decide about *his* job offer, *her* job offer. Time to decide about Jillian Devane's offer. Time. Annie felt the pack of lies closing in on her. Her thoughts dark and hidden, she was slowly working herself into a hole. "Yes," she muttered and sipped her coffee. She winced at the black and bitter taste. She'd forgotten to add cream and sugar.

"I still have the job as mountain guide, right?" Lacy asked Malcolm.

"If you want it, but what are you going to do with Emma Jane?"

"Oh, she'll come with me!" She tapped a row of fingers to his shoulders. "You know, they make those backpacks now where you can carry your baby on your back as you hike."

"You're going to let her carry the baby up the mountain?" Cal asked.

Malcolm laughed. "Have you ever climbed with Lacy?" He wrapped an arm around her and said, "Emma will be safer on her back on a mountain rock than in a stroller on a sidewalk any day of the week."

Lacy beamed like a puppy with two tails. Lifting her coffee cup, pinky outstretched, she sipped, then yanked the cup from her lips. "Oh, look—it's Troy!" She waved him over.

Troy swaggered over in a near-arrogant stride. Decked out in his customary T-shirt and jeans with the addition of a denim jacket, the boy oozed confidence and ego. Cal spoke first. "Hello, Troy."

"Afternoon."

"Care to join us?"

"Naw, but thank you." He flicked a glance toward the lunch counter where Casey was working. "I'm here to see Casey."

Of course he was. Thoughts of Cal faded as a pair of oversized sunglasses near the entrance seized her attention. Jillian Devane scanned the restaurant. When she saw Annie, she smiled. Annie's heart stopped then thwacked hard against her chest. *Please don't come over here, please don't come over here. Not with these people around me. Not Lacy and Malcolm and Cal.*

Annie swallowed against the batter of pulse. Jillian was headed straight toward them.

Chapter Fifteen

"All this talk of riding is making me jealous," Malcolm said, oblivious to the approaching disaster. Pale blue eyes crinkled the corners of his tanned skin. "Let's say you and I go for a ride, Lacy."

She blinked. "But you don't have any horses. How are we gonna ride?"

"Delaney said we could use her horses any time we wanted, remember?"

"Which will only be temporary," Cal put in. "Soon enough you'll have a whole stable full of your own. Another one was born just the other day, in fact. A real fine boy with a sturdy build. Named him Vegas."

Malcolm brightened. "You did?"

Cal nodded. "Delaney supplied a list of names, so we're running down through 'em."

Overcome by pleasure, Malcolm didn't notice Jillian until she was upon them. But serpents had a way of moving fast on unsuspecting prey.

"Well, isn't this a quaint gathering."

Nerves formed a noose around Annie's heart. If Jillian mentioned the property sale she'd be toast. Spying the disgruntled look on Lacy's face, Annie added, make that burnt toast.

"Is there no other place to eat other than this *restaurante*?"

"We only frequent the best places, Jillian," Malcolm said a tad snidely. "You should know that better than anyone."

Jillian smiled at him, raking a lascivious gaze over Troy. Annie tensed. Did Troy realize he'd absently given the woman a return onceover with his girlfriend in eyesight? Jillian gave a gentle shake to her hair and opened the collar of her leather jacket as though inviting him to linger in her splendor. Dressed more casually in painted-on jeans and stilettos, Annie wondered if Jillian had anywhere to go. What did she do all day?

"So tell, me *cariño*, where is Nick hiding himself these days?"

"Traveling as usual," Malcolm replied.

"Where to now?"

"Exotic locations."

"I hear he's in South Africa," Jillian said.

"South Africa?" Lacy blurted. "What's he doing there?"

"Business," Malcolm said evenly.

"So far away..." Jillian said, then wrapped her gaze around Troy. Dropping her attention down the length of him, she pursed her lips. "Perhaps I'll find other distractions while I'm in town."

"And why are you in town, Jillian?" Malcolm asked.

Annie held her breath. *Don't answer that.*

Artfully avoiding Annie, Jillian responded, "You *would* like to know my intentions, wouldn't you?"

Bland and detached, Malcolm didn't rise to her bait. Even the pale blue of his eyes proved an opaque shield to what his true feelings must be—if any of what Lacy said were true. "Only in so far as they pertain to me."

"And you think my plans pertain to you?"

"Unfortunately, they usually do."

Jillian slid a hand up to rest on her narrow hip. "In due time you will know. Until then I intend to enjoy myself in your small country town."

"Be careful," Malcolm mocked. "You might not want to leave."

Her eyes became slits. Drawing a fingertip beneath Troy's chin—a move so deliberate and so quick the boy didn't have time to respond—Jillian smiled. "As if that would be a problem."

Involuntarily Annie whirled to check on her daughter's whereabouts. Her heart fell. Sure enough, Casey stood behind the counter, jealousy and hurt exploding in her sullen gaze. Jillian noticed the same. Annie flicked a hot and angry glance toward Jillian. If the woman didn't want to be here, why was she trying to buy the land? Why fight so hard to convince Annie to sell? There were other mountain ranges, other creeks and streams. Flashing a glance toward the front door, Annie glimpsed Jack Foster entering and groaned inwardly. It was becoming a downright family affair around here today!

Pulling the sporty sunglasses from his eyes, he located the group of them in seconds. A positively mischievous smile crept onto his lips as he headed over, pulling up next to Jillian. Jack eyed her openly as a man would when presented with a beautiful woman, to which she did likewise. Standing together, Annie thought they made a handsome couple. Jack's youthful good looks had only matured in their appeal. His hair remained full and brown, his skin scarcely lined, but his dark brown eyes spoke of a man at home in the country, a mountain adventurer through and through. He didn't take life too seriously, merely a man looking for a good time. Funny, but compared to Cal's more refined features, Jack seemed the cowboy and Cal the city slicker. "Hello, brother."

"Jack."

"Jack Foster—I didn't know you were in town," Lacy said, looking to Cal for an explanation.

"Jack's home for the holidays," he revealed, as though it were a warning rather than small talk.

Oblivious to the tension piling onto the table between them, Lacy asked, "Wow, how long has it been, twenty years?"

Jack sent another ogle Jillian's way before saying, "It's been too long is what it's been, though you don't look a day older than seventeen."

Lacy rewarded him with a coquettish grin and a small wave. "Oh, Jack, how you *do* go on. I'm old and married now." She turned in her seat and placed a possessive hand on Malcolm's arm. "This is my husband, Malcolm Ward. Malcolm, this is Jack Foster, Cal's brother."

Malcolm's black brow rose in surprise. "Cal's brother?" He extended a hand to Jack. "Nice to meet you."

"Jack hasn't been around for a while," Cal said, and Annie could sense a torrent of emotion churning through him.

"He was married to Delaney," Lacy informed Malcolm then looked up to Jack. Her gaze cooled as though she suddenly remembered why he left. "Aunt Frannie told me you moved up north years ago."

"Is she around?" Jack asked. "I haven't seen her, yet."

As if annoyed the focus had been withdrawn from her, Jillian cleared her throat. "Jillian Devane." She offered a hand to Jack who accepted it easily. "I'm a developer friend of Malcolm's."

"Pleasure to make your acquaintance." He lifted her hand to his mouth and kissed it.

The move appeared unimpressive to Jillian, yet she smiled. "Are you here for lunch?"

"I am."

"Would you care to join me?"

Jack grinned. "I never say no to an invitation from a beautiful woman."

Lacy bristled but Annie could care less. Good riddance was all she could think. Take Jillian as far away from this table as possible, though she found it curious Cal remained standoffish to Jack. Cal's parents and brothers seemed fine with his presence in town, surprise or otherwise. He didn't drink during his visit, he contributed genial conversation. Annie didn't get it. Why was Cal displeased by his brother's appearance?

Once again, Annie wondered about Jack's reference to the accident. When she had asked Cal about it, he'd been evasive, vague. He told her he'd been involved in a car accident, broke his arm but nothing he couldn't get over. He also mentioned it was none of Jack's business. Which seemed odd, considering the man was nice enough to ask.

Jack focused on his brother. "Catch you around, Cal."

"Sure," he mumbled.

"Shall we?" Jack gestured for Jillian to lead the way.

"Catch you around," she mimicked, directing her reply to Troy with a wink.

Annie bristled, angry for her daughter as much as put off by the rudeness Jillian displayed.

"Later," Troy said, and followed them over to the lunch counter taking up residence at the opposite end. Casey went to him immediately, a wary gaze split between Troy and the new couple in town.

"I didn't know you had a brother," Malcolm said.

"He has three," Lacy piped up. "Didn't I tell you?"

Malcolm smiled in amusement. "You must have missed that detail in your genealogical account of the town's occupants." At her blank look, he pinched her chin. "Maybe I forgot. Anyway, it's nice to meet your family, Cal." Cal nodded but didn't voice the same. Malcolm turned to Lacy. "And he's Delaney's ex-husband, you say?"

"He is. I told you about him, didn't I?" Darts were shooting from her eyes, willing him to understand the situation without her spelling it out for him in front of Cal.

"It's okay, Lacy," Cal said. "Jack has his issues. It's no secret in town."

The lights went on for Malcolm and his gaze sharpened. "Oh, I'm sorry."

"Cal and Jack are nothing alike," Annie pitched in.

Cal placed a hand to her arm. "You don't have to stick up for me, Annie. I can fight my own battles. Jack was abusive to Delaney and she walked out on him—nothing less than he deserved. He left town and headed north, been living in Nashville ever since. I'm not sure why he's back or for how long." Glancing over his shoulder at Jack and Jillian yucking it up, he added quietly, "But I hope not long."

"Cal," Lacy said, disbelief and disappointment swirling in her tone. "You don't mean that. He's your brother."

"I'm sorry, Lacy, but Jack has already proven he's willing to cause trouble. Blood kin or not, I have no use for a man of his caliber."

Chapter Sixteen

"May I have this dance?"

Perched on a high top chair, his wife Lacy Owens Ward giggled. "Of course, silly. Who else am I going to dance with?"

Dressed in a long-sleeved fitted black dress, her figure barely showing her pregnancy, Malcolm slid a glance around the lounge of Whiskey Joe's and said, "I daresay any one of these gentlemen would love the chance to swing you around the dance floor, should the opportunity be given." She dished out a playful grin. "But they'll have to step over my lifeless body to get there."

Accepting his assistance as she descended to the floor, she remarked, "Would you really fight for me?" Almost five months pregnant yet she refused to abandon her towering black heels.

"You know I would." Malcolm drew her close but not too close. He didn't want to squish the baby between them. "In a heartbeat."

"I believe you would," she declared imperiously, then allowed him to escort her to the dance floor where they joined a dozen other couples already in motion on a wooden dance floor. It was surrounded by maroon carpeting flecked with beige, a scatter of wood high-tops placed around its perimeter. The air was stale with smoke, most of the occupants dressed casually in jeans. It was wholly different than Los Angeles where bars were sleek and open, simple lines, steely colors, filled with people dressed in the latest trends. And no one smoked. Not indoors, anyway.

The song playing was a country pop tune unfamiliar to Malcolm. But then again, most of the songs played in Tennessee were unfamiliar to him, though he was learning to recognize a few. Sliding a hand behind her back, he grasped her right hand, pulled her close and glided her about the dance floor. He'd been living in Tennessee for six months, yet he still considered southern California his home. It's where his family lived, his parents occupying the same house where he was born. But Lacy was pure country, and a future with her meant a future of country music and gospel. Both fine additions to his collection of music.

Lacy gaped at him, becoming acutely aware of the couples around them. "Malcolm, what are you doing? This isn't a slow song. People are staring at us."

"Don't care." She tried to wriggle free, but he held firm. "A woman in your condition needs to be held."

She flipped her face and glared at him. "I'll have you know I'm in perfect dancing condition."

Malcolm grinned and pulled her closer. "Yes, you are. Now calm down. You're throwing my rhythm off."

With a final struggle, Lacy surrendered. "Oh, poo. You're no fun."

"On the contrary," he replied, dipping his head for a kiss, "I'm built for fun."

"Well, you can be, I'll give you that. But I'm going to give you a lesson in line dancing the instant we get home." She glanced around them, mortified to be slow-dancing a fast song. "This is ridiculous!"

But Malcolm was only half-listening, his attention diverted by a new entry into the lounge. Troy Parker. As the boy sauntered inside, an unsettling déjà vu settled in. Was he alone? Malcolm watched the door. Seconds passed, but no Casey. "Troy's here," he announced quietly.

Lacy whirled. "Where?"

"And he's alone."

"I'm sure he's meeting Casey. The two are *always* together."

Unnoticed as yet, Malcolm tracked Troy's movements. He went straight to the bar but didn't seek out a bartender. He appeared content to linger in place. "I hear he's doing a fine job over at Cal's ranch."

Lacy nodded. "Delaney said the same thing."

"Maybe she'll hire him on at the stables."

Lacy squeezed his hand. "That's a *great* idea. You're brilliant, Malcolm!"

He smiled down at her. "That's what they pay me for."

Jillian Devane waltzed in and Malcolm cursed under his breath.

"What?" Lacy whirled and saw her, stiffening within his arms. "What is *she* doing here?" She turned on Malcolm. "I don't like her at all. She is nothing but trouble."

"You can say that again."

Jillian was headed for Troy, exaggerating the sway of her hips in her skintight jeans and stiletto heels, her leather jacket the only part of her attire that seemed to fit in. When the boy saw her, he straightened. The two exchanged words, drawing glances from several nearby men. Jillian tip-toed a finger along Troy's shoulder, fiddled with the neckband of his T-shirt beneath his jean jacket. Troy stilled, fully engrossed with the woman before him. He didn't pull her hand away, didn't step aside. He said something to her, but Malcolm had no way to make it out.

Jillian leaned into him, her fingers expertly tracing a line from his collarbone to his shoulder. Malcolm closed his eyes. *Don't do it, Troy*.

"What does she think she's doing?" Lacy cried under her breath.

"Seducing a young man."

She smacked him. "Do something!"

Malcolm held Lacy firm until the song ended, then released her. Instinct told him to intervene, but Troy was an adult. And a bull. "Something tells me Troy wouldn't appreciate my interference," he replied, steering Lacy back to their table, his mind running through outcomes.

Jillian ran a hand down the length of Troy's chest and Lacy gasped. "You can't let her run her hands all over him like that!"

Troy didn't seem to mind. As he watched the events unfold from across the lounge, it occurred to Malcolm the boy looked hypnotized by her presence. He wasn't smiling, wasn't moving. Troy simply stared at her. Even from this distance, Malcolm could see a building desire. Troy's gaze was transfixed on Jillian's mouth as she spoke. She leaned her breasts into him and whispered something into his ear.

Troy jerked away from her.

Malcolm's gaze darted to the entrance in time to see a crushed Casey halt in her tracks, her face wrenching in hurt before she turned and ran. Jack Foster dodged to one side as he entered, clearing the way for the departing girl. Troy bolted after Casey, leaving Jillian standing alone, a satisfied smile slithering onto her glossy lips. When she spotted Malcolm and Lacy, her satisfaction turned triumphant. *Damn her for toying with the boy.* Jillian knew what she did to men and didn't care who she hurt in the process.

"Should we go after them?" Lacy asked.

Malcolm shook his head. "It's not our battle."

"But Casey..." Lacy's voice broke, tugging at his heart. "Did you see the look on her face?"

"I did." New feelings rumbled through him, ugly feelings, protective feelings. If Casey were his daughter, he'd run after Troy and give him a good pounding. Strange, but something about living in Tennessee brought out the animal in Malcolm. In Los Angeles he'd never felt the urge to fight, not once. Since he'd been here, he'd been in one fist fight and felt primed for another. He looked down at Lacy. Then again, he'd never had a woman he felt was worth fighting for, and in his eyes Casey was an extension of Lacy. Reining in his emotion, Malcolm restrained his tone, "Let them hash it out. We'll help clean up the mess later."

Outside, the slap of cold air snapped Troy to his senses. What the hell had he been thinking, letting that woman go on for as long as she did? "Casey!"

"Leave me alone!" she cried. "I never want to see you again!"

A couple walking into Whiskey Joe's stared at the two of them, the man showing signs of intervention. Ignoring the accusatory stares, Troy barked at him, "That's my girlfriend." The man backed off but kept an eye on the situation. "Dad gum, Casey—stop!" Easily catching up with her, he grabbed her by the shoulders and stopped her short. She was shaking, and Troy hated himself for being the cause. "I didn't do anything, I *swear*."

"She was hugging you!"

"She wasn't *huggin'* me."

"Yes she was!" Tears streamed down her face. Streaked black with mascara and eye liner, she looked like something out of a horror movie. "How could you do this?" she yelled. "First that Loretta woman and now her? I thought you *cared* about me. I thought we were *together*."

"I do, Casey, you know that. We are." He whipped a hand toward the lounge. "That woman was only trying to cause trouble."

"And you were *letting* her."

"I was doing no such thing. She was trying to come onto me. What was I supposed to do, throw her off of me?"

The scowl ingrained on Casey's face told him *yes*, that's exactly what he was supposed to do. Kick her clear out of the bar. "Dad gummit." He loosened his hold, allowing her to yank free. She took a step away from him, glaring at him with a level of hate Troy couldn't believe possible. He clawed a hand through his hair, wanting to rip it out. "I'm *sorry*."

"You sure are sorry!" She tried to sound cruel but her voice cracked. A fresh wave of tears burst free and she hugged arms to her body.

He reached out for her. "C'mon. Let's forget this ever happened."

"Are you crazy? I can't forget that you flirt with other women."

"You have to, Casey."

"I don't. I don't have to do anything. I thought you loved me Troy, but you don't."

"Casey, I *do* love you."

Casey's face twisted in a vile expression of disgust and disbelief. "You're a liar and a cheat."

Anger fired through his veins. "No, I'm not. I *mean* it. I love you, Casey. Haven't you figured that out, yet?"

"I don't love you, I hate you. I never want to see you again." Casey turned and ran, and this time he let her go. He could see her car, see that she got into it safely. Red taillights shot on and the car jerked out of its space. Casey tore out the parking lot so fast Troy feared she might hit something! He dragged his hands down his face, sadness pouring into him. It flooded his soul. Casey said she hated him. Maybe she really did.

What possessed him to let that woman touch him when he knew Casey could walk in at any time?

But Troy had never seen a woman so beautiful, so intense—and so forward. He didn't like her, but desire had pulled at him when she pressed her body to his. She had no shame, no inhibition. It was something in her eyes. They were strange, golden. He couldn't look away. Or maybe it had been her voice, low and sexy, whispering things his mind couldn't help but imagine. Was it his fault she came on to him? Would another guy have reacted differently?

Troy glanced over his shoulder at the blue neon sign, *Whiskey Joe's*. Lighting up the front of the cement building, the letter "e" blinked on and off. No sense in going back in. There was nothing of interest for him in there. Everything he cared about just drove out of the parking lot and out of his life. Disgust roiled in his gut. Because he was a dog. A selfish dog taking pleasure in another woman's flirtations.

Troy wrapped a hand around the back of his neck and hung his head. Need coursed through him. He needed Casey, needed her connection. He needed the sweet love he knew she felt for him. He wanted tonight to be special. Thanksgiving had been a horrible letdown for her. She'd hated it. He'd hated it. Everyone probed and pushed. No one could leave well enough alone. *It's not too late. You can still go to college.*

He didn't need college to do what he loved. He needed his woman by his side while he worked the job he loved. He needed her support, her belief in him. But she had left him. Lifting his head, he stared into the black of night. Loneliness snaked in. He needed a drink.

Chapter Seventeen

Sitting alone in a corner booth, the restaurant fairly clear at this hour on a Sunday afternoon, Casey was lifeless, her expression dull, lackluster. The girl looked as if someone had died. Delaney's heart caught. *Was she okay? Had something horrible happened?* Hurrying over, Delaney exclaimed, "Casey, what's the matter?" The girl looked up at her but didn't say a word. Delaney dropped to a seat, urgency clawing at her. "Has something happened?" Casey gave a tiny, pathetic nod. "What?" Delaney asked, pulse thumping in her chest at the lack of information.

"I broke up with Troy."

She broke up with Troy. Relief streamed through Delaney's body, clearing out the panic. It wasn't anything serious. Well, serious to Casey. Delaney reached a hand across the table. "I'm sorry." Tears swamped Casey's eyes. Delaney wanted to know what happened, she wanted to demand details, but the utter despair staring back at her prevented even the first probing question.

Casey looked away. A heavy tear pushed free, rolling down her cheek. The diner walls echoed family and kinship, red-checkered curtains and bright red booths emphasized a mood of jovial hospitality, none of which spoke to a girl nursing a broken heart.

"Do you want to talk about it?" Delaney asked, unable to squelch the mother in her. If it were Felicity sitting here, she'd offer an ear and a shoulder to cry on. She'd want to know everything so she could begin the process of healing.

Caution entered Casey's gaze. "I don't know..."

Delaney smiled. "I'm a good listener. I care about you both."

Casey lowered her gaze and Delaney held herself in check. She did care about Casey whether the girl believed it or not. She held no ill will toward her and Troy—well, he was like one of her own.

"He was with that Jillian woman."

The name cut her in two. "Jillian?"

Casey nodded. "At Whiskey Joe's. They were together."

"Oh, no." Delaney replied, upset that Troy would let himself be drawn in by that creature, while at the same time, it didn't surprise her. Jillian was here for one reason and one reason only: destroy Ladd Springs and everyone around it. Dialing back her personal feelings, Delaney asked, "Are you sure? It sounded like you and Troy were doing so well, and if you ask me, I don't think that woman is his type." Casey smacked her with a knowing glance before turning away and Delaney felt the blunt force of truth. Troy had been with Loretta. Why not Jillian? Although she hated the reality of the male libido, it was the quiver to Casey's lips that broke Delaney's heart. "Oh, *sweetheart.*" She rose from her seat and changed sides, pushing onto the bench with Casey. Slipping an arm around her, she instinctively pulled her close. "It'll be okay," she assured her, knowing no such thing but understanding the girl needed comfort, needed to believe in hope of some kind. Casey dropped her forehead to Delaney's shoulder and began to sob. Narrow shoulders shook as her muffled cries increased.

Fran stepped out of the kitchen and caught sight of them, but Delaney warned her off. They needed to be alone. Casey needed to be alone. Fran respected the request and kept her distance, though she was clearly upset by the scene. Casey was her great niece. She was family, which meant it was her duty to come to her aid.

Smoothing a hand over raven-black hair, Delaney lingered on the notion. Casey was *her* family, too. First cousin, once removed. Or were they second cousins? Delaney didn't know and she didn't care. Casey was family and without Felicity here, the girl felt like a daughter. She was going through a hard time and needed the comfort of someone who cared. Taking in the diner, mostly vacant after the Sunday supper crowd, Delaney wondered where Annie was. Did she know her child was hurting? Had she offered the support Casey so desperately needed?

Delaney didn't have a lot of answers. What she did have was a warm body and a ready ear, and if that's what Casey needed at the moment then that's what she'd provide. She'd call Annie later and let her know—if she didn't already—and if she became angry over Delaney getting in her business, then so be it. Casey was fragile. Only six months since Casey's overdose, Delaney feared the breakup with Troy could cause a relapse. Teenagers were sensitive that way. They lived and died by their relationships, and if Troy had really rejected her the way she claimed he did, then Casey was ripe for a bout of depression.

Jillian. The mere thought of the woman made Delaney's skin crawl. She was out to cause trouble and Delaney didn't like her being here one bit. She was selfish and ruthless and vindictive. She was out to hurt Nick and that alone was enough to warrant ill-will. Though if Delaney were sitting in church, she'd have to admit that part of her was jealous. Jillian was a beautiful. Nick had obviously thought so, dating her for over a year. They'd been lovers, a couple.

Delaney closed her eyes, shoving visions of the two of them together from her mind. Could Jillian get him back? Could she wield whatever powers she used on Troy to get Nick back into her arms? A shudder raced through her. Tightening her hold on Casey, she knew that Jillian was not only beautiful but worldly and rich—everything she was not. A sharp longing stabbed at her. She wished Nick wasn't so far away. He'd called this morning, promised he'd be home soon. He was still in Africa but getting on a plane in the morning to come back home. Delaney's heart swelled. He'd used the word *home*. Home—as in the two of them being a family.

Nick had proposed but she had no ring. He was looking, he said, for the perfect diamond for the perfect woman, insisting only the best would do. Nerves percolated deep in her belly. He insisted they marry during the grand opening of Serenity Springs in a lavish show of their partnership going forward. Absently, she fiddled with the gold pendant at her neck. Nick had it designed for her, made from the gold they discovered on the property. It was a wishing well, a symbol representing the power of the mind, their hopes and plans for the future.

Part of her liked the idea of hosting their wedding during the grand opening. It would publicly signal the beginning of their future together. Another part of her felt swallowed up, buried by the development going on around her. Workers scoured the property like ants, grading the land with heavy machinery, combing sections of dirt to leveled perfection. They were discreetly marking hiking trails, ensuring guests would not get lost as they explored the mountainous land of Tennessee. They were creating a Meditation Trail, setting the groundwork for a riverfront restaurant Malcolm planned to call On the Fly. He even planned to build a fishing hut and place it steps below the restaurant, along the river's edge so guests could catch their own meal!

Then there was the hotel. Delaney couldn't imagine how he was going to fit a fifty room hotel in the space he'd carved out, plus a spa down the hill, but he seemed confident it could be done. But it wasn't her concern. She was in charge of the horses, given free rein with regard to how she wanted the stables built. It was a thrilling prospect and one she dove into with joy. Working with an architect, she had designed them with all she could ever want or need. From quality to convenience, Delaney tried to think of everything. She couldn't wait to share her passion for the animals with guests from all over the world.

Serenity Springs. It was an overwhelming, yet intriguing prospect to watch the transformation from wooded landscape to Harris Hotel. She wanted to discuss the hotel name with

Nick when he returned home. She had an idea and hoped he'd go for it. A squiggle of nervous excitement scraped her sympathy for Casey. *Home.* Everyone needed a place to call home. Delaney gave a gentle squeeze to Casey. "Are you hungry?"

Casey sniffled and shook her head.

Delaney stroked her arm, settling her gaze on a plate of cold food before them. With French fries visibly hardened, yellow cheese congealed to a meat patty, the meal was totally unappealing. "You have to eat."

"I'm not hungry," came the mumbled reply.

"Wanna go for a walk?" Walking always made Delaney feel better. "We could hike through the property, talk about what you want to do with your land."

Casey lifted her head, her bleary-eyed tear-stained face inches from Delaney's. "My mom wants to sell."

Delaney expelled a breath. "*What*?"

"We can't afford to build a house on it."

"But you can't sell—that's Ladd land. It's been in the family for generations."

Casey slumped back onto her shoulder, rolling her head to face outward toward the restaurant. "I don't want to be a Ladd. I hate my father."

Delaney grunted. A thousand thoughts flashed through her mind's eye like a bad horror movie. Jeremiah was a louse. He was an arrogant, self-centered, egotistical man who cared nothing about his family. She could understand Casey's feelings toward Jeremiah, but Annie going to sell? After how hard she fought to get the land, claiming she wasn't interested in money, only the legacy due her daughter? Delaney had believed money was Annie's intention from the start. She had no desire to mix with the Ladd family, no desire to live on the land. She wanted the money.

Fury branded Delaney's heart. No. Absolutely not. She would not let Annie sell. It took everything Delaney had to allow Felicity to sign those papers granting half of the property to Casey. She only did so because it was the right thing to do. Casey was Jeremiah's daughter and thus entitled to the family legacy that was Ladd Springs. Annie wasn't entitled to a *cent*. Besides, who would she sell to?

A sudden fear thrashed her bones, her muscles went slack. There was only one person possible. Jillian Devane. *It explained her presence in town.*

"My life sucks."

The frank comment pulled Delaney back to Casey with sketchy focus. "No, Casey, don't say that. You've hit a rough patch, but you'll get through it, you'll see." Delaney prayed it was true. She prayed Casey would not take this as a reason to take drugs again to drown her numb sorrow. Drawing the hair away from Casey's face, Delaney gazed into blue eyes and realized the pain went deep. This was no ordinary teenage crush. This was serious—at least on Casey's part. Delaney hoped Troy felt the same. He couldn't be interested in Jillian. Not really. Could he?

"Hi, Dell."

Jerking her head up at the sound of the male voice, she gasped. "Jack."

"Long time no see."

A torrent of emotion choked the words from her. She couldn't speak. She couldn't breathe. Jack Foster was standing before her, in the flesh. His wavy brown hair was cut shorter now, but his eyes were the same. They looked at you and through you. Ten years and everything came flooding back to her—the fights, the alcohol—even his cologne was familiar, a musky, earthy scent that incited a visceral recoil. Delaney swallowed back a host of feelings—anger, confusion, curiosity, disbelief—and asked, "What are you doing here?"

Jack smiled, sporting the same mocking gleam she remembered during their bouts. It was a look of sheer contempt, a look that demeaned and ridiculed. "It's Thanksgiving, remember? I'm here to see the family."

Delaney couldn't refute the notion, though she bet the Fosters weren't overwhelmed with joy. Mrs. Foster, especially. She hated the way her boys sullied the reputation of their family during their younger days while Mr. Foster abhorred the lack of discipline. To him their behavior represented a lack of respect for the community, a community he served proudly with his bank. "I meant standing at my table," she said, embarrassed she sounded so weak.

Beside her, Casey's tears had subsided as she stared up at Jack with an odd mix of interest and distrust. Did she realize this was Felicity's father?

Anxious for him to leave, Delaney added, "Unlike your family, I'm not interested in catching up on old times."

He chuckled. "Nice to see you, too, sweetheart." Jack overtly checked out her legs beneath the table. "I gotta admit, you look good. Still as hot as ever."

"Make yourself useful and disappear, Jack." She drew Casey closer to her. "Can't you see we're not interested in company?"

Tapping Casey with a thoughtful gaze, he said, "How's Felicity?" When Delaney didn't respond, he pressed, "She in town? I'd sure like to see her."

Casey registered his identity, turning to Delaney with a look of shock.

"She's away at college," Delaney replied.

He nodded, as though approving. "Don't tell me she didn't come home for the holidays." Delaney remained stone-faced but Casey's change in expression gave it away. He thrust her a self-serving smile. "That's what I thought. Well, listen, tell her I'm in town, will you? I'd like to see her while I'm here."

When hell freezes over. Delaney would rather spit nails into his coffin than allow him to hurt her daughter again. And hurt her, he would. The last time Jack contacted Felicity was to deliver a lecture on how he wouldn't pay a dime toward her college tuition. She'd have to earn scholarships like he did. Which was a load of bull. His father's friends sponsored most of those scholarships to get in Gerald Foster's good graces. None of which were necessary, anyway. The Fosters were worth plenty.

"You know how to find me," he said affably. "I'll make my schedule flexible to see my daughter."

Bile rose in her throat. The man made her sick.

Jack winked. "Try to smile, Dell. That scowl makes you look old."

Chapter Eighteen

Annie paced her living room as she awaited Cal's arrival. His phone call this morning sounded uncomfortable, awkward. Was he coming to press her on the issue of employment with Serenity Springs? Did he want her to take the job, thus clearing the way for him to accept the position as General Manager?

She knew Cal wanted the job and she knew he wanted her consent. They'd been discussing a future together in round about ways, and Cal had made it clear he wanted Annie to be a part of his life—a big part. A nervous tremor wound through her. She wanted the same. Cal was coming to mean a lot to her. A very lot. But if she sold Casey's half of Ladd Springs it would cause friction. It would prove a sticky-wicket between her and Lacy, Malcolm, Nick, Delaney...and Cal, if held title as General Manager. It would be uncomfortable at best, outright hostile at worst. Annie paused. Did she want to be a part of Serenity Springs? Did she want to tie her future to that of Delaney and Lacy?

Annie jumped—"Oh!"—startled by the ring of her cell phone. Pulse racing, she scooped the phone up from her sofa table, staring at the screen in disbelief. *Delaney*? With a reflexive press of her thumb, Annie answered. "Hello?"

"Annie, its Delaney."

Smoothing a hand down the side of her head, she nodded. "Yes, what's up?"

"I spent the afternoon with your daughter. She's in a bad state."

Annie dropped her hand, her breath escaping in a rush. "What?"

"Are you aware of her breakup with Troy?"

Annie's heart leapt into her throat. "Breakup?"

"Yes, they broke up last night. Apparently Troy was messing around with Jillian Devane and Casey caught them."

Annie reached out for the couch to steady herself. "Jillian Devane? What would he be doing with her?"

"Same thing as any other red-blooded man. If she was offering, he was taking."

"I can't believe it," Annie muttered more to herself than Delaney, although no sooner had the words erupted from her lips than did visions of the two at the diner flooded through her mind. *Troy and Jillian*? She dropped to a seat. "I don't know what to say."

"Speaking of unbelievable things, I can't believe you're considering selling Ladd Springs."

Adrenaline surged through Annie's weak limbs. "*What*? Who told you that?"

"Casey."

Casey? Casey was sharing their private business with Delaney? Since when were the two of them close enough to share personal information? And if Delaney knew about the potential sale, could she stop it? Could Nick?

"Is it true?" Delaney demanded.

Through a fog of bewilderment, her strength draining fast, Annie envisioned Delaney's high and mighty expression through the phone connection. Delaney thought she was catching Annie in the act. "No," she spat, "it's not true."

"Then why would Casey say it?"

"Gerald Foster offered to buy the land from me," Annie lied, anger welling quickly at a lie she felt powerless to control—but dammit she wouldn't let Delaney have the upper hand with her!

"Gerald? What would he want with the property?"

Annie allowed the significance to sink between them before responding, "I think we both know the answer to that one," then took pleasure in Delaney's silence. About time someone gave it back to her, and Annie was glad she had the honor of dishing it out. Regaining her wits, she went on, "As for the sale of Casey's property, it's none of your business what I decide to do with it, one way or another."

"It sure as hell is my business. I gave it to her!"

"Operative word, *gave*." Annie savored a smug smile. "The property belongs to Casey, not you. When and if we decide to sell, you'll be the first to know."

"Annie, I *swear* if you sell that property to Jillian Devane, I will have your hide, you hear me?"

A swarm of angst fluttered in Annie's breast, she flung her gaze about the room. *Delaney knew about Jillian?* But how? Even Casey didn't know about the deal they were discussing. Annie had purposefully kept that detail secret—from everyone. Had Jillian told her? Fear slid down her spine. No, it had to be a coincidence. A wild guess on Delaney's part and nothing more. Jillian Devane was a smart woman. She knew there'd be a fight if anyone got wind of the sale beforehand. Throttling a fresh slew of nerves, Annie said, "Thank you for letting me know about Casey, but I'm finished with this phone call."

"I'd watch her closely, if I were you. She's vulnerable right now."

On account of her drug problem. "Yes, thank you, but I don't need help raising my daughter."

Before ending the call, Delaney cracked, "Oh, and for the record, Nick didn't have anything to do with Jeremiah's beating."

Annie latched a hand to the couch. "What?"

"Casey told me you think it was Nick behind the beating, but it wasn't. It was Ernie."

"Ernie?"

"Yes, *Ernie*. He went God knows where to call in some kind of thug attack in an effort to stop Jeremiah from causing trouble. So next time you're doling out the blame, leave Nick out of it."

Annie clenched the phone at her ear. *Ernie had Jeremiah beaten and robbed?* "I don't believe you. Why would Ernie do such a thing? And how would *you* know, anyway?"

"He confessed to me at the hospital before he died. The man hated his son and I can't say as I blame him, the way Jeremiah was treating him." Delaney released an exasperated sigh. "Ernie thought he was doing the town a favor by running him off. It's twisted, but it's the truth."

Casey walked in the front door and Annie's thoughts swerved to a halt. "I have to go," she said and ended the call. Pushing away from the couch, she hurried over to her child, shoulders sunken, eyes dead. "Sweetheart, what's wrong? What happened?" Annie didn't want to let on what she knew. She wanted Casey to share it with her like she had Delaney.

"Nothing."

"Nothing?

"I want to be alone," she mumbled and walked past her mother en route for her bedroom.

Crushed, Annie could only watch her go. *Nothing*? She could share her heartbreak with Delaney and not her own mother?

The betrayal whipped up a tornado of emotion. Anger, jealousy, hatred and resentment swirled together in a funnel of hurt and disbelief. Casey had chosen Delaney over her. She had opened up and shared her pain with her but wouldn't reveal the first detail to her own mother. It was a poke in the eye and Annie had had enough. She was tired of Delaney's intrusive personality and her know-it-all attitude. She probably needled it out of her daughter, then acted like Casey had shared it of her own accord. Annie's temper teetered on the edge of control. The woman was a witch. A selfish witch. Why, Annie had a mind to sell the property just to spite her.

Cal hesitated outside Annie's front door. Glancing down the deserted second-story corridor, he pulled at his jacket collar as misgiving kicked up a dust storm in his gut. He needed to talk to Annie, but doing so in public wasn't advisable. The news wasn't good. It was real bad and he felt partly responsible, but it was what it was, and he wasn't going to play games with her. Annie was a sensible woman. She understood that people made choices. Sometimes good ones, sometimes bad ones, but they made choices and they had to live with them. Whether they wanted to or not. It was a lesson he'd learned the hard way. Cal rapped on the door, the cold metal bruising to his knuckles. Moments later, Annie opened it. "Hi, Cal."

Although she was expecting him, her pretty blue eyes weren't nearly as eager as he'd hoped. Just as well. He'd be erasing the joy from them right soon, anyhow. "Hi, Annie." She stepped aside. Cal made sure to be quick about it. It was freezing outside and he didn't want any more frigid air running into her apartment than need be. Annie closed the door behind him. "Thanks for having me over,"

"Cal," she said, a small smile rushing to her lips, "you know I'm always glad to see you."

He nodded, a twitch nervous. He hoped that remained true after what he was about to tell her. "Is Casey home?"

Annie nodded. "She's in her bedroom."

Cal cursed the luck but didn't let on. "Well," he began, careful to keep his voice low. "I need to tell you something and it's best I get right to it."

Concern rippled across her features. "What's going on?"

"Troy was fired today."

She grasped her neck. "What?"

He nodded. "Beau called me and I had to agree with the decision." Though it hurt like hell. Troy had been his recommendation. He believed in the boy but now...

"What for?"

Cal took a few steps toward her but stopped. He understood this was a touchy subject. "He'd been drinking."

The color drained from her face. "He was drinking on the job?"

"No. But he showed up late with alcohol on his breath." *Seeping from his skin* was the way Beau put it, but Cal didn't need to paint a picture any darker than it already was. "I think he must have been hung over, but I wasn't there. They called me first thing, seeing's how I'm the one who recommended him for the job."

Anger scorched her reply, "And he blew it."

"He did."

Fury trickled into sapphire eyes, chilling them with a rage he'd yet to witness in her. "I knew that boy was no good, right from the start."

"Now I wouldn't go that far. He made a mistake—"

She bristled, sending prickleys across his skin. "Mistake? You call getting drunk and showing up for work hung over a *mistake*?"

As a matter of fact, he did. Done it himself on a number of occasions and every single one of them had been a mistake. "He's been doing a fine job—"

"Until he decided to blow it, deciding that drinking was more important than holding down a job." Before Cal could reply, Annie whirled and strode across the small living room. She marched from one end to the other, torching the air between them. "Casey is better off without him. He's a low life, a loser." As though realizing her daughter might overhear, she stifled her tone. "She can do a heck of a lot better than Troy, I'll tell you that. I'm almost glad he was fired. Now she'll see him for what he is."

"Don't you think you're going a little too far?"

"Too far? Do you know he was messing around with that Jillian woman and Casey caught him? Did it right in front of her."

The revelation cut Cal at the knees. "*Troy*?"

"Yes. And now he's drinking?" Annie locked her arms over her chest. "Casey is better off without him. She's at a sensitive point in her life and he's no good for her. Trash, is what Troy Parker is and I intend to keep him as far away as possible. For good."

Cal dragged a hand through his hair, his mind sifting through the new information. In the weeks that he'd known and worked with Troy, he'd seen a fine young rancher in the making. Troy had a wild streak a country acre wide, but he was solid when it came to horses. He knew his stuff forward and backward. The animals were an extension of him. His

Daddy didn't have a better ranch hand, and if it were up to Cal, he would have given the boy a second chance. He paused on the female angle, more than a little stumped. "I don't know about this Jillian business, but I can tell you the boy's not trash. He's made of solid material and has a bright future ahead of him."

"Not drunk, he doesn't."

While Cal couldn't disagree with her there, he believed people needed space and time to work through their issues. They needed to grow and develop. Mature. Particularly a strong-minded proud boy like Troy.

"Troy will never amount to anything, and I won't stand by and let him ruin Casey's life right along with his own."

Cal stepped forward. "Now c'mon, don't get *sideways* on me. He was drunk. One time. It doesn't mean he's going to make a career out of it."

Anger broiled in her eyes. For a second Cal feared she might lash out and strike him. "This isn't his first time and I doubt it will be his last. Mark my word." She jabbed a finger toward him. "Troy Parker will get drunk again and who knows what kind of trouble he'll cause."

In the sweep of the moment, Cal realized what his ex-wife must have gone through all those years ago. Getting drunk did cause trouble. It undermined the trust and confidence of those around you. No matter how hard you tried to rationalize or explain your way out of it, drinking hurt the ones you loved. Looking into Annie's eyes and struggling heart, Cal realized forgiveness was a hard battle to win. "He's just lost his way is all. Today isn't the rest of his life. He can be better than this, just give him a chance."

"He's going nowhere fast and taking Casey with him." Annie stopped, the light catching her face in a twist of revulsion. "Have you forgotten what I told you about Casey? That she is susceptible—vulnerable?"

"No. I haven't. And it's for her sake that you've got to keep it together. Casey loves Troy. This setback will hurt, but you've got to help her through it."

Annie glared at him, contempt hardening her gaze, sharpening her edge. She was stressed, worn out, wielding a sword he wasn't accustomed to being on the wrong end of. "I'm sick and tired of people lecturing me about how to raise my daughter. I'm the one who's been taking care of her, watching over her. She's young, impressionable. She doesn't know what love is. She only knows emotion—emotion that drives her to make poor choices. And I'd call drinking more than setback. Alcohol and drugs destroy lives, Cal. They almost killed Casey and until you've walked a day in my shoes, you have no idea what I'm going through."

"I understand more than you know." From *both* sides of the equation. Caroline left him because of his drinking. His daughter Emily disowned him because of his drinking. His drinking nearly cost him his life and the life of another.

Cal bowed his head. It was a wound that bled every day, a scar that dug deep under his skin. But he was different now. He was sober almost eleven months, and he was going to prove to Emily that he was worth a second chance. Her mother might be a lost cause, already taken up with a new man, but his daughter *couldn't* be. Losing her would be like losing a chunk of his heart.

Cal raised his head and faced Annie directly. If he could do it, so could Troy. "People can change, Annie. All they need is someone to believe in them."

Annie lapsed into silence. She didn't share his opinion. She believed Troy was all he was ever going to be. Cal hated the wall rising between them. It was thick and heavy. Impenetrable.

"I think you should leave."

The quiet dismissal cut like a knife. Haunted by memories of another woman uttering those exact words, Cal hesitated. At some point Annie would have to know what he'd been through and where he was going in order to understand him, to love him. If they were going to have a future together, she'd have to know. She deserved a man with no secrets. Once everything was on the table, she could make her decision from there. But now was not that time. The icy flecks in her cold blue eyes warned she was not in a listening mood. "I'll go." Heart splintering, Cal turned, holding her in his gaze. "But you haven't heard the last from me on this subject."

Chapter Nineteen

Troy sat in his truck and waited outside the diner for Casey to finish her shift. The last customer had left almost an hour ago, which meant Casey wouldn't be long now. Staring through the diner's windows, he searched for sight of her. Fran was hard to miss, running in and out of the kitchen, around the restaurant as employees swept and mopped. Casey might be sitting down, rolling silverware for tomorrow's service. She might be cashing out. Troy helped her close a couple of nights so he knew what to expect. Green numbers glowed on his dashboard—nine-thirty—he figured she should be walking out any minute.

Since he was parked next to her car, she would have no choice but to face him. Troy didn't expect her to be happy to see him. It wasn't like he hadn't tried another way. He'd called her cell phone but she didn't pick up. He drove by her house but realized her momma probably wouldn't let him anywhere near her. Once she heard why he was fired, Miss Annie would barricade the doors and windows.

He didn't blame her. Casey's overdose would make any mother fear her daughter's involvement with him. He didn't blame Casey, either. She'd been hurt by what she saw. *I don't love you. I hate you, Troy. I never want to see you again.*

But she couldn't mean it. She was mad, hurt. She couldn't stick to it, could she?

Troy hoped not. He loved her. He really did and he'd never let that Jillian woman ruin the best thing he had going. He'd already lost the second best thing he had going. Shame dribbled into his chest as he recalled the disappointment in Mr. Foster's eyes. Showing up to work with a hangover had been the stupidest thing he could have done. Troy knew the rules. He should have called in sick. Most days he worked on his own, a distance from the house. How was he supposed to know Mr. Foster was going to show up?

He showed up because Cal told him what a fine job Troy did with the foal. Mr. Foster had come to thank him. He had come to show his appreciation, but before he said the first word, he knew. The old man could smell Troy from ten feet away. *You're fired.* Troy's gut wrenched at the memory. Quick, to the point, no questions asked. The evidence undeniable.

Drinking a fifth of whiskey will do that to a guy. The sweet liquor doesn't stay in your stomach but sinks into your skin. You can't wash it away. It has to work itself out and that takes time. Troy understood the man did what he had to do. The rules had been stated up front. Drinking wasn't tolerated. From what Troy had heard, Mr. Foster's sons drank enough to fill the rivers of Tennessee. They'd been wild as stallions giving the old man his fill. His was zero tolerance.

A policy he was going to adopt. Gritting his teeth, Troy stared into the diner. He was finished. No more alcohol. No whiskey, no beer, he was done with it all. Zero.

Two dark-coated figures crossed the front windows. Troy's heart skipped a beat, his eyes glued to the smaller one as Jimmy Sweeney pushed out through the front door, stepping aside for Casey to pass. Jimmy put his arm around Casey and led her across the deserted parking lot, their path lit by a yellowed streetlight. Troy's heart squeezed. They walked toward him at a pretty good clip. His breathing grew shallow. Would Casey make a scene? Would Jimmy?

Troy waited. The red neon light atop the diner went dark. Seconds later, the interior lights went out. Only the night remained between them. Pinned to his seat, Troy couldn't move. Twenty feet away Casey slowed. Through the darkness, they made eye contact. Troy's heart fell. As expected, she was *not* happy to see him.

Jimmy caught on and stilled. A skinny dude, Troy could take him without thinking. If Jimmy tried to stop him from talking to Casey, Troy would lay him out. Flat. Casey picked up her step and Troy pushed out his through his door. Limbs shaky, he hung by his truck. "Casey."

Familiar blue eyes drilled into him. "What are you doing here?"

Troy's pulse kicked into his throat. "We need to talk."

"I have nothing to say to you."

Jimmy withdrew his arm from her shoulders.

"I need five minutes," Troy said.

"No."

"Five minutes, Casey. No matter what you think I've done, we're worth that much, aren't we?" He could see her wavering.

"Want me to wait?" Jimmy asked her.

She glanced up at him and Troy's heart thumped wildly. Casey was *his* woman! His temper fired hot but he extinguished it. Stop. *Wait.* "Give me five minutes," he pleaded. "Five minutes and then I'll leave if you want. I'll do whatever you say, but I need five minutes. *Alone.*"

After a few agonizing seconds, Casey nodded.

Jimmy hovered close and Troy wanted to belt him one. *You heard her*, he wanted to growl. She wants to talk to me.

"I'll see you tomorrow," Jimmy told her, the concerned look in his eyes grating on Troy. Dad gum—it wasn't like she should be afraid of him!

Preoccupied with Troy, Casey mumbled, "Okay."

Training his gaze on Troy, Jimmy walked to his car four spaces over.

Go on, Troy thought. She's safe with me. Waiting until Jimmy was inside his car, Troy turned his focus to Casey. The hurt in her eyes broke his heart. It was fresh and raw. He'd done that to her. Well, *he* didn't. That Jillian woman did. "Casey," he began, not sure how to proceed. Flicking a glance to Jimmy's departing car, he breathed easier. At least they were alone. He could talk freely. "There was nothing going on between that woman and me. She was only trying to make trouble. Ask Delaney, she'll tell you. She's been tryin' to cause trouble for everyone."

Casey was listening but made no outward attempt to confirm the same.

"I lost my job today," he confessed. Tears swam into her lids at his revelation. He failed her. But he had to come clean, she'd find out anyway. "After you left me, I got drunk. Really drunk." Pity stirred in her eyes, angering him, but he continued, "Mr. Foster came to the stables and when he smelled alcohol on me, he fired me on the spot." Casey remained fixed in place, rigid, unyielding. Other than her tears, she appeared cold, uncaring. "I'm not complaining or anything," he continued, "I know I did wrong. But it happened."

Casey didn't respond. She simply stared.

"Dad gum, Casey. Say something."

"What do you want from me?"

"I want to be with you."

"Why?"

"What are you talking about? Because I love you, that's why. You believe in me." Realizing that made her sound like a fool, he quickly added, "And I messed up. I messed up big time but I won't again." Casey crossed arms with an exasperated shrug. A tear fell and she glanced away, but Troy felt her opening to him. "I swear I won't. I've quit drinking. That Jillian woman don't mean anything to me. You do." He stepped toward her. "I love you and I want to be with you. Don't you want to be with me?"

"I don't know what to do."

"Be with me." She turned to him and a round of tears broke free. "I need you, Casey. I'm gonna quit drinking. I'll get another job. But I need you with me." Casey wasn't running away. She was listening, clearly thinking it over. "If you're not with me," he said, "none of it will be good. I'll hate my life."

Her body slackened and Troy knew he had won. This time. Pulling her to him, he inhaled the scent of her, a mix of fry oil and shampoo. There were no arms sliding around his waist. No smile or sweet words. Troy didn't kid himself. He was on fragile ground. Casey stayed put, but this might be his last chance.

He was going to make it a meaningful one.

They left her car at Fran's and drove to a field near his house. The hills were soaked in moonlight, the sky so clear, Troy could have driven out here without his headlights. Beside him, sitting on the center seat and tucked within his arm, Casey's body was warm. Troy wanted to lay under the stars with her. He wanted to tell her how he was going to make it up to her. They were a couple again and he wasn't going to mess it up. He never wanted to see the pain in her eyes again. Casey was more than his girlfriend, she was his *friend*, the kind who listened and supported a guy even when he messed up. She told him not to worry about the Fosters. There'd be other jobs and she'd help him find them.

Pulling off the road, he cut his headlights and drove down a gravelly road overgrown with weeds. Seldom used, it led to an open field not visible from the road.

"Where are we going?" she asked.

Troy hugged her to him. "There's a meadow on the other side of these trees. I thought we could watch for shooting stars."

Casey smiled. He couldn't care less about looking at a bunch of white dots in the sky, trying to catch a few that streaked across, but she seemed to really enjoy it, pointing out stuff like constellations and telling him all about them. Troy was impressed by her knowledge, but truthfully couldn't make out half of what she was pointing at—though he never said so. He nodded and pretended to think they were really cool. If she could support him and his desires, he could support hers.

After driving around a bend of trees, Troy parked. He pulled a blanket from behind his backseat, and picking a spot between his truck and the trees, spread the blanket out across the grass and sat, pulling her down with him. Taking her in his arms, Troy laid her down and rolled over on top of her, keeping her warm as best he could. Nuzzling in the crux of her neck, the soft strands of her hair, he inhaled the scent of her, sweet and feminine. He didn't mind the scent of fried food that lingered in her clothing. He wasn't smelling her clothes, he was smelling her skin. Her soft skin. Casey was soft and sweet and made him feel strong. Pulling back, Troy sought her eyes to capture her feelings. "I love you, Casey."

She gazed up at him with a delicate smile. "I love you, too, Troy."

"I'm never gonna let you down again."

She nodded, but the uncertainty in her gaze tugged at his heart. Casey wasn't sure about him. She was going to give him a chance but she wasn't convinced. Not yet. "I won't," he said, then dipped down to kiss her. Her soft gasp roused a need. Deep and stabbing, it startled him with its intensity. Troy kissed her harder, faster, his heart moving through the kiss from deep inside his chest to deep inside hers. Casey looped her arms around his back and kissed him like he was the most important thing in the world, like she'd die without him.

Casey made Troy feel powerful. She made him feel worthy. It was a feeling he wanted to live forever. Burying himself in her he kissed her lips, her cheeks, moved down her neck, back up again. Her slick mouth welcomed him without question. She wasn't tense, she wasn't hesitant, she was with him. Desire surged. Love gushed. He'd never felt this way about a girl before. He'd had a crush on Felicity, but they never talked like he and Casey, never shared their private feelings. How could they?

Travis was always in tow and three was a crowd. In a weird way, he was thankful Travis and Felicity got together. It gave him the chance to be with Casey and what he felt for her, Troy doubted he'd ever feel again. His gaze met hers, searching for confirmation. Did Casey feel it? Did she feel the same things he did?

"Casey," he said huskily, his body and mind warring for control. He was supposed to be looking at stars with her. He was supposed to be oohing and aahing as she pointed, but he couldn't think of anything but her. "Do you love me?" She nodded. "Do you love me as much as I love you?"

A slow smile wound from her lips to her deep blue eyes. The air was thick with the quiet. Too cold for no-see-ums, the temperature silenced the katydids. In the wash of moonlight, Casey's pale skin was lit with a vulnerability that pulled at him. Clear of blemishes, her face was like porcelain, fragile against the jet black of her hair. She peered up at him with more love than he deserved. *Casey loved him.* She loved him no matter what and he loved her. Tracing her brow, he kissed it, kissed her forehead, kissed her nose. She moaned softly, hardening his lust with a quick and urgent need. "I'm going to make it up to you, Casey. I'm going to make you proud of me."

She brushed the hair from his eyes, outlined the small scar on his cheekbone with her fingertip. "I'm already proud of you."

He shook his head, his heart wincing. He was nothing to be proud of—not yet. "No, I have to earn it. I'm going to show you that I can be who you think I am. Just give me time and I'll prove it."

She smiled, a gesture so tender it stole his breath away. Casey couldn't see anything but the good in him. She saw him for the man he could be, the man he was destined to be. "I'm gonna make you so proud..."

Troy couldn't finish the sentence. Casey placed a finger to his lips, because she didn't need to hear anymore. She didn't care. Troy's heart swelled. Recalling the foal he helped deliver and how he'd wanted to share it with her, he bet she'd be great with horses. Maybe one day, they could have a horse of their own. Deliver it together, raise it, train it to be the finest stallion that ever walked Tennessee. Vegas' slick black muzzle and distinctive white star came to mind. The foal was a beauty—a big one. He was going to make Miss Delaney a fine stallion one day and while Troy wouldn't be taking part in his life, maybe he and Casey could start their own ranch. A tenderness moved deep inside him. Someday, maybe even a family.

Troy's heart was pumping so hard, he swore she could feel the pounding. Cupping her neck, he kissed her gently on the lips. "I want to make love to you," he whispered into her mouth. Casey stilled beneath him. "I want to love you and show you that can trust me."

Casey stared at him, but something in her gaze softened. Opened. In that moment, everything changed between them. Casey didn't resist. Her body relaxed. Nothing stood between them but love. "Will you?" Her consent was barely a movement. Troy felt it more than he saw it, but it was there. "I love you, Casey. I'll always love you."

Casey closed her eyes and gave herself to him. He'd been forgiven.

Chapter Twenty

Casey burst into the apartment, catapulting Annie's pulse. She ran to her bedroom and slammed the door, the force nearly jolting Annie from the couch. She raced down the hall. "Casey?" She knocked briskly, a punch of adrenaline stampeding through her chest. "Casey, what is it?"

"Troy's *gone!*"

Alarmed by the panic in her daughter's voice, she demanded, "What do you mean, gone?" When Casey didn't respond, Annie tried the door knob. Finding it unlocked, she pushed it open. Casey was splayed across her bed, her face buried in her pillow. Instinct propelled Annie to her side. "What happened?"

"I saw Felicity at the diner," came the muffled reply. "She told me. Travis told her."

Annie placed a hand over her forehead. Gone, as in *missing*? Or packed up and left? "Did you call him? Is he okay?"

"Yes."

"And?" Annie pressed, growing more impatient by the second.

Casey rolled over to her side. Eyes teary, she murmured, "He left."

"Left?" The word felt inadequate, incomplete, though Annie feared she knew the reason. "Did you talk to him?"

"He wants to prove himself."

"Prove himself? To who? Why?" Annie asked, hating the despair in her daughter's gaze, the utter desolation.

"He wants to show everybody he's not a loser." Casey's blue eyes sharpened with lethal precision. "People like you."

Annie swallowed hard. "Casey."

"It's true, isn't it? You never cared for Troy. You don't like the fact that I'm seeing him, admit it."

"I didn't like the fact you were wrapping your life around his, but that doesn't mean I have anything against Troy. I only care about what happens to *you*."

Annie sank to the edge of Casey's bed. Cal's words reverberated in her skull. *Casey loves Troy. This will hurt, but you've got to help her through it.* "I know you care about him."

"I *love* him!"

Annie nodded mindlessly. If she could erase the pain in her daughter's eyes with words, she would. If she had a magic wand, she would brush the hurt away like a snow flurry against a warm windshield, a heartache that didn't stick. If she could, she'd wipe all evidence of the boy from Casey's heart. But she couldn't. Life didn't work that way. Love didn't work that way. Sometimes love hurt. Sometimes it set wings to your soul and other times it sucked you down whole. Love was unpredictable. Unfortunately, Troy wasn't. "Does this have anything to do with what happened yesterday?"

Casey looked away, clearly surprised by her mother's knowledge of events. "I don't know," she said, predictably dodging the reality of her boyfriend's poor choices. "He told me he needed to make some changes, needed to get his head straight. He said it was going to take time and I should be patient, give him time to show people he could do it." Raw anguish rolled through her gaze. "But I didn't expect him to leave. I didn't know he meant move out of town!"

"Oh, sweetheart, I'm sorry."

Casey rolled off the bed and stomped to her dresser, turning her back on Annie.

Giving her child the space she needed, Annie held her tongue. She didn't go to her and hold her, fold her in the embrace she knew the girl needed. She didn't offer any soothing words to ease her pain. Annie did nothing. She sat and she waited. Casey would have to open the door and invite her in.

Moments passed and Casey's shoulders began to shake. Annie heard the sniffles and knew the hurt was flowing freely. "I don't get it," Casey mumbled.

"Get what?" Annie ventured softly.

"He was doing a great job. Why did they fire him for something he did off the job?"

"Because Mr. Foster has specific rules against it."

Casey spun around to face her. Black liner created ugly streams down her cheeks. Anger scratched through innocence. "But it's not fair. His sons drink. Why should he fire Troy and not them?"

Annie couldn't dispute the point. It didn't make sense to her, either, but she wasn't about to question the man on his business practices. Troy knew the deal going in. He should have controlled himself. He had no one to blame but himself. "They're his sons. He's not going to fire them."

"So he takes it out on everyone else?"

Annie shrugged. It was a teenager's logic. "Maybe. Or maybe he's trying to do better."

"By firing the best ranch hand he had?"

Staring at the incredulous look on her daughter's face, only one question remained. Annie didn't want to hear the answer, but she had to know. "Were you with Troy when he was drinking?"

"No."

"You weren't with him? Not at all?"

Resentment strummed the air between them. Casey zeroed in on her mother, a mix of hate and understanding scoring her weary eyes. "I wasn't drinking. I don't drink. He went out and got drunk *because* of me, not with me."

"Because of you?"

She nodded, bombarded by a fresh onslaught of tears. "I accused him of being with that woman. I told him that I hated him and I never wanted to see him again." Casey's voice trembled as she explained, "He was upset. He got drunk. But he said he didn't do anything with her," Casey added quickly. "She came on to him. He had nothing to do with it."

"And you believe him?"

"Yes. Aunt Lacy was with Fran today and told me she watched the whole thing. Troy didn't do anything." Casey hugged her body as if supporting it from toppling. "That woman came on to *him*, not the other way around."

Annie breathed in deeply. One less mark against his record didn't make for a clean slate. One way or another, Troy was on a downward spiral. First it was his job in Murfreesboro, now his position with the Fosters. While he might not be on the prowl, he most certainly was not in line for a promotion. Exhaling in a heavy stream, she peered at her daughter. "So what's next?"

She might as well have kicked the floor out from under the child. Casey looked dazed, clueless, as if the question had never crossed her mind. "I don't know."

Annie contemplated the road ahead, Casey's future, her future. The two of them had some decisions to make. The two of them could move, start fresh. They could sell the property and take the money to begin their lives anew. Troy wasn't here. There was no reason for Casey to stay. Annie could help her daughter start over, maybe even attend college.

Cal's image popped into her mind's eye. Visions of his smiling face doused her heart. Cal wanted to commit his future here. He wanted to be part of Ladd Springs, of Serenity Springs. It was a place where Annie wasn't welcome. "You still have your job at the diner," she said, hoping it would be seen as a positive in her daughter's column.

Casey unwound her arms with an utterly beaten look. "Great."

"Have you given any more thought to going to college? With Troy gone, maybe it will give you something to fill your time."

"He said he'd be back."

"Be back, when?"

Casey wiped her eyes, her cheeks, then swiped a hand under her nose. She walked toward her mother and slumped to the mattress beside her. "He didn't say."

Annie wanted to scream at the top of her lungs, *Does he expect you to wait for him? Does he expect you to stop everything until he gets his act together?*

Over Annie's dead body. She would *not* let Casey sit home, whittling her time away as she waited for Troy Parker to grace her with his presence. She had to move on with her life. She had to find her passion, follow her dreams. It was the same thing Annie needed to do. Scraps of her last conversation with Cal broke in but she pushed them aside. Cal had found his way. She needed to find hers.

Dropping elbows to knees, Casey plunked chin to her hands and stared at the floor. "I probably couldn't get into college."

Hope detonated in Annie's chest. Did that mean she would consider trying? "Of course you could. Your grades in high school were good."

"C's. Most of them were C's."

"Only during your senior year. Before that you earned A's and B's."

Casey snorted.

"You could get into college, no problem. If you want, you can begin with the community college." They take everyone, Annie thought, the idea quickly gaining steam. Casey could attend the local college and then transfer to another school, a university. Or, better yet, they could sell the property and head to Chattanooga, or Knoxville. Thoughts of her mother and Felicity instantly nixed both locations. Maybe Memphis or, shoot, who said they had to stay in Tennessee? Annie loved the mountains. Perhaps Ashville would be a nice place to start over. Surely they had good schools there. "You could get your grades up after a semester or two and then apply to a four-year school."

"I don't even know what I'd do."

But at least she was thinking in terms of doing *something*. It was more than Annie had hoped for, and she wasn't about to push the subject. Cal was right about one thing. Casey's heart had been broken, and it was Annie's job as her mother to see her child through it. And see her through it she would. Better yet, she would see Casey through her heartbreak *and* work to see that college became a reality. First thing in the morning, Annie would call Ms. Devane. She would get the paperwork moving and sell the property. Jillian was offering twice what Cal could get logging and if Annie played her hand right, she could negotiate a higher offer. Her preliminary review of the online listings suggested Ms. Devane was on the low end of the market. She obviously had money. There was no reason Annie shouldn't get every penny she could out of the woman and then let her worry about roads and permits as she built her hotel.

As for the competition, Harris Hotels would have to fend for themselves. Annie was becoming convinced Jillian Devane wasn't quite the menace everyone was making her out to be. If she'd tried to ruin Nick before without success, why should they be worried about her now? Besides, Jillian wasn't Annie's problem—Casey was. With a gentle hand to her daughter's back, she whispered, "We'll get through this. We'll get through this and send you to any college you want." When Troy's ready to come home, he can wait on *you* for a change.

Later that night, seated alone in front of her computer, Annie stared at image after image on the screen, the lot of them beginning to look the same. Scrolling through photos of rolling hills and pasture for nearly two hours would do that to the eyes, eyes that were beginning to glaze over. Annie blinked and turned away from the monitor. She set her pen down and closed her notepad. One thing for sure, Ms. Devane was a thief. Glancing back at the screen, a particularly gorgeous piece of wooded land was featured front and center on a real estate website. Annie deemed Ladd Springs to be twice as nice as that one. Sure, the one listed had a house and pole barn, but if she deducted a hundred thousand for the structures, she still ended up with hundreds of thousands more than Ms. Devane was offering. Annie Owens might not be in the business of real estate, but she could research, same as anyone else.

According to the numbers listed on the internet, Casey's half of Ladd Springs was worth a heck of a lot more than five hundred thousand. It was closer to a million, maybe more. Blowing out her breath, she stood abruptly. And she would not be taken by some highfalutin' real estate developer lady who marched into town throwing money at her. If Jillian Devane wanted the property as bad as Lacy claimed she did, then she would have to pay for it. All Annie had to do was come up with a price. Turning off the computer, she retreated to her bedroom. Passing by Casey's bedroom door, Annie felt a stab of longing. Casey should be looking forward to college, a wonderful and exciting life, not tying her entire future to Troy. This should be an exciting time in her life, not depressing.

Annie entered her bedroom and flicked on an overhead light. She needed a change, too. She was tired of struggling, tired of working day after day and the occasional weekend only to barely scrape by. It wasn't fair. When she turned on the light for her bathroom, her gaze went to the line of nail polish bottles neatly organized atop her vanity, bright and colorful against the off-white countertop. Nails didn't pay the bills. She enjoyed the work, but the money wasn't enough to get ahead. It was enough to survive but that was it. No matter how hard she tried to save, she couldn't manage to get beyond paying the bills and actually grow her savings. Logging would give her an enormous sum of money *and* keep the property, but Ms. Devane's offer was double that amount, maybe more if Annie could convince her that the property was worth it. Selling would change their entire lives. They could move to a bigger city, Casey could go to college, Annie could work in a high end salon...

But it would mean leaving Cal. Annie dropped a hand to her vanity. A man she believed could be the one. Mr. Right, if such a thing existed. Gazing into the mirror, Annie saw a woman alone. An aging woman, a woman who'd been alone for most of her life and who desperately wanted change. She'd like to be with Cal. She'd like to think a future with him would be a happy one. They understood each other, grew from the same roots. It seemed a good fit. Cal didn't have a stake in Delaney's hotel business. Would he really care if she sold the property to Jillian? Would he mind if they sold and moved to a bigger city? Chattanooga was only an hour away. He could find a good job, remain close to his family. Hadn't he been telling her he was looking for a change? He mentioned using some of the timber money to build a home on the land, but Annie didn't care about staying close to Delaney. She didn't need to tie their futures together. She needed to stay close to Casey.

Annie scrutinized the reflection of her eyes. Dark circles were beginning to form, her mascara looking heavy and harsh against the pallor of her skin. She was tired. Change would do her good. Would Cal object to her selling?

Ignoring the sliver of answer that tiptoed through her heart, Annie washed her face and went to bed.

The decision had been made. Armed with recent land sales in the area, Annie called Jillian Devane to inform her of her decision. She was selling, but she wanted eight hundred thousand dollars for the property. It had been a bold move on her part, but to Annie's surprise, the woman didn't blink. *You drive a hard bargain, Ms. Owens. Draw up the paperwork and I will pay you eight hundred thousand dollars cash.* She'd been subtle, mincing her words with precision, but Annie could hear the excitement in her voice. The woman was *thrilled*.

Annie shivered as a burst of wind tumbled a pile of fallen leaves. The air was cold, clouds low and heavy. It would make a few people unhappy to learn of the sale, but they'd have to get over it. This was about securing her future. Theirs was set. Thoughts of Lacy and Delaney came to mind, their men, their wealth. It was time she found her own happiness. While she couldn't shake the feeling she was slinking around, making deals with the devil, she couldn't ignore the mind-boggling sum, either. *Eight hundred thousand dollars.* She never dreamed of seeing that much money in a lifetime, let alone one afternoon. One very cold afternoon.

Pulling her coat tightly to her body, she plowed ahead. Mr. Dakota said he could have the papers ready for signature by lunch time. She couldn't believe a major transaction could be handled so soon, but he assured her it was no problem. All she had to do was sign on the dotted line and the deal would be done.

For the first time in months, Annie felt light of mind. She felt good, energetic. The chilly air bit at her cheeks, but she didn't care. A decision had been made. It was a decision that freed her heart. After spending so much time worrying about how to pay for the property, she never had the opportunity to enjoy the fact that it was theirs. With the sale, Casey would be able to enjoy the benefits of being financially secure, and Annie could take her percentage as trustee. Mr. Dakota said there was nothing wrong with it, so long as Casey didn't object. It was a consent Casey had given more readily than Annie expected.

Grateful things were beginning to roll their way, Annie was already thinking in terms of investment. The sum of money was enormous—easily able to cover Casey's college expenses, a little house for the two of them wherever they landed. Gerald Foster could help direct her as to which investments she should choose, how to keep the money safe long-term. As soon as Annie thought of him, his offer to purchase nipped at her conscience. He'd wanted first dibs. He'd wanted the chance to buy the land from her before anyone else. Running back through the conversation, Annie tried to recall if she'd agreed. *Had she?*

Annie couldn't remember. The Thanksgiving supper had been nothing but a blur of "meet the family" and "what accident?" She was still curious about what really happened, if there was more to the story than Cal was letting on. It sure felt like it, but now it seemed like none of her business. She and Cal might be finished once he learned of the sale. She expected him to be upset with her, but she took strength in the knowledge that she had done what was best for her and Casey. If he had any serious intentions of being with her, he was going to have to accept the fact that she was a grown woman with a mind of her own. She didn't need his permission to sell—or his approval.

Wrapping a gloved hand around a heavy vertical bar that was the entrance to the Dakota Law Firm, Annie hoped it wasn't the end to their relationship. She hoped Cal meant what he said about moving with her.

Jillian Devane stood in the small lobby, her presence consuming the modest setting of the Dakota law firm, a single couch, two wingchairs, a potted plant and a mass-produced framed landscape print hanging on a wall lined with wainscoting. Draped in a full-length chocolate silk coat and matching hat, her black hair combed in a sleek swath down her back, Jillian smiled. "Good afternoon, Ms. Owens."

Momentarily stunned as the reality of her actions hit home, Annie hesitated. "Hello."

"You're right on time," she noted in a tone Annie felt to be somewhat mocking.

She cleared her throat, "I do like to be punctual."

Mr. Dakota walked out through his open office door with a friendly smile. "Hey, Annie."

Dressed casually in a plain white dress shirt and black slacks, the lawyer wore no tie or jacket, something Ms. Devane probably found lacking. But Mr. Dakota was a country lawyer, and in these parts folks didn't waste time on formalities and pretense. They focused on getting the job done. Annie stepped forward. "Hi, Mr. Dakota."

"Call me Hank."

"Hank."

Looking between the two women, he asked, "Ready?"

Jillian practically purred, "*Yes*."

Pulling the gloves from her hands, Annie nodded. "Let's do it."

Chapter Twenty-One

A looming sense of dread settled over the table as Nick Harris received an update on the situation. Delaney, Malcolm, Lacy and Cal huddled together at Fran's Diner, each and every one feeling the impact of his displeasure. Malcolm was steeped in concern, Lacy sat supportive by his side while Delaney sat like a bundle of nerves and resentment. Cal had worked his way through nearly half a bowl of Fran's boiled peanuts. Nick Harris hadn't been in town for a twenty-four hours and his anger was palpable. Not exactly the circumstances Cal would have chosen for his first meeting with his new boss, a man who fit Annie's description snug as a glove. Part lumberjack, part international businessman, Nick's six-foot four stature and dark brown hair was surly and foreboding and could rattle even the bravest of men in a dark alley.

"What the hell has been going on since I left?" Nick demanded.

"Jillian Devane, that's what," Malcolm replied.

Nick stared at his partner, dumbstruck. "Do you think Annie will sell?"

Malcolm looked to Cal, as did the others. It was Annie's decision, but he was the one working to help her make it. "I don't know. I don't think so, but Annie has a mind of her own. If the number's high enough, she might."

"I knew she was only after the money," Delaney interjected.

"Now hold on," Cal said. "Annie's worked hard her whole life. She's taken care of her daughter, and there's nothing wrong with wantin' to do better by herself."

Delaney glared at him. "You're preachin' to the choir, Cal. My life story reads no different."

"And you sold out," he reminded quietly, heedless to the scorch of reprisal staring back at him. Delaney had a reputation as a spit-fire but she wasn't anything he couldn't handle.

"It's not the same—"

"How much is Jillian offering?" Nick jumped in, redirecting their focus. "Can we up the offer? Make a deal with Annie so sweet, she can't resist?"

"Maybe I can talk to her," Lacy piped up. "Maybe I can get her to realize that Jillian is no good and she's only using her."

Nick seemed doubtful. "Money is money. Annie doesn't have a vested interest in Harris Hotels or Ladd Springs."

"Well, she *should*. Casey's a Ladd, isn't she?"

"And thrilled to be one," Delaney mused soberly. Dropping an elbow to the table, she plunked her face into her palm. "Casey hates Jeremiah."

Cal agreed. From what Annie said, Casey despised her father. There was no reason for her to find any sentimental value in the property. And with Troy gone, she was going to be hurting something fierce. The two were ripe for picking up stakes and moving on.

"I say we make an offer," Malcolm submitted. "If Annie is willing to sell to Jillian, she should be willing to sell to us. Can you talk to her?" he asked Cal.

"I can try." Though he was uncertain as to whether they were actually on speaking terms at the moment.

"Try," Nick reinforced. "Find out what Jillian's offering and double it."

Delaney's expression took a hit. "*Double it*?"

He nodded. "I know Jillian and I guarantee she's offering pennies on the dollar for what the land is worth."

"Don't you think Annie would know that?" Malcolm looked between the men. "She has to have someone helping her with the deal. An agent, a lawyer? Surely they'll advise her if it's a lowball offer."

"She's working with Dakota," Cal said. "I found out over Thanksgiving."

"Is he ethical?" Malcolm asked.

"I haven't dealt with him in years, but my Daddy trusts him. They've had a lot of dealin' together at the bank."

"Can you call him?" Nick asked. "Get information on any deal she might have working?"

"I don't think you'll get anywhere," Malcolm returned. "Attorney-client privilege should prevent him from discussing the matter."

A privilege Cal knew could be stretched and bent around these parts. Legal jargon might hold up like a steel cage in California, but around here, people discussed business without thinking, assuming everyone knew about it already. There were no secrets between friends and family, and that accounted for most of the town.

"Well, we need to do something and we need to do it fast," Nick snapped.

"I hear you," Cal replied, cutting him some slack. Under the circumstances, Nick was under a lot of pressure. His hotel plans were well underway and if Jillian purchased the adjoining property, she could make his life miserable.

"And I mean fast. You don't know what this woman is capable of."

"He does," Malcolm said.

Cal nodded, and glanced around the restaurant, the normalcy of the lunch crowd disquieting him. Local folks were oblivious to the danger that lay ahead, the havoc one woman could play on their town. After Lacy spotted Jillian Devane outside the Trendz salon, Malcolm had warned Cal to keep an eye out for trouble. Jillian was a serious threat, he'd told him, explaining how she'd destroyed a competitor in South America through dubious means. A group out of Asia beat her in a deal for a tract of prime oceanfront land, snapping the land out from underneath her shiny black heels. Jillian bought the adjacent property, put up a small building and sat on it for two months. Tragically, the structure burned to the ground, taking hundreds of acres with it. The nearby hotel was evacuated, a sizeable chunk of its land scorched clear to the shore-line.

On word of the disaster, Jillian feigned shock and despair, but Nick knew better. Jillian had orchestrated the fire, alluding to the incident in subtle terms, suggesting it was karmic justice, a concept she whole-heartedly supported. But Nick recognized the deception behind her thin mask of sympathy. For him, it had been the beginning of the end to their relationship.

Which made Cal feel better about the man. He'd come to know and respect Malcolm, but his time in Arizona taught him there were developers who didn't care about the land they developed or the people they sold it to, no matter how loud they professed to the contrary. They were interested in money, nothing more and nothing less. Cal couldn't work for a man like that, not in good conscience. Straightening in his seat, he said, "I'll talk to her. She's a reasonable woman. She'll understand what's at stake."

Cal waited until Annie returned home. Parked outside her apartment complex, he watched from afar as she parked, walked up the staircase and entered her home. He gave her a few minutes to settle in before climbing out of his truck and ascending the stairs himself. He didn't expect her to be happy to hear from him but she would. He had to dissuade her from selling to Jillian Devane, whether it cost him her affection or not. Wild flames raging through forest land exploded in his mind. The town's well-being depended on it.

Mildly winded, he knocked on her door.

Annie appeared before him, clearly surprised. "Cal? What are you doing here?"

"I hope you don't mind me showing up on your doorstep without calling first, but I have to talk to you."

"What is it?" She stepped aside, letting him in. "Is everything okay?"

Cal felt like a heel, a henchman doing his master's bidding. But it had to be done and he was the only one to do it.

Squaring off with her, he asked point-blank, "Are you selling the land to Jillian Devane?"

Annie hesitated, but the jerk in her gaze told him all he needed to know. His posture slackened. "Why, Annie? What happened to the logging?"

"Jillian offered a lot more money than I'd ever realize from logging."

"But you'll lose the land entirely."

Annie stepped away from him, hovering by the dining room table. "Casey doesn't want it. She's through with the Ladds, the Parkers..."

Cal followed her, but hung back. "Is this about Troy and Casey?"

"Please don't tell me you're going to stick up for him again. He dumped her, Cal. She forgave him and he dumped her. Dumped her flat and broke her heart."

Cal understood broken hearts all too well. But broken hearts could mend. Troy could mend. If Annie sold to Jillian, the land they both knew and loved would be destroyed. His new beginning would be destroyed along with it. "I should tell you that Nick has made an offer to buy it from you."

"Nick? Why would he want to buy it when he already has half of Ladd Springs?"

"To prevent Jillian from getting it."

She blew out her breath and crossed her arms. "I think Nick is making a big deal out of nothing. If he can't stand the competition, he should get out of the business."

"It's more than competition."

She stormed past him and took up position on the opposite side of the couch. She turned. "Really? Because from where I'm standing it looks like a man afraid that a woman is going to upstage him."

Cal hated the distance she was putting between them. He didn't want to make accusations about a person, even a woman like Jillian, but Annie needed to understand what was at stake. "She wants revenge, Annie. The woman is buying the property to destroy Nick."

"So I've heard," she said, rolling her eyes.

"If you know what she's after, why would you help her?"

"Because I need the money, Cal. Casey wants to go college, she wants to start fresh, maybe even get out of this town and find her future in a bigger city. This is my opening with her and I'm not going to blow it."

The knife to his heart was quick. Cal was all too familiar with blown chances. He understood Annie was working under powerful pressure. "I understand."

"Do you? Because it sounds like you're fighting me on this, Cal. I thought we agreed that I needed a new direction, a change in my life. This offer to sell is that chance."

"But Nick can buy it."

"Your daddy said he wanted to buy it, too, but I doubt they're willing to pay me what she's offering."

"How much?"

"Almost a million dollars." Cal let out a low whistle. "That's right." Annie had declared the amount almost victoriously, but he knew the woman only offered the amount to ensure her revenge. If what Malcolm said about her family wealth was true, the sum was a penny in a beggar's tin can. "I hardly think Nick has the kind of money to waste on buying more than six hundred acres of land he doesn't need, competition or not. Jillian Devane in Tennessee is something he's going to have to live with."

"It's not competition when a person resorts to arson."

Annie paled. "Arson?"

Cal nodded. He hated to cast people in a scandalous light when he had no proof, but Annie left him no choice. He had to get her to understand what was really going on, how they could lose everything if she sold to Jillian, his new job included. "According to Malcolm, Jillian lost out on a real estate deal in South America several years ago and was spittin' mad. Another company purchased some land she wanted and laughed in her face as they built their hotel. She bought the adjacent land and built a small building. Two months later it burned down and took half the hotel property next door with it."

Annie gaped at him. She was listening. She understood the ramifications. Encouraged, he felt a blast of confidence. "Jillian Devane willfully burned hundreds of acres of beautiful land, Annie, because she wanted revenge—revenge for losing out on a sale." Cal paused, allowing it to sink in. He had Annie's complete attention and he aimed to use it to get her to see the consequences of selling. Annie brought a hand to her forehead.

Cal's heart squeezed. She must be imagining the same thing happening to Ladd Springs, hating the thought as much as he did. He dropped his voice, "This woman wants that revenge again, and I'd hate to see the same thing happen here."

Annie took two steps and fell into a heap on the couch. Dropping her face into her hands, she shook her head. Cal saw it as his opportunity and went to her side. Annie had heard him. His mind eased. She knew it wasn't the right thing to do. She wouldn't sell to Jillian Devane, not at this point. Sitting beside her, he placed an arm around her shoulders. "She's not a decent woman." Annie clamped her hands tightly to her face and Cal's spirits fell as he realized she must have been looking forward to the money. It had to be more than the logging, or else why would she sell? Cal rubbed a hand up and down her back. "If you want to sell, Annie, Nick offered to buy the land," Cal said. "I know he'll pay a fair price."

Annie returned a muffled, "I can't sell it to him."

"Sure you can. Or maybe you might want to keep it." His hand paused. "If Casey wants to go to college and you don't like the logging idea, we can come up with something else." Like marriage, he wanted to say. Cal wanted to marry Annie, and as her husband he could easily pay for Casey's college, could pay to build a house on the land, too. Envisioning Casey studying from a desk in her bedroom in their new log cabin home, Cal's hope swelled. Annie was proud and independent, but she couldn't tell him no if they were married. He pulled her to him, relishing the scent of her, the feel of her soft body next to his. He hummed against her silky hair. "We can work it out, Annie, I know we can."

Abruptly, she lifted to face him. A horrible feeling overcame him as she said, "No we can't. I've already signed the contract to sell to Jillian."

Chapter Twenty-Two

As Annie idled at the salon, a shiver raced through her. Most of the women had gone home for the day, only the receptionist and one stylist remained, but she was packing up her things. "Are you sure you're okay to lock up?" Bobbi Jo asked again, digging through her purse for her car keys. "I don't mind staying."

Annie smiled. She appreciated the girl's enthusiastic attitude toward her growing responsibility. It was a sign Bobbi Jo took her job seriously and would make a great assistant manager one day. "I'm fine," Annie told her. "You go on."

Bobbi Jo waited for her hairstylist friend to join her up front. The two gave one last questioning look. "If you're sure?"

"I'm sure." And ready to get this over with. Jillian Devane was meeting her here under the guise of scheduling a time to go over the survey for the property, the preliminary boundary lines. It was the one thing Ms. Devane insisted upon before closing. She wanted a completed survey of her own. Probably to locate the closest property line to the new Serenity Springs hotel, enabling her next fire to hit as close to home as possible. *Home.* It was Delaney's home. Felicity's home, land Annie and Lacy had enjoyed as kids. Imagining it black and crispy was hard to digest. It left a bitter taste, a traitorous feeling in her gut. She and Delaney had their differences but they were part of the same community, shared a history, a hometown. That meant something. Annie expelled a sigh. It was coming to mean more than she believed possible.

Escorting the girls to the door, Annie pretended to lock up behind them. She waved through the glass door, forcing a smile to her lips. *Bye-bye*, she mouthed. With a swift glance at the wall clock, she prepared herself for Jillian Devane. She would be here in ten minutes. Glancing around the salon, a slew of nerves tumbled through her. She had to convince her to cancel. Annie had to make her see it wasn't worth the effort and that she would do everything she could to stand in her way. Cal said the law was on Jillian's side, that Annie had no right to cancel. But if she could appeal to the woman in her, make her think this was about her daughter, maybe she would sympathize. Maybe she would see it wasn't the right thing to do.

Jillian didn't need to know that Annie knew about the fire. She was a mother interested in her child, not a woman trying to save her family's land. Casey's land. Casey's family. Thoughts of wildfire blazed through her mind. Viscous images of terrified animals and charred tree trunks, acres upon acres scorched because she had been short-sighted when it came to building Casey's future. Casey didn't need money or land—she needed love and compassion. She needed her family. Sadly, it was the only part of the picture Annie had missed. Family meant more than blood kinship. It meant solidarity.

The light rap at the door stopped Annie's heart. She turned to see Jillian Devane stroll inside. Circling the receptionist desk, she stood feet from Annie. "Couldn't this have been handled with a phone call?"

"Like I said, I needed to discuss the survey with you."

Cold eyes appraised her with no small amount of skepticism. "I'm a very busy woman. I have people who take care of these things. Can't your lawyer handle this for you?"

Dressed warmly in her fur coat, an earthy tan turtleneck cradled up around her neck, Jillian displayed a disposition that was anything but warm and cordial. She was stern, businesslike. She was treating this call as a nuisance detail she'd rather not be handling. "I'm sorry, but I'd rather discuss it with you personally." A swarm of nerves undermined her confidence but she pushed past them. "I want to cancel our deal."

A flicker of anger danced behind Jillian's tiger eyes. "Do you understand that you cannot?"

"I'm appealing to your sense of compassion." Jillian almost laughed, jarring Annie to realize the absurdity of her request. A woman willing to burn down a hotel didn't tote a bag of compassion. She nursed a heart of stone. What was she thinking? A budding desperation drove her forward. "My daughter doesn't want to sell. She's decided she wants to stay here and go to college. And since it's her property, I thought it only fair to grant her wishes."

Jillian's frosty glare matched the cool drips of blue lighting overhead. "She should have thought of that beforehand."

"I'm asking you to cancel. There are other properties. You can still compete with Harris Hotels if you buy a different one. I'll even help you find it," she said, the lie automatic.

"I do not want other properties. I want the one I have."

"Well, I'm not selling it anymore."

"Oh, but you are."

"I can back out."

"If you back out, I will sue you for default."

"Go ahead. I don't have anything to sue for."

"You have the property."

"It's not mine—it's Casey's! She has a right to say no. She can object to the sale—Mr. Dakota said so!"

It was the first crack she had detected in the woman's iron façade. Unwittingly, Annie must have hit upon something. "You are legally entitled to sign for her until she is of age thirty. The contract is solid," Jillian insisted, her eyes flat as a shark's and just as dispassionate.

Annie wracked her brain for a way out, an escape clause—something that could prevent the sale from going through. If it did, the destruction of Ladd Springs would rest on her shoulders. It would be her fault. "I'll have her contest it." Yes, that's what Jeremiah had planned to do to Felicity's title. He was going to contest it, fight it, tell a judge it wasn't legitimate. She could do the same thing, right? "We'll contest this sale and fight you in court."

Jillian slipped into an indulgent smile, a gesture that held complete contempt. "Your talk of legal matters sounds very compelling, Ms. Owens, and you're right. You may choose to take this to court." Her gaze went dark, but her pupils held a white glow. "But I'd advise you against it." Jillian neared and Annie felt her lungs collapse. "If you fight me on this and I warn you, I will exact my revenge on *you*." Annie flinched. "I am not a woman to toy with, do you understand?" Annie nodded, despite herself. Flames licked at her imagination as the threat seared onto her psyche in very real terms. "I will close on this property in one month's time. I expect the survey to be completed upon my return from Brazil."

She was leaving? An abrupt relief swept through Annie, filtering through her limbs.

"Do we understand each other?"

"Yes." She nodded like an obedient child. "Yes."

"Good."

Cal parked outside the old farmhouse that had been Ernie Ladd's home for as long as he could remember. The ridgeline of mountains called to the boy in him, the scent of pine pulling memories and joys of days gone by. Overhead, the setting sun glazed puffy white clouds, the blue sky melting to purple-gold as the temperature dropped quickly. It was a gorgeous evening taking shape, another crisp autumn night. If only he could take Annie into his arms and snuggle up by a fireplace. He was aching to hold her, make love to her. He was tired of proper distance and decorum. He wanted her close to him, by his side, in his heart. Cal wanted Annie in his life for good. But first, they had to solve the problem of Jillian Devane.

Walking toward the cabin, he observed a wooden structure rundown by time. More than weathered, it was worn from neglect and a cryin' shame, if you asked him. This property was one of Cal's favorite places, always had been. Inhaling the sight of thick forest around him, a river curving around and under the entry bridge, the expanse of meadow seeping into a distant line of trees, Cal thought Ladd Springs was a beautiful tract of land. It was Tennessee living in its purest form. While his family-owned ranch land was groomed to perfection and lined with miles of fencing, the main house bordered by expensive landscaping and flowers, the Ladd property remained fairly close to its original condition. Other than all the survey flags placed about the perimeter, the flattened earth to his right, the heavy equipment parked in neat rows off to the side, waiting for the crew to return. Cal smiled inwardly. Annie was right. Nick and Malcolm had been busy!

Turning, he sought a trail that he knew led to the stables. Nothing more than a tunnel of green, the path wound alongside a creek the entire way back. If followed past the stables, folks would stumble upon the earliest Ladd homestead, the house Grandpa Ladd inherited from his daddy and grandfather before him. Cal remembered it well. Bigger than Ernie's shack of a home, the Ladd estate had been two-storied and built on the edge of a forest overlooking a field of rolling green. It was a wide field where horses once grazed to their heart's content, along with a mess of goats. Originally constructed near 1800, the home had severely aged from its previous grandeur by the time Cal and his brothers stormed the scene.

Cal remembered the place well because he and his brother Jack used to set designs on catching one of old man Ladd's horses. They had their own horses, but their father only allowed them to ride under his supervision—a restriction the Foster boys didn't take kindly to, he and Jack in particular. Riding was in their genes, in their blood. They didn't want to wait until Daddy gave the okay, so the two of them would hide on the edge of Ladd forest, inserting themselves between the shadows of trunks and leaves as they crafted a plan. They'd fix their eyes on a target, discuss the best way to wrangle an animal under their control, and then one of them would bolt out of hiding and work to get a running jump. Invariably the horse would wise up and take off. Warmed by the memory, Cal chuckled. One time, Jack nearly got kicked. They didn't know it at the time, but the Palomino was in foal and a bit particular about who she'd let ride her. Jack didn't mind a lick. He brushed off the dirt and went back into hiding, setting his eyes on the next prize. Cal heaved a sigh. Those were good days, he thought, bothered by the difference between then and now with regard to his brother, Jack.

"Hey, Calvin!"

Cal turned to see Albert Ladd waving to him from the porch. Decked out in blue denim coveralls and white T-shirt, the older man was round as a melon. Albert's dark hair was longer now and appeared to have thinned, but that was to be expected. Cal hadn't seen him for what, going on twenty years?

"Hey, Albert!" Cal waved and walked over in short order. Taking the steps two at a time, he shook hands with the senior Ladd. "I didn't know you were home."

"I'd been nappin'."

Cal smiled. "Nothing wrong with a little slumber. How the heck have you been?"

"Well, I guess all right." He lowered his gaze and said, "Since Ernie died and all."

"I know. I was sorry to hear about that Albert. Ernie was a good man." There'd been no public funeral. Delaney kept it small and personal. Actually, from what Annie said, Ernie was buried somewhere behind this cabin. It had been a last request of Ernie's. Delaney's mother was buried there, and Ernie said he wanted to be with her, in heaven and on earth.

"Took good care of me."

"I'll bet he did," Cal said and wondered who was taking care of him now. Delaney lived in her mother's hideaway cabin up the hill. Did she look after him? Settling his gaze on Albert's hang-dog look, the tattered wool coat falling from his shoulders, Cal imagined she did. Who else?

"What brings you out?" Albert asked genially.

"I'm here to see Delaney. Annie Owens told me she lived here. Up in her momma's old cabin." He gestured toward the tiny log home barely visible from the porch.

Albert nodded. "She's a good girl."

"Always was a fine young lady, from what I remember."

"She has a daughter, you know."

"So I hear."

"Came home from college, she's growin' up so fast." Albert smiled. "A real angel, that girl, used to come play her flute for me and Ernie every night before she moved off to Knoxville."

Cal let out a low whistle. "I'll bet that was a heavenly sound."

"You know it was," Albert replied wistfully, lumbering toward a rocker. "Sweeter than God's own orchestra, I tell you. Even came down and played a spell for me before she left." He lowered to a seat and took to informing Cal of the news of the day, catching him up with Ladd business, any town gossip he'd heard.

As Cal listened, visions of his past floated in. Standing on Ladd property brought back memories of Delaney and Jack, Annie and Jeremiah, even Casey and Troy. Young lovers who ached to be together but eventually tore each other down. It wasn't the way love was supposed to work. Love was supposed to strengthen you, lift you higher than you could climb alone. But relationships didn't always work out that way, his marriage a case in point. Cal had loved Caroline with all his heart, but he couldn't hold onto her love on account of his drinking. He'd tried to make amends, but some things couldn't be forgiven.

When Albert paused long enough for him to cut in, Cal said, "Well, Delaney's waitin' for me." He didn't want to be rude, but he didn't want to churn through the past, either. His life was about looking forward, not back.

Albert shooed him off the porch. "Then you better git. Don't want to keep that one waitin'."

Cal chuckled. "Well, if you don't mind..."

Albert nodded. "Good to see you again, Calvin. Don't make a stranger of yourself."

"I won't. I'll be sure to stop by again soon."

Cal tipped his head and went in search of Nick and Delaney. Bombarded with memory as he crossed the rickety creek bridge, he dropped his gaze to the rushing water below. Greens and browns were a blur beneath the rapid flow of water, the evening sunlight catching in eddies as it swirled around rocks. He paused. His family's property didn't have near as many water features as the Ladds, and after working over a decade without any whitewater to speak of, Cal understood the value. Water was inherently calming. Fast-flowing, it calmed what stirred you, washed over your spirit until you were cleansed. When Cal first gave up the drink, he'd ached for a stream to calm him. Looked high and low for some kind of water to speak to his soul, remind him of who he was and what he needed. Phoenix had rivers but they weren't like home. Maybe because they weren't surrounded by the lush green mountains he loved. Maybe it was the color, but something about sitting near the Arizona water didn't feel right. This felt right.

"Cal."

Cal lifted his head and found Delaney standing near the bridge. She wore no more than a scratch of makeup yet her skin was tanned and healthy-looking, despite the fog of fall that had descended on the town. Though she was almost forty years old, he had to admit Delaney was still a looker, the jeans and jean jacket suiting her well. He wondered at the foil-covered dish in her hands but didn't ask. It was none of his business. "Hey, Delaney."

"What are you doing here?"

He smiled. "Looking for you and Nick."

"Did you talk to Annie?"

Cal appreciated a straightforward approach. It was nothing less than he'd expect from Delaney Wilkins. She married Jack when she was young and feisty and it seemed that part about her hadn't changed. But Annie was right about one thing. Delaney had hardened. She wasn't the idealistic young girl who fell in love with his brother, wanting nothing more than to dote on him, run with him, share her life with him. Cal believed she would have, had Jack not hit her. The abuse had left its mark not only on Delaney, but on the entire Foster family. But unlike him, Jack had not changed his ways and Cal wasn't sure he ever would. "The news isn't good."

Distrust gathered instantly in her gaze and she drew her dish close to her body. "She sold, didn't she?"

"She did."

"That selfish—"

"Stop right there." Cal held up a hand. He wasn't about to listen to Delaney tear down the woman he loved. Her suddenly edgy stance looked as if she was prepared for battle—a battle he would fight and win. "Annie did what she thought best for her and Casey. I can't hold followin' her gut against a gal."

Delaney narrowed her gaze. "You're giving her too much credit, Cal. She intended to sell that land the minute she got her hands on it. It's always been about the money with her."

A strange anger unfurled in him. Cal took a step toward Delaney and lowered his voice. "Delaney, I'm going to tell you something and I'm only going to tell you once. You tie that tongue of yours in a pretty package and stick it in the back of your throat when it comes to Annie, 'cause I don't want to hear another cross word about her come out of it, you hear?"

Delaney opened her mouth...and slowly closed it.

Cal smiled, unsettled by the thrash of feelings in his chest. "Annie's had a hard go of it and she's managed to keep it together. That's sayin' something."

"And I haven't?"

"You left Jack for a free roof over your head and the knowledge you had a legacy to look forward to. Annie was abandoned by her mother and the father of her child, then had to scrape by for everything she has. She's built a fine career for herself, and where her heart could have been tarred black, it remains clean and pure of motive." Delaney clamped her mouth shut but he could see an objection exploding behind her fiery brown eyes. And that's where it should stay. "So we're clear..." He honed in on her. "I won't stand by and listen to you speak disrespectfully about the woman I love." Catching sight of movement from the corner of his eye, Cal looked up in time to see Nick Harris jump free of the wooded trail that meandered down from Susannah's old cabin. Even from this distance the man's over six-foot broad-chested stature was imposing, appearing at home in the forest wearing jeans and a plaid shirt. Delaney followed Cal's gaze but remained mute. Nick closed the distance in seconds. Noticing Delaney's odd expression, Cal's gaze darted between the two of them.

"Everything all right here?" Nick asked.

"Real fine," Cal replied, silently tagging Delaney for a response.

"Fine," she agreed. "Except that Annie already signed a contract."

Anger deepened the tanned lines around Nick's black eyes. "Are you sure?"

"Unfortunately, yes," Cal said. "We were literally a day late."

"Damn."

Cal understood it was a setback—a major one—but he would not let them take it out on Annie. She was an innocent. She had no knowledge of Jillian's history of arson, her depth of bitterness and desire for revenge. And that was their fault—his, Nick's, Malcolm's. None of them had bothered to share the details with her, and they should have—the minute Lacy told them about Jillian's visit to Annie's salon. "She didn't know about the arson. She didn't know the severity of the situation. And considering the iffy relations between land owners..." He tapped Delaney with a brief glance. "You can't blame a woman for wanting to sell and start fresh."

Nick looked to Delaney but didn't defend her. As well he shouldn't, Cal mused. Delaney had a lot of good traits, but when she didn't like a person, she sharpened her claws and stood poised for the kill.

Delaney grunted. "I've gotta go."

Cal watched her as she headed straight for Albert's cabin. When she jogged down the steps empty-handed a few minutes later, he realized he'd been right—she was indeed the one taking care of Albert these days. Yes, Delaney Wilkins was a good woman. Hard-headed, but with a heart pure as gold.

"I guess it's time to pay a personal visit." Cal turned, surprised. Was Nick watching after Albert, too? "Jillian has to be stopped."

Cal nodded. *That made more sense.*

Nick heaved a sigh and asked, "You coming?"

"Where to?"

"Cougar hunting."

Chapter Twenty-Three

Annie swung open the door to Fran's, the clang of bells jarring to her mood as she entered the diner. She'd blown it. Totally blown it. She had foolishly tried to reason with Jillian Devane and instead of convincing her to cancel, she'd pasted a target on her head. A big, fat black X that shouted, *Come and get me*!

How stupid could she be? What part of her thought it was possible that a woman capable of burning down a hotel would listen to reason and sympathize? It was ludicrous, nuttier than a three dollar bill.

"Hey, sugar!" Annie barely returned her aunt's wave.

The non-response was like a magnet. Fran hurried over and took hold of her arm, "What's wrong, Annie Grace? You look like a bag of shock's been dumped on you."

About to dismiss it as nothing to worry about, Annie abandoned the effort, certain Fran would see clear through it. "I'm in a mess of trouble, Fran."

"Trouble?" Blue eyes hollowed with fear. "What's wrong? It's not Casey, is it?"

Annie shook her head. Spotting Casey in the kitchen with Jimmy Sweeney, she was grateful the boy was proving a positive distraction for her daughter. He was Candi's nephew and not free of emotional issues himself, but he'd given up his Goth gear over the summer and was working to "walk the trail" with the rest of them. Casey seemed to like him. Even talked about how he was helping her understand Troy's departure. It didn't bring him back, but then again, Annie wasn't sure if she wanted Troy back. It seemed he always ended up hurting her daughter and as far as Annie was concerned, the more distance between them, the better. But she didn't have time for Casey's troubles. She was mired in a mountain of her own. "I've sold the property to the entirely worst person I could have."

"Who?"

"Jillian Devane." At Fran's blank look, she clarified, "The foreign woman who's been running around here lately."

Comprehension formed shadows in Fran's wise old eyes. "I knew she was no good. What's she want with your property, anyway?"

"To get back at Nick Harris." Again, Fran wasn't privy to the details of Nick's past and Annie waved her off. "Trust me when I say it isn't pretty."

"Well then, don't look now, but ugly just walked in."

Annie gulped. Sure enough, Jillian Devane waltzed inside the diner. Her pulse scattered as she recalled the threats. *Was she following her*? Spying on them?

Jillian walked over. "Ms. Owens," she said, "so nice to see you again."

"What can I do you for?" Fran asked, her tone noticeably cold.

Unaffected, Jillian replied, "I'd like a coffee to go. I have a long drive to the airport and I don't want to fall asleep on the way."

Fran checked with Annie, silently asking if she was okay alone with the woman. Annie nodded. "Coming right up."

Trying to avoid looking directly at Jillian, Annie kept her attention on the door. Bells announced Nick and Delaney's arrival. Jillian's eyes lit up, focusing on them immediately.

Annie wanted to crawl under a booth. Surely the two of them must know. Cal had to have told them, though she wasn't sure. She hadn't spoken to him since last night when he tried to console her. Who knew who he'd told in the meantime? Curiosity moved Annie a few steps closer as she watched the scene unfold from a distance. What were they saying? Were they discussing her?

Jillian slid her hands up Nick's chest and leaned into him—to Delaney's utter horror—and Annie swore the woman was about to slip open a button on his plaid shirt. In an unlikely show of cowardice, Delaney remained frozen in place. Annie was appalled. *Did Delaney not see what the woman was doing?* Annie was happy to see Nick slowly remove the slender hands from his chest. He was having none of her games. "Not this time, Jillian," she heard him say. "Cancel the contract or I go to the authorities."

She responded like a satiated cobra. Propping an elbow on a crossed arm, she tapped a finger to her lips. "For what purpose?"

"We both know very well what went down in Sao Paulo."

Jillian's demeanor cooled. "*Amorzinho*, I don't have any idea what you're talking about."

Nick smiled. "Don't forget who you're talking to, Jillian. I know what happened, and I will push it if you don't cancel your contract with Annie Owens." As if on cue, he looked directly at her. A reflexive hand went to her throat.

"What's going on over there?"

Annie jumped. "Oh!" She whipped her head to the side. "Aunt Fran—you can't sneak up on people like that."

"I'm sorry, sugar, but that looks like a showdown gearing up to match the likes of Cleopatra." She searched Annie's gaze. "What's going on?"

The bitter scent of black coffee rose from the Styrofoam cup in Fran's hand. Covering her nose to ward off the stiff aroma, Annie whispered beneath her hand, "I think Nick is trying to save me from myself."

"What?" Fran zapped Annie with a sharp glance. "You're plumb not making any sense."

Annie waved her to hush as Nick said, "Cancel or I make the call."

Jillian laughed in his face, pulled the fur collar at her neck. "You always did entertain me with your bravado, *Nico*, but there is no way I'm going to cancel my deal." She glanced over her shoulder, snaring Annie in a smoldering warning. "I've come to love this place you call Tennessee and can't wait to return from my business trip to close on my new home."

"Play it your way, Jillian. But when I'm finished with you, you're going to be sorry you didn't heed my advice."

"Perhaps." She curled a finger around his collar, then promptly slid it free. "But only because I will miss the sound of your sexy voice. You will be here waiting for me, won't you?"

Annie was floored by Delaney's absolute submission to Jillian Devane's advances against her man. For as long as she could remember, she had never seen Delaney back down from a fight. Man or woman, didn't matter. Delaney was tough and hard, and while it had caused more than a bushel of trouble between them, Annie thought this was a time she should use some of that attitude to her advantage.

With a flutter of long brown fingers, Jillian waved good-bye, then sought Fran for her coffee.

"The Queen is waitin'," Fran grumbled under her breath, but dutifully brought the cup to Jillian. As she withdrew her purse to pay, Nick said, "It's on me." Jillian's arched brow lifted in pleasure. "Consider it my consolation gift."

"Until we meet again, *amorzinho*." Blowing him a kiss, she walked out the front door, opened by Cal Foster on his way in. When he spotted Nick and Delaney just inside the door, a stupefied look came over him, which solidified when he saw Annie.

Annie almost giggled at the absurdity. If she weren't the cause of all this horrific strife, she would have laughed openly. But she was. And it was really horrific. Heaving a sigh, she waited for Cal's approach.

He paused by Nick and Delaney. "The dragon lady was here?"

"She was."

Casting a wary gaze toward Annie, he asked, "Did she say anything about the property?"

"Only that she won't cooperate voluntarily. But she will, you can count on it."

Cal didn't appear convinced but didn't argue the point. Instead, he came to her side. Brushing a light kiss to Annie's cheek, he held her in his gaze, his eyes soft and gentle. "How are you?"

"Not great," she said, but better now that he was here. "I feel so responsible for this horrible situation."

"It's not your fault, Annie."

"It is," she said, grateful Cal remained by her side. Even knowing how she felt about Delaney and Nick and their hotel and his desire to work for them, he remained firmly entrenched in her camp and it meant a lot to her.

Loyal. Devoted. Honest. Those were the words that described Cal Foster. He remained her staunch ally and for that she loved him. Annie stilled as the sentiment wound deep in her heart. *She loved him.* Sneaking a peek at him, she savored the new emotion. She'd been so busy struggling for the rights to Ladd Springs, struggling to work with her emotionally charged daughter, pay the bills, build a future that she'd completely overlooked the man by her side. Well, not completely. A wave of pleasure rolled through her. She'd enjoyed having him by her side and hadn't missed his clean-cut good looks.

Delaney fiddled with a gold pendant at her neck and Nick placed a finger beneath her chin. When he leaned down to kiss her, Annie experienced a sharp desire for the same. She turned to Cal, but his eyes were glued to Nick and Delaney. Annie's heart hit the floor. She could have really used a hug right about now, but he seemed more interested in what they were doing. Cal slid a hand around her shoulders. Or was he? "Don't look now, but the lid might be about to blow."

"Huh?"

Jack Foster strolled into the diner, standing shoulder-to-shoulder with his ex-wife and her new boyfriend. Annie dropped her head back. If only Fran's diner weren't so popular!

"Hi, Delaney."

"Jack."

"Was that Jillian I saw walk out of here?"

"Wouldn't know and don't care." The blistering tone perked Annie's attention. The old Delaney was suddenly back?

Jack smirked. Oblivious to the identity of Nick Harris, he extended a hand. "Jack Foster, Delaney's ex-husband."

Nick looked to Delaney for confirmation. Cal cursed under his breath. "I might have to step in."

She clutched his arm. "Do you think that's a good idea?"

"Jack's been drinking. I can see it from here."

Maybe oblivious had been the wrong word. Could Jack be looking for a fight? Annie simmered in a well of memories. Jack was definitely the type to provoke a brawl but she'd bet Nick would prove victor.

"Nick Harris," he replied, and Annie swore she saw the hand by his side ball into a fist.

Annie held Cal back. "Delaney won't let it get to that," she advised, one eye locked onto Delaney's face. She was very aware of what was transpiring. Tension altered her posture, vigilance moved into her eyes.

"Keep moving, Jack. We don't want any trouble with you."

"Trouble?" He feigned a hurt look. "Who said anything about trouble? I'm here for food." He looked around, his gaze landing briefly on Annie and Cal. A malicious gleam came alive in his dark gaze—tripping Annie's pulse—but he returned his focus to Nick and Delaney. Giving Nick the onceover, he asked Delaney, "This your new man?"

"Delaney and I are engaged."

"Engaged? Well, what do you know, you're actually going to give it another try?"

She cocked her head. "Surprising, isn't it? After my first one went so well."

"No need to bring up stale bread, Dell."

"I don't call striking a woman stale bread," Nick said. "I call it assault and battery."

It was the first wrinkle in Jack's smug demeanor. He leaned toward Nick, heedless of the near half-foot difference in height. Jack wasn't a tall man. He was tough, appearing more so in his black jacket and jeans, but he wasn't tall. "Don't get cute with me. Our marriage is none of your business."

"Anything that concerns this woman concerns me."

"Ah, hell" Cal muttered and went to intercept his brother. Annie didn't follow, content to watch the fireworks from a distance. "Jack, how about you leave these two be?"

Jack knit his brow. A cutting smile took hold of his mouth. "The man is insulting me, brother. You know I can't let that pass."

"Sure you can. Besides, Fran doesn't need you messin' up her diner. If you're not careful, she'll be handing you the mop."

Jack surveyed the restaurant for sight of Fran. She stood behind the food counter, staring him down. Annie was proud of old Fran. She didn't shy away from ill-mannered customers, though she seemed content to let Nick and Cal handle this particular one.

"On second thought," Jack said, "I think I'll grab a quick bite to eat with my kin."

"Good idea."

"Nice to meet you, Nick." He emphasized the name. "Best of luck to you. You're going to need it with this one."

Cal shadowed his brother as he walked toward Annie. Probably didn't trust him not to take an impromptu swing. If there was one thing she remembered about Jack from high school, it was his itch to scrap. Reason or no reason, he was always looking for a fight. He and Beau were the fighting Fosters. Cal and Clint were the sweet talkers, invariably pulled into their brother's disputes.

"Hi, Annie."

Up close and personal, Annie easily detected alcohol on Jack's breath. "Jack."

"What were you doing over there?" Cal asked him. "Can't you leave Delaney alone to find a little happiness?"

"Happiness?" Jack whirled his head like a bobble doll. "Is that what she's doing? Looks to me like she's gold-digging again."

"Jack."

"You know Delaney never loved me. She only wanted me for the money."

"You know that's not true."

"Hell it ain't. Ask her uncle. He'll tell you."

"Ernie is dead."

The news caught Jack on the chin. "Dead? Really? What finally killed him?"

"Cancer."

Jack blew a soft whistle. "Damn. Something gets us all in the end, doesn't it?"

Obviously, Annie thought. She could read the same thing in Cal's eyes though he didn't bother to voice it, either. Seizing on Cal, Jack said, "You know, it makes me think of those folks in your accident." Annie sucked in her breath. Cal's expression went slack. "You ever talk to the family?"

"I don't," Cal said, avoiding her direct gaze.

"Why not? After all," Jack swung his head around like a drunk off-balance. "You do owe it to them to check in and make sure they're doing all right, don't you? I mean..." He smiled, but it was a mean one. "It's your moral obligation."

Edging a distinct shoulder between them, he replied flatly, "I've settled my debt."

Jack laughed. "Money does come in handy, doesn't it?"

"We're leaving now, Jack." Grasping Annie's arm, he glanced toward Nick and Delaney, who were settled in a booth. "I'd leave that man alone, if I were you," he advised his brother. "I think he can take you and I'd hate to have to explain to Daddy how Jack hasn't learned to control himself."

Jack scowled. "I don't need your threats."

"But you need Daddy's money, don't you?"

"You're a bastard."

It was Cal's turn to smirk. "One with a bank account."
Cal steered Annie toward the door before Jack could say another word.

It's your moral obligation? What did he mean? Annie
wondered. Cal was the one hurt. Questions tumbled through
her mind. Was someone else hurt, too? It didn't make sense.
She was going to have to ask Cal about what happened and
this time insist on more detail.

As they passed Nick and Delaney, Annie's heart
pinched. Delaney looked so sad. Whatever Nick had said to
her wasn't pleasant. Was he concerned about Jillian burning
his land? Did he confess it was a real possibility, now that she
had sold?

Allowing Cal to lead her out into the cold night air, Annie battled a pile of mixed emotions. The red neon glow of
Fran's Diner cast Cal's face in an eerie hue. "Annie, we need
to talk."

"Yes?"

Cal placed heavy hands on her shoulders. "I need to tell
you what happened the night of the accident."

Startled by the despair in his voice, Annie changed her
mind. She didn't want to know.

Chapter Twenty-Four

Cal hoped Annie would understand. He hoped it wouldn't end the light in those beautiful blue eyes, the ones she shone on him every time they were together. "But not here. Can I drive you to your place?"

"But my car?" Startled, Annie looked behind her.

Cal followed her gaze to a little white sedan parked in the center of the lot. "I'll drive you back." He didn't want her driving without him. He needed to be with her. Jack's impromptu visit had set him on edge. It brought back memories he'd rather forget but didn't have the luxury. You alter the course of a man's life and it changes you. On the inside. It changes your DNA.

In Cal's case he was going to use that change to make himself a better man.

"Okay." She nodded. "Okay."

Cal led her to his truck and drove her the short distance to her home. He hated the awkward silence that filled the cab, but it couldn't be helped. Annie held his hand and that was enough. They were connected. It was a connection he'd have to trust.

Unlocking the door to her apartment, she flipped the light switch and he helped her out of her coat. "Can I get you something to drink? Coffee? Water?"

"No, thank you." Gesturing a hand toward the sofa, he asked her to sit with him. She did. With more than a little trepidation, he noted in dismay, but she did. Cal inhaled deep and full and settled in for what might be his last evening with the woman he loved. But Annie deserved better than a man who kept secrets, a man with a past. Not that he could change a thing, only hope she had enough forgiveness in her heart to spare him. Cal took her hand in his own, cradled it, admired the soft skin and fine manicure. Annie was a beautiful woman but more, she was a smart woman. A capable woman. Two perfect qualities for a partner in life. Staring into a mountain of question, he began, "The accident Jack's been referrin' to...I wasn't entirely honest when I told you it was no big deal."

Alarm scored her eyes. "Were you hurt worse than a broken arm?"

"Naw." Shame filled his soul. "I walked away from the accident with barely a scratch and an arm that healed just fine."

"Then what?"

As he looked into Annie's eyes, vivid images flooded his mind. It was evening, the hour when a summer night's was just settling in. The roads were slick from the rush hour traffic. It had been raining, not heavy, but steady. Misty. He'd had a great day at work, stopped by his favorite watering hole on the way home, had a few drinks. A few. The irony struck him again how he hadn't been drunk, only under the influence. Now, if it had been on a weekend, when he and his buddies got to serious drinking, things might have been different. He shook the hypothetical away. As always, he reminded himself, it didn't matter. A mangled car was a mangled car. "I was involved in a car accident. A bad one. It was after work one night, it was raining." The storm clouds of concern gathering in her expression were meant for him. They shouldn't be.

They should be for the man who lost his legs. "I hit a car."

She gasped, flinging a hand to her mouth.

"I was turning right, traveling into his lane. He was driving at a pretty good clip, but my truck was bigger and the impact rolled his like a tin can." At the tremor in Annie's hand, he lowered his gaze. He couldn't bear the growing terror in her eyes. It reminded him of the terror he felt walking over to the crumpled vehicle. "He ended up flipping onto the median. I jumped out, of course, and tried to help..." His voice fell away. But the man was in bad shape, his body contorted unnaturally within the confines of his seat. Cal allowed the usual shudder to pass through him. No one should have to witness a human being twisted like that. It stuck with you. Became a part of you. "I called the police. The ambulance came. They airlifted him to the hospital."

"Oh, Cal," she cried, squeezing hold of his hand. "I'm so *sorry.*"

"Don't be sorry for me." Cal raised his head to face her head on. "Be sorry for the man I hit. He'll never walk again."

The declaration stopped her cold. He felt her retreat. Mild, but it was there just the same.

Guilt ripped a hole in his gut. As it should. "The police questioned me. I told them I'd had a drink after work. It was a lie. I had more than one. I had a few." And while he believed he could handle them, Cal knew the police wouldn't understand. They wanted to test his breath. He'd refused. "They took me down to the station. My lawyer showed up and took over from there. I didn't hear about the man's condition until two days later." Even today, when he thought of the consequences, Cal had trouble breathing, trouble moving, like an elephant sat on his chest. The guilt stuck with him, ate at him. "I went to see him afterward, but the family threw me out." Tears pricked behind his eyes. Cal would have probably done the same thing had it been his family member lying in that hospital bed.

"Did you go to jail?"

"No. The official findings were mixed. Some witnesses on hand said he ran a red light, others said a yellow. A few said I ran the stop sign. Between six different eyewitnesses, they couldn't come up with an absolute cause." But his wife had. Caroline pegged him with the accident the minute he arrived home. *You'd been drinking, hadn't you*? He didn't lie. She could smell whiskey on his breath and it was all she needed. She kicked him out of the house that day.

Visibly unsettled, Annie asked, "Why didn't you tell me?"

"Because I was ashamed. Because I felt responsible."

"But the police said—"

"I'd been drinking, Annie. If I blew when they asked me, to I would have failed the breathalyzer." Annie slowly closed her mouth. Her withdrawal was sudden and distinct. "I'm not proud of my actions. Whether I caused the accident or not is irrelevant. If I hadn't been drinking, my reflexes would have been quicker. I would have noticed that car and stopped. But I didn't." He bowed his head. "I kept going."

A long silence stretched between them. Annie removed her hand from his, clasping her knees in a statue of thought. She didn't leap to his defense, didn't wrap her arms around him in comfort. She sat immobile. Isolated. Cal didn't blame her. He wouldn't blame her if she threw him out on his backside, now that she knew. It's what his wife had done. And Annie wasn't his wife.

A deep sadness filled him. At this point she might never be. "There's something else I have to tell you." Panic tore through her blue eyes, her beautiful blue eyes that deserved to shine with joy, not pain. "I have a daughter."

She expelled her breath. "A *daughter*?"

"Her name is Emily and she's eleven. She lives in Arizona with her mother."

"Oh my..."

Cal understood. It was a shock to her system. He'd never mentioned the first word about having a child. But he had to be sure that he and Annie had something important before he shared that part. It was the ugly part, the tortuous part. But it was the most important part of all.

If Annie couldn't handle the issue of Emily, deem him worth the effort to fight for her forgiveness, than he needed to know that before tying her up in it. "The accident was front page news. Her mother left me, and to this day Emily won't speak to me." Annie's expression embodied the pain and suffering he felt. As a mother, she understood. Probably far better than he. "Emily's the reason I quit drinking, Annie. She's the reason I left Arizona. But I'm not letting her go. I'm here for a fresh start. I intend to prove myself worthy of being her father, a man she can trust and admire." He peered at Annie's hands clenched in her lap. So close, yet so far. "If you and I have any future together, you need to know what I'm up against. It's a battle I can't fight alone."

Cal allowed Annie to digest the information. She'd need time, he figured, to fully absorb the significance of his situation. It was time he'd gladly give, should she ask for it, but Annie wasn't rushing to his side. Her hands were gripped so tightly, Cal thought she was going to break her fingers. He heaved a sigh. Did he expect any different?

"Cal, I don't know what to say."

"Say this isn't the end for us. Say you'll work through it with me."

"But there's so much, so much I didn't know, that I need to think about..."

He nodded. "I'll give you time. Just ask me, I'll give you all the time you need."

"What's happened to the man? Do you check in on him, like Jack said?"

It was a fair question. Jack had raised the issue, it was only fair he come completely clean on the count. "The man didn't have insurance. His car was covered, but not his health. After being cleared of wrongdoing, receiving only a citation for running a stop sign, I told my lawyer I wanted to pay for the man's care. He advised me against it, said it would make me look guilty. But hell, I'd already been smeared all over the newspaper. My boss nearly fired me over the incident, my wife left me, my daughter disowned me, what more could they do? So I told him to pay it. Pay whatever it took to get the man mobile."

At the queer look in her eyes, he explained, "I have money, Annie. Not from my Daddy, but from my investing. It's been a hobby of mine and it turns out I'm pretty good at it. I paid the man's hospital bill, paid for his rehab, a fancy wheelchair, but when the family found out, they cut me off. Told my lawyer to cease and desist, so to speak."

"*What*? Why on earth would they do that when they didn't have money to pay for it?"

"They believed the accident was my fault and didn't want to accept tainted money."

"That's absurd."

Cal shrugged. "Is it? They're proud people. I would think that's something you'd understand." The comment iced further protest. Not wanting the conversation to die, he continued, "I still check in. They have a daughter, little older than Emily. She goes to a different school. Loves ballet. I sponsor a scholarship at her local school of dance. It's the least I can do."

"Have you tried contacting your daughter? Emily?" she asked tentatively, as though learning to say a new word.

"I have. But I have to go through her mother and her mother is the one puttin' the brakes on our relationship. She's still angry, stuffing the child's head with negative thoughts. At this rate I might not be able to talk to her until she's of age."

"Oh, Cal, you can't let that happen. She's at a very impressionable age. You have to get to her now, before it's too late."

The urgency he heard in Annie's voice set his spirit afloat. "Well, I don't know exactly how I'm supposed to do it, with her momma acting as block and all."

"You have to figure a way around her."

Annie's determination tugged at his heart. "I'd like to believe there is one, but I'm not sure how to find it."

"We'll find a way. We have to. Casey is proof in point, isn't she? A girl needs her father. She needs his love and guidance. You can't give up on her."

Cal only heard "we." *We'll find a way*. Reaching over, he unlocked her hands and held them firm. "Does that mean you'll give me another chance?"

She looked at him, confused. "Another chance?" When he nodded, her eyes sparked with realization. "Oh, *Cal*." Her expression fell. "You never lost the first one."

The statement roused a raw need in him. *You never lost the first one.* Annie hadn't given up on him. She hadn't forsaken him. One mistake, one awful mistake that changed his life and the lives of others yet she forgave him. "I love you, Annie." His confession sucked the air from the room. "I love you. I want you to be my wife."

"Cal," she said breathlessly.

"Do you love me? Could you love me?"

A smile pulled at her mouth. "Don't you know?"

He shook his head. Not really. Not in her own words. Cal touched a fingertip to her mouth. "Tell me."

Tears glistened as she nodded. "I love you. I love you with all my heart."

They were the sweetest words a man could hear. He slipped a hand behind Annie's neck and pulled her to him. Tense, unsure, he brushed his lips over hers until the stiffness eased. Cal kissed her and she responded, exquisite, gentle. Accepting. His heart trembled as he felt himself on the edge of something extraordinary. Annie Owens was taking him in. She was taking his love, his troubles, his promise of a rocky road ahead and doing so with a tenderness and determination he didn't deserve. Cal's desire mounted. She was giving him the gift of her love. It was a gift he was going to earn, he would prove himself worthy. And with a soft swipe of his tongue, Cal's insides fired with a hunger that pulled deep inside him. Running his fingers through the silky tendrils of her hair, he probed deeper, stronger, seeking to lose himself in her grace. It had been too long since he'd experienced the love of a woman. The true love, the unconditional love.

A love he needed something fierce.

Cal pulled away. A small sigh escaped from Annie. In the quiet of her living room, the pale lamp light painted her face with an even greater vulnerability than his own. Cal ventured, "That was nice."

Her eyes fluid with emotion, Annie looked as if she were crossing a bridge. Suspended over fast-moving water, afraid she might trip and drown. But she wouldn't. Not with him by her side. He rubbed a thumb over her cheek, mesmerized by the feelings streaming through him, between them. "You have no idea what you mean to me, Annie." Her eyes darted back and forth across his. "I need you. I need you to get through this life of mine, to get to the other side of happy."

"Cal, I'm the one with the needs. You've done so much to help me, yet look how I've repaid you. I've probably cost you the job with Serenity Springs. It was everything you wanted and I've ruined it."

"You haven't ruined a thing. Serenity Springs will be fine, with or without me."

"What if she burns the place down?" It was a tormented whisper. "What if she ruins the land? I'll never forgive myself."

"She won't. Nick and Malcolm will beat Jillian. I don't know how yet, but I've learned to judge a man's character by my gut and Nick and Malcolm are solid. She's messing with the wrong men, I can tell you that much."

Annie seemed eased by his assessment, but Cal could feel a world of guilt remained. It was squeezing the joy from her eyes, the joy he so desperately yearned to see. "You've got to believe me, Annie. We'll find a way. With you by my side, I'm not worried about anything."

A tortured smile formed on her lips and he kissed it free. Softly, open-mouthed, he massaged the worry from her, from himself, from their growing love. Annie surrendered to him, stirring him deeply. At her mild shiver, he murmured, "Are you okay?" She nodded. Looping his arms beneath her, Cal hoisted her from the sofa and carried her to her bedroom. Casey was at the diner. He'd seen her with his own eyes and knew the place wasn't due to close for several more hours. They'd be alone. Together. It was all he needed.

Chapter Twenty-Five

Annie paced the salon, aware employees were tracking her progress with silent concern. No one said a word to her, but all watched her walk back and forth, into the lounge, out of the lounge. It was as if they understood her heart was heavy, her mind a wreck, each giving her the time and space she needed to work through her troubles. Casey's breakup was now common knowledge. Everybody knew her daughter was vulnerable, especially being alone during the holidays. It wasn't right.

Most sympathized and told Annie to hang in there. *It's a tough age. She's working through the pain. She'll come around.* None of them had a clue as to her real troubles. No one knew about the impending closing, the day when Casey's share of Ladd Springs officially changed hands. Only she did. Jillian Devane had called this morning, announcing she was back in town and ready to close on her new property. Four weeks of absence had been erased in the space of one message, one the receptionist was happy to relay. *Jillian Devane would be here at close of business.* And what time was that, Annie had asked? Bobbi Jo had looked at her strangely, but answered the stupid question. Five o'clock, of course.

Annie had a five-fifteen appointment but it was off the books, a favor to a friend who couldn't afford the full fee. It was a service she routinely offered, one the salon owner didn't mind, requesting it not be recorded so she could keep her books straight.

Five o'clock. Doomsday. Annie's mind emptied as she entered the employee lounge, her nerves whittled to the bone. If it weren't for Cal, she'd have come completely unraveled by now, but with the help of his steady hand and presence of mind, she kept it together—until she received the phone call.

Harris Hotels had exhausted their resources, searching for a way to cancel the contract. But thanks to her wonderful lawyer, Hank Dakota, the contract was solid. Signed, sealed and delivered. The survey had finally been completed and they were ready to close. Cal had stalled for as long as he could, but there was no getting around it. Mr. Dakota had to call and inform Ms. Devane the necessary paperwork had been completed and she could close at any time.

Jillian was coming to the salon to discuss the matter. Annie swerved to a halt, drawn to the wall clock. Four fifty-five. Cal was in Chattanooga with Malcolm. He'd formally accepted the position as General Manager of Serenity Springs and was working with Malcolm on hiring an assistant chef. Annie paced. Why did it have to be today? Couldn't Bobbi Jo have told Jillian eight o'clock? *Quitting time tonight is eight o'clock*! she wanted to shout.

Her pulse thumped in her throat. Maybe she could run an errand and return at five-fifteen. She needed eggs. Annie stopped. She didn't need eggs. There was a full dozen sitting in her refrigerator. Last minute shopping? Certainly there must be a gift she needed to buy. She resumed motion but froze. The bell for the salon's front door sounded. *Was she here*? Annie raced to the door and cracked it open far enough to peek through. Moving so the angle was right, she strained to see the front desk. Her heart detonated, pulse hammering wildly. On the other side of the salon's Christmas tree, she could see her. It was Jillian.

She was here!

Bobbi Jo dutifully walked through the salon, headed her way. Annie ran from the door, stopped, whipped around. Cabinets lined the walls, a round table sat in the middle, there was no place to hide. No rear exit to escape. *Think*, Annie. Think!

Seconds later, the lounge door swung open. "Annie, there's someone here to..." Bobbi Jo's voice fell away. "Annie?"

Hidden away in the color closet, Annie could envision Bobbi Jo looking around the empty room. "Annie?" Bobbi Jo's voice neared the closet and Annie held her breath. Crammed between shelves and door, she couldn't move even if she wanted to. "That's weird," Bobbi Jo muttered mere feet from the closet.

Annie heard the lounge door open and close but remained in place. It would be just her luck that Jillian would insist on seeing for herself—because she was a smart woman. She knew when she was being avoided. The door to the lounge opened again and Annie froze. Oh no, please don't be Jillian. Annie already felt like an ignorant fool for dodging her in the first place but to be caught in the act would be humiliating! But the insane logic still appealed to her. Jillian couldn't close on the property if she couldn't find her. The closet door swung open. A stylist shrieked. Annie's pulse kicked as she smacked a finger to her lips. "Shhh...!"

Reeling from the shock of finding a woman in the color closet, the poor stylist was too stunned to utter a word. Annie willed her to keep quiet, and the girl nodded. The frightened-doe-look in her eyes made Annie feel like a bigger fool. Wait until it got out that Annie Owens had lost her mind. The town would have a heyday with that one.

Annie emerged from her hiding place. "I'm sorry to have scared you," she said, her apology sounding pathetic even to her own ears. "But I had to...I had to..." Annie dropped any effort at explanation. Would it matter?

The wild look in the girl's eyes negated all reason to continue.

Annie went to the door and pushed it open a hair, checking to see if Jillian had left. No sight of her, but Annie didn't want to chance it. She was probably waiting outside for her to show up. Annie groaned aloud. "How do I get mixed up in these things?"

"Can I get my color now?" the girl asked timidly.

"Yes, get your color."

Keeping a wide berth around Annie, the stylist rummaged through bottles and bowls and excused herself. "Thank you," she murmured and bonelessly slipped out the door.

Annie tugged at her blouse, shook her hair. She couldn't believe she'd been reduced to hiding in a closet. It was idiocy. Lunacy. Maybe she was crazy. Like Aunt Fran used to tell her when she was agitated as a girl, "Go on and hide your crazy and start acting like a little lady." Well, her crazy was alive and well, but it didn't matter anymore. It was over. Jillian would sue Annie if she didn't close. She had signed on the dotted line and Jillian Devane would take her for everything she was worth—which was the property.

Annie felt the land run through her fingers, a dream she'd never realize. Cal could support them, but Casey's rightful inheritance would be gone. Because of her mother's short-sightedness. The employee lounge door opened, slow and easy. Bobbi Jo poked her shiny brunette head inside. "Annie?" She looked at her. "Are you all right?"

"I'm fine." She slumped to a seat at the table.

Bobbi Jo eased into the room, holding onto the door as she closed it behind her, like she was afraid to startle Annie with any quick movements. "Are you sure?"

"I'm sure." And she didn't like being treated as a senile old woman by an eighteen-year old beauty queen. She was fine. Insane, but fine.

"Okay. Did you know you have a five-fifteen appointment coming in?"

"I know." She slapped a hand to the table and asked, "Is that woman still here?"

"What woman?"

What other woman would she be talking about? "The woman who came looking for me."

Realization slowly came to life in Bobbi Jo's brain as she made the connection. "Oh...*that* woman."

"Yes, that woman. Is she gone?" Annie asked, her earlier embarrassment dissipated. Go on and let Bobbi Jo and everyone else think she was crazy. It was over. She was done with it—so long as Jillian was gone, she would be fine.

"Yes." Bobbi Jo blinked big green eyes. "I think so."

"Will you check for me, please?" Annie didn't want to be rude, but she did have a client coming in who she needed to prepare for.

"Sure." She nodded briskly. "I'll do that, right now."

Annie waited the few minutes it took and rose when Bobbi Jo returned, announcing, "She's gone. I walked outside and looked up and down the street, just to be double sure."

"Thank you," Annie said, a tired resignation unfurling within her. She was too old for this silliness. But when one acted silly, silly is what you lived with.

Annie pushed in through the front door of Fran's Diner. Tired, weary from the stress, she was relieved to find the restaurant near empty. Tuesday nights weren't Fran's busiest, requiring only two servers. Tonight those servers were Casey and Jimmy. The two leaned against a wall by the kitchen entrance, chatting quietly as they waited and watched for customers to need them. Casey waved to her mother. It was a small gesture but a sign the two were making headway. Her daughter approved of Cal, which made Annie's decision to accept his proposal all the easier. She smiled inwardly, waggling her ring finger. She was still getting used to the feel of a ring on it.

Strolling over to the teens, she asked, "Pretty slow tonight, huh?"

"It's been dead," Casey replied glumly.

"We had a small rush around five but ever since it's been pretty quiet," Jimmy said.

"Can't rake in the tips when there aren't any customers." Both agreed with a nod. Annie looked around, searching for Fran. "Where's Aunt Fran?"

"In the back. Dishwasher is busted."

"Oh." Annie scanned the diner, wondering if she was even in the mood to eat. She wasn't hungry, stress and anxiety weaving through her stomach with thoughts of the looming closing. At least she had Casey on her side. Her daughter didn't care one way or the other what happened with the property. Sell it, log it, whatever, though she was warming up to the idea of attending college. Annie looked at Jimmy. Long, wavy black hair barely combed free of his eyes, his lanky build and awkward angles were those of a boy who hadn't quite filled in to his manhood. He was the reason Casey was reconsidering. Said he'd take a few classes with her, "just for kicks." Annie hoped it was for more than "kicks" but according to Candi, Jimmy had no ambition. There was nothing he was dying to do, nothing that set fire to his heart. He had no passion, no enthusiasm. He was coasting. Though next to Casey he seemed pretty energetic. These days she was slow as a pour of sweet sorghum. Annie sighed. Hopefully something would catch his attention other than her daughter. Watching the two of them together, it occurred to Annie that Jimmy might be harboring a sweet spot for Casey.

At the clang of bells, Annie turned. It was none other than Delaney Wilkins. *Yay*, Annie mocked privately. But upon seeing the glazed-over look in her eyes, something pulled Annie to her. Delaney wasn't a happy woman these days. Nick was gone more often than not. Albert was proving to be a full-time job. Add the fact that Malcolm had put her in charge of the stables and you had for one stressed-out woman. Annie thought Delaney would have loved working to develop the stables, but according to Lacy, the perfectionist in her seemed to be undermining the process. She was overwhelmed. The charge had shot clear out of her and she simply went through the motions these days. Up in the morning, check on Albert. Off to town, close out her bookkeeping clients. Back home for lunch, check on Albert, off to work on the stables. Cook food for Albert, hand deliver it to his cabin. Miss Nick every step of the way. On and on it went, Lacy said, with nary a break for fun. It was a lifestyle Lacy couldn't hack for one hour let alone day after day, week after week, but Annie understood the monotony of obligation. It's what you did when people were relying on you to survive. Like Annie, Delaney held her head high and kept on chugging, despite her personal desires to the contrary.

Maybe it was time someone gave her an atta boy for her efforts. With a surprise spring in her step, Annie set off for Delaney. As she neared, the familiar animosity wriggled into Delaney's gaze. Muted against the pale blonde strands falling loose around her face, the soft blue of her sweater, it was there just the same. In a purposefully meek tone Annie asked, "What brings you to the diner this hour?"

"Albert wants pie."

She couldn't suppress a chuckle. "Pie?"

"Pie. The man has a perfectly good blueberry pie sitting on his kitchen counter, but he wants peach pie." She grunted and rolled her eyes as if the mere thought exhausted her. After a brief pause, Delaney brushed long sweeps of hair behind her ears and settled on Annie. Surrendering her typically sharp tongue, she remarked, "I don't know how Ernie put up with him all these years."

"I'd venture to guess it wasn't by spoiling him."

Caught off guard, Delaney took a step back. "Spoiling him?"

Annie laughed freely, warmed by the hate-free exchange happening between them. "Ernie would have told him to eat his blueberry pie or shut his pie hole."

The comment drew a reluctant smile from Delaney. "You remember Ernie well."

"Not as well as you, but I do remember that he was a simple man with a simple mindset, and I don't see him spoiling anyone." Annie paused. "Except maybe Felicity." Delaney's expression softened at the mention of her daughter. "I was always surprised he didn't buy her a car or pay for her college. Never made sense."

"Ernie wasn't interested in making sense. He was a creature of habit."

"That he was. And temper." While it surprised Annie to learn Ernie had it in him to physically harm his own flesh and blood, even if at second-hand, it brought a measure of closure for her daughter. Casey had often wondered if it had been Troy behind Jeremiah's beating. The police seemed to think he had motive, though Annie said it was probably Nick. He was the one with the strongest motive. Money.

In the lull when the usual distance started to fill the space between them, something snapped inside of Annie. "I'm sorry, Delaney."

"Sorry?" Suspicion knocked confusion into her gaze. "About what?"

"About the property, about Jillian. About all of it. I've made a mess of things and I'm sorry." Knowing Cal's support was behind her bolstered Annie's ability to own up to her mistakes. If he could do it, she could do it. "I had no idea what the woman was capable of, but even so I should have respected the family legacy and kept it in Casey's name, no matter what."

Delaney stilled. An open line extended between them. "A woman has a right to sell her land, Annie. It's nobody's business how you run your life. I should have respected your decision."

Annie couldn't believe what she was hearing, but pounced on the opening. "Delaney, I was only trying to do what was best for Casey." The words tumbled out of her mouth. "It's been so hard and the bills, I just—"

Delaney held up a hand. "You don't have to explain yourself to me. I've learned a few hard lessons about struggling myself these days. With Jack in town it's made me take stock of where I've been and where I'm going. Things aren't as simple as I thought. Add the fact that my life seems to be ruled by duty and obligation with my man nowhere to be found and I understand 'doing what you need to do' a whole lot better."

Annie felt a surge of respect for the woman she had disliked for so long. The concession felt real, like Delaney meant it from the heart. "It's hard to go it alone, isn't it?"

"That it is." Delaney said and for a moment, Annie felt like they were allies. "I was happy to hear about you and Cal. Haven't given you a proper congratulations." Delaney tipped her head. "He's a nice guy. One of the few Fosters I like. Hope you two find a lifetime of happiness together."

"Thank you." Noting Delaney's ring finger remained absent a diamond, Annie didn't want to rub Delaney's nose in her joy.

Delaney glanced at Casey. "She sure could use some stability in her life. The loving guidance from of a man like Cal will go a long way to set her on track. Too bad he doesn't have kids of his own. He'd make a great dad."

Annie agreed, though didn't reveal the fact that Cal had a daughter of his own. That was something he had to do on his terms. Warmed by talk of her future with him, she said, "Casey and I are lucky to have him."

Annie's joy was short-lived. Noticing her abrupt change in expression, Delaney turned. Annie mumbled, "That woman is like a bad dream."

"Try nightmare."

Annie braced herself as Jillian approached. It was the hour of reckoning.

"Ms. Owens," she purred in that practiced fake way of hers. "So glad I found you." Completely ignoring Delaney, Jillian prodded, "Did you forget our appointment this evening?"

"I didn't forget. I had more important things to do."

Jillian smiled smooth as silk, a smile full of arrogance. It turned Annie's stomach. "I'm sorry you wasted your time on a return trip to Tennessee, Ms. Devane, but as I indicated before, I've changed my mind on selling."

Jillian stepped closer. "As I've indicated before, Ms. Owens, I will sue you and take my property in court if I have to."

Annie linked her arms over her chest. Shifting her weight from heel to heel, she said, "Go ahead. I'd rather take my chances in court then knowingly make a deal with the devil."

Squinting heavily-mascaraed eyes, Jillian said, "You country people are so trite."

Annie bristled at the insult, as did Delaney, but to their credit, both women remained in control. A courtesy this woman didn't deserve. "You're entitled to your opinion, Ms. Devane, but the fact remains. I'm keeping the land."

"You are mistaken," Jillian tossed back, but she was clearly losing her cool. All ease had been erased from her bronzed complexion, her flinty cat eyes flashing in anger. "I will prevail and make you pay dearly."

"Not so fast, Jillian."

Nick's voice cut the room in two. He strode toward them and Delaney's entire demeanor transformed. The edginess disappeared, replaced by naked longing. "Nick!"

Dressed in an expensive leather jacket and dark blue jeans, he came to her side and she hugged him close. It was the first time Annie had firsthand insight into how much Delaney missed Nick during his travels. "I've come to inform you that the game is over, Jillian. You will not be the new owner of Ladd Springs."

Chapter Twenty-Six

Jillian linked her arms over her chest, a hot jealousy rising to her eyes at the sight of Nick and Delaney embracing. "If it isn't Mr. Knight in Shining Armor."

Nick brandished a sardonic smile. "Sorry. That fellow is a fairy tale. I'm the real deal and your deal is done."

"What makes you think I will walk away from the most beautiful property in Tennessee? The land so close to my greatest *love.*" She thickened her accent on the last word, clearly for Delaney's benefit.

"I just flew home from a meeting with your father. Took me all night and a day to get here, but when the woman of your dreams is waiting patiently, a man likes to hurry." He squeezed Delaney to his side and she smiled like a schoolgirl, the pale blue of her sweater taking years from her face.

"What business do you have with my father?" Jillian asked, caught like a trout on the fly.

"I shared some information with him regarding an awful fire a few years back. A fire to which I have proof of origin." Jillian's eyes closed to slits. "You see, bribery is rampant down in your neck of the woods, and if you search hard enough, you can find someone willing to talk for the right price. I know you set that fire and I know you paid to have the proof destroyed."

"Like you said, no proof."

He grinned. "Don't need it. One voice recording replayed for your father is all it took."

Jillian lashed out but Nick was quick—grabbing her hand midair. "Now, now, now, landing yourself in jail for assault and battery would not make your father happy."

Jillian yanked her hand free. "You don't know anything about my father," she hissed.

"I know he's running for office and taking no chances his daughter might prove a liability to him." Raising his hand from Delaney's waist, Nick set it on her shoulder. "You should call him. I think he wants to use your prowess for his campaign."

Annie looked for the whip of a tail behind Jillian—the woman looked ready to pounce!

"You will be sorry, *amorzinho*, for interfering in my business affairs."

"Seeing as how I'm about to be married, I think you should refrain from calling me lover." He wrinkled his nose. "It makes you look desperate."

Jillian gritted her teeth and turned on her heel, warning, "You have not heard the last from me."

Nick heaved a sigh. "Unfortunately, I believe you."

Annie watched, along with Nick and a dumbstruck Delaney, as Jillian Devane exited the diner. She felt like jumping up and cheering, but was more interested in the semi-proposal she just heard. Seemed Delaney was interested in a follow-up as well.

Nick turned Delaney to face him. "You will marry me, right?"

Delaney's mouth fell open. "Yes, but I thought—"

He tapped a finger to her lips. "I said I wanted to wait until I found the perfect diamond." Nick reached into an inside jacket pocket and withdrew a petite black velvet box. "I have." He opened the box. Annie and Delaney gasped in unison. "Do you like it?"

It was the biggest, fattest, squarest diamond Annie had ever seen. It had to be three carats, maybe more. She flashed a glance to Delaney. Could she wear a diamond so big?

Delaney's hand was locked on her throat. She looked between the diamond and Nick, Nick and the diamond. "It's beautiful, but it's so big..."

He dropped his head back with a hearty laugh. "Since when is that a bad thing?"

She stared at him and uttered, "Seriously, it looks too heavy for my finger."

"Shall I have them cut it in half?"

Delaney slugged his shoulder. "Nick, be serious."

"I am." Removing the ring from its case, he took her finger and slid the glittery rock in place. Delaney was trembling. "Fits perfectly," he pronounced.

Annie's gaze shot to the bells clanging loudly at the front door. A whoosh of relief and elation rushed through her. Cal and Malcolm had arrived home with Lacy in tow.

Decked out in a full length black coat, his wife swathed identically, Malcolm stopped short. "When did you get in, Nick? You told me you weren't due for another hour."

Nick lowered to one knee and casually replied, "I might have exceeded the speed limit." Then to Delaney, "With our friends as our witness, will you grant me the highest honor and become my wife?"

For the first time in Annie's whole life, she watched Delaney turn red as an apple. She stammered, "Yes, you fool, I'll marry you. Now get up, you're embarrassing me!"

"It's about time," Malcolm said.

"Hey, not everyone flies off to the Vegas at the drop of a hat. Some of us need planning."

Everyone laughed, including Delaney. Annie peered over her shoulder to behold the shining eyes of her daughter. Her heart lurched as the girl dashed into the kitchen, a bewildered Jimmy slow to follow, but follow he did. Casey was thinking of Troy. Jimmy might have become her lifeline, her support, but Troy remained her true love. It was a title no one else had the power to assume at the moment. Oddly, it was Jimmy who held the power for Annie. Without him she and Casey would not be working their way back to one another, a process painstakingly slow but worth every step. Jimmy kept Casey on the straight and narrow. Jimmy made her daughter laugh. Annie's heart sank into the pit of her stomach. If only she could repay Jimmy somehow, let him know how much she appreciated what he was doing for her daughter, for the two of them. A thought struck. Candi could make it happen. She'd know what he'd enjoy.

Cal pulled up to her and slid an arm around her shoulders. Reaching up, Annie clasped his hand. Pressing into the soft suede of his coat, the warm line of his body she thought, one day Casey would find someone to love, someone as decent and committed as Cal. Troy had done her wrong. He'd made promises and broke every one, but that didn't mean she couldn't learn from her mistakes. Like her, Casey could learn how to spot the wrong one and hold out until the right one came along. Until then it was Annie's job to see that Casey was happy. And she would. She'd help her make good decisions regarding her future, her self-esteem. She'd teach her how to recognize a good man when she saw him. And she'd teach her the value of family. More than blood relatives, Annie would teach Casey the value of a strong family. It was a lesson she'd learned a lot about lately and it was time she shared it with her daughter. Annie squeezed Cal's hand as she watched Lacy fawn over Delaney and her ring. "That's some kind of Christmas gift."

Cal leaned over and brushed his nose against her hair, tickling her ear. "You wait until Christmas morning, hear me?" A tiny thrill zipped through her. "Then we'll talk about comparing gifts." As Delaney marveled over her diamond, holding her finger at arm's length while Lacy ogled it, Annie wondered what he could possibly mean. She already had a ring. What could be better than that? Cal said to the group, "I think we might want to warn folks visiting the hotel there's something in the water around here that make men want to marry!"

"Well if they didn't grow them so hot around here"— Malcolm hugged Lacy to him—"we might be able to resist."

"I say we bottle and sell the stuff."

Nick chuckled at Cal's suggestion. "How about we get the hotel built first, shall we gentlemen?"

"It's as good an idea as any," Cal volleyed back.

Nick brushed Delaney's hair over her shoulder. "I'm planning a Grand Opening Day celebration wedding event and I refuse to wait a day past Memorial Day."

Cal raised his brow. "You two gettin' hitched on opening day?"

"That we are."

Delaney looked to Annie, then Cal, a mischievous spark in her eyes. "Care to join us?"

She could have vacuumed the sound from the room. For a second no one said a word. All eyes turned to Annie. Several customers turned heads her way. She erupted with a nervous laugh. "Why not? Let's do it!"

"Only we might have to postpone it a day or two."

Nick looked at Delaney with a stern eye. "Are you trying to squirm out of it already?"

"No. But Ashley won't take kindly to you upstaging her big Memorial Day party."

"Good grief—I almost forgot. She'd have my hide!" he exclaimed and Delaney smacked his arm.

"She won't give you any pie for your hotel, either."

"Pie?" Fran breezed out of the kitchen. "Someone need a slice of pie?"

Delaney and Nick exchanged a guilty glance. "Nick here was wantin' to know if you'd consider sharing your peach pie recipe for the new hotel," Cal interjected.

"Share my recipe?" Fran waggled a finger. "Not on your life, but I might sell you a few!"

The group of them laughed uproariously. Nick moseyed near Fran and wrapped an arm around her shoulders. Gathering her close in an almost conspiratorial manner, he said, "You drive a hard bargain, Fran. We'll buy your pies on one condition."

"One condition?" She eyed him warily. "What's that?"

"You let me buy some from Ashley, too."

Lacy covered her mouth with a giggle. When Aunt Fran looked on the verge of saying no, she squealed, "C'mon, Aunt Frannie—you have to sell us your pies! You have to!"

Fran broke into a grin. "Lord a'mercy how can I say no to pregnant woman? Of course I'll sell you my pies!"

"Thank the Lord," Cal whispered to Annie. "I thought for a second there I was gonna have to enter into secret negotiations."

Annie smiled. "She'd have come around." And suddenly, the sentiment gave her pause. *She'd come around.* Like she had. Like Delaney had. She snuck a glance upward at Cal, his soft profile, features she was beginning to know by heart. Her stomach flipped. Would Emily come around? Would she let go of the hurt and entertain a fresh start with her father? With her? Could she forgive him and accept him, mistakes and all? Mild-mannered, heart of gold, he was worth a second chance wasn't he? Her gaze drifted back to the couples making plans for an upcoming hotel, upcoming weddings, and she lingered on the narrowing divide between her and Delaney, the healing wounds between herself and Lacy.

Didn't everyone deserve a second chance?

Chapter Twenty-Seven

Mid-February Annie was amazed by the progress of Serenity Springs—make that Hotel Ladd. Delaney had convinced Nick to change the name, leaving only the spa to reflect the original title. Annie thought it was a nice gesture on Nick's behalf. It ensured the land remained tied to its heritage, a reflection of generations gone before and still to come, and placated Delaney's growing angst over losing control. After all, this was a business to Nick Harris. For Delaney and Felicity, it went deeper. Ladd Springs was their legacy.

Sections of the hotel looked fairly complete. The buildings were up, the landscape was in. Employees spent all day on site, training for their new positions. Cal was like an old riverboat, steady as she goes. On site he kept the pace smooth, the tempo upbeat, kinda like a factory in motion. Behind the scenes he worked through problems until he found a solution. He never raised his voice, merely guided people in the direction he wanted and away from that he didn't. Malcolm worked mostly with contractors and designers, applying the finishing touches to his masterpiece. From what Cal said, the design aspect was all Malcolm. From the indulgent spa to the riverfront restaurant and each and every trail in between, everything creative was Malcolm.

Except the stables. Those belonged to Delaney and was the place she lived these days. She worked night and day, but somehow, Annie didn't think the word work ever crossed Delaney's mind. Horses were her passion. She lived and breathed them, cared for them like they were her children. One day, while waiting for Cal to finish up, Annie decided to explore, following a trail that led to the stables, and what she saw took her breath away. Once the wooded path hit a clearing, a gently rolling meadow stretched between her and a pristine line of corrals. A sloped gravel road, lined by white fencing led the way, and when she arrived hilltop the smell of leather and wood engulfed her. There were no horses or hay as yet, only bridles and leads, saddles and pads. Annie recalled the scent and how it reminded her of everything Tennessee, everything country. Delaney had created an ambiance as warm and welcoming as a country campfire on a crispy-cold night. When Delaney discovered her, she had graciously given her a tour.

"Annie?"

She turned at the sound of Cal's voice. "Yes?"

"What are you doing standing out here all alone?"

"Just enjoying the scenery."

He jogged down the front steps from the main hotel, a log structure practically built into the mountainside. Massive beams ran floor to ceiling and crossed lengthwise to support an A-line roof and walls of windows. Malcolm insisted every wall be a window for an inside-outside sensation. Wanting no barrier between his guests and the land outdoors, he had even gone so far as to line every bathroom in river rock and included open-aired, spring fed steam showers. When Annie had asked him what he intended to do when it rained or snowed, he simply smiled, pushed a button, and an ingenious automated cover slid into place. *"Voilá."*

Annie shook her head. Malcolm was not only creative, but the man harbored a technological affinity as well. Sliding doors weren't his only marvel of machinery. He rigged all the sprinklers to use rain water and recycled hotel water to irrigate the landscape. By utilizing a high-tech filter, he claimed the water was practically as pure as the springs by the time it hit the leaves outdoors. His compost bins were another ingenious feat. Strategically located throughout the property, the food waste his guests discarded was composted for use in the hotel's herb and vegetable gardens to grow the next batch of culinary creations.

"Are you ready to take a look at the spa?"

Anticipation skirted through her. "I am."

Cal took her by the hand and guided her through a covered walkway that followed the mountainside and into the spa. Another feat of gorgeous design by Malcolm, the spa had been worked in and around mountainous rocks, over and above a rushing creek. It was the same creek that used to run behind Ernie's cabin, long since destroyed and replaced with an adorable rustic shack where they housed historical items from the area. That was Cal's idea. A history buff, he convinced Malcolm and Nick their guests would love a quaint trip into the history-rich past of Tennessee, complete with Indian relics, tokens leftover from the old mining days and of course, tales of gold fever that wracked the land, including right here in Ladd Springs. For added mystique, an authentic graveyard lay within view—home to Susannah and Ernie and any number of Ladds to come. Cal assured them that after a visit here, those pretty gold pendants they had in the gift shop would sell like hotcakes.

Opening the door for her, Cal asked, "Have you given the salon your notice?"

"I have," she said, with no small amount of ambivalence. Annie had been torn up inside when she told the owner she was leaving. Trendz had been her professional home for almost ten years, and it felt like she was leaving home when she told them she was joining the staff at Serenity Springs. Annie grinned inwardly. Make that running the Serenity Springs spa. The nail department, anyway. Walking into her section, her jaw dropped. "Do you need five stations?"

"Yes ma'am. We aim to have manicures, pedicures, waxing, the works."

Annie laughed. "But do you think you're going to need them at one time?" She looked at a row of fancy leather chairs wrapped in plastic, sleek stone sinks behind each, complete with built-in wooden racks for her selection of nail polish, a stack of drawers to house her manicure tools. A line of pedicure chairs lined the opposite wall, outfitted equally well. Unlike the stark contemporary décor of Trendz, the pale cream walls and recessed lighting matched the supple vanilla leather of the chairs to give this area a calming aura. Polished pebblestone floors lent a natural, earthy feel. It was unfinished, but she could easily envision Malcolm's intent.

"We plan to run at full occupancy."

"All the time?"

Cal grinned. "All the time."

She shook her head. "You're going to have your hands full."

He slid them around her waist and nuzzled her ear. "I hope so. We're going to need a few kids to fill that house."

Grasping hold of his arms, she reveled in the feel of him, the peace she felt in his presence. Enfolded within his embrace, she immersed herself in the scent of his cologne, a subtle fragrance with a mildly woodsy spice. Thoughts of Christmas morning floated to the forefront of her mind. Cal's gift to her had been architectural drawings. It wasn't what she expected to find when she unwrapped the enormous gold-papered box with the glittery red bow, but then again Cal was proving to be anything but ordinary. He told her it was a dream home, a place he'd always wanted to build in the mountains but had no one to build it with until her. A slew of warm memories inundated her. He promised she could change anything she wanted, but after perusing the pages, Annie didn't want to change a thing. She loved it, but it was what he said to Casey that touched her heart the most.

There was a private detached cabin included solely for her. Said he understood living with her momma wasn't ideal for a young woman on her own, and he believed she needed her own space. Annie thought Casey was going to jump from the couch and hug him. She didn't, but Annie could see the appreciation bursting in a gaze straight from her heart. Cal had given her the greatest gift of all. Independence.

And despite the fact that her life was beginning a beautiful new phase, something had been gnawing at Annie and she needed to get it off her chest. Turning within his arms, she peered up at him. "Cal?"

"Yes?"

"Can we invite Emily to the wedding?" Cal went rigid. "I mean it. I think it might be a nice outreach, don't you?"

Sadness poured into hazel eyes, his features etched by time, a time greater than his years. "Annie, I think it's a real sweet idea, but I don't think she'll come. I've called her twice and her momma won't let her talk to me."

"Why don't we go see her in person?" His Adam's apple logged up and down. "Would you, Cal? Would you take me out there to meet her? It's a lot harder to say no to person when they're standing right there in front of you."

"I don't know, Annie. That might be asking a bit too much of her."

"Will you at least consider the idea?"

Visibly relieved, he nodded. "I will."

She kissed him. "Thank you."

After they investigated every nook and cranny of the new nail salon, Cal took his time escorting Annie back to the lobby. He idled around the path, indulging in a spout of a waterfall escaping from a crack in the rocks. It was spring water, one of the many natural outlets on the property. Ladd Springs earned its name for a reason. "Have you given any more idea to where you want to live?"

It was a question she'd been anticipating but had no answer. "I have."

"And what do you think about my suggestion?"

"Building on Casey's land?"

"We could offer to buy a section from her. With that and the money from the logging, she would be set for quite some time. You don't think she'd object, do you?"

"No." Not really, though it was probably not the right time to broach the subject with her. Lately, she'd been moody, ornery. Annie took it as a sign she was ready to move on from Fran's and choose a real direction for her future, partly due to Cal's promise of building her a space of her own, partly due to Jimmy's eagerness over the whole college adventure thing, as he called it. Casey didn't talk about Troy anymore. Never mentioned his name, perhaps dropping any and all hope for his return. Annie believed her daughter had finally come to accept that it wasn't meant to be and it was time for her to move on with her life. Annie was thankful for the change but saddened at the same time. She wished her daughter could look ahead with a bigger sense of excitement, but instead Casey appeared to become a cold realist. If she needed a degree, she'd get one, so long as Jimmy went to school with her. They were talking about starting this summer, with a few science classes of all things.

But Annie wasn't about to argue. Jimmy had done right by Casey and their friendship was something Annie valued. Delaney's input with Casey helped too, and these days, Annie would take any help she could get. It was ironic, but where Delaney had been her biggest opponent when it came to recognizing Casey as family, she now stood as her biggest ally. She seemed to want nothing more than to see Casey and Felicity grow close, paving the way for the next generation of Ladds. She gulped. Grandchildren.

"Are you opposed to the idea?" Cal asked.

"No. It's just a reality I'm still getting used to."

Cal hugged her to him. "Don't take too long. I'm getting' mighty impatient to settle down and get cozy by the fireplace." His slightly crooked smile made her laugh. "What? You can't blame a man for wantin' to snuggle with his woman, can you?"

A flush of warmth rose to her cheeks and she pushed into him. "No."

"Well, alrighty then. Get busy with your thinkin' and give me an answer soon, will you?"

Annie felt the buzz of her cell phone within her coat. As she reached for it, a swarm of angst streamed through her. Lacy was due to deliver any day now and was to call the minute she went into labor. Annie pulled out her phone, concerned to see Casey's number on the screen. She was supposed to be at work. Annie pressed the phone to her ear. "Casey?"

"Mom."

"What's a matter, honey?" She glanced at Cal. "You sound sick." He released her and immediately she felt the loss of his body heat. "Is everything okay?"

"I'm pregnant."

Annie felt the blood drain from her head. She gripped the phone. "Pregnant?"

Cal returned a stunned look.

"What am I going to do?" she cried.

"I don't know..." Annie closed her eyes. She could only pray it was Jimmy's.

# # #

The End

Frannie's Boiled Peanuts

1–2 lbs. green peanuts (fresh from the garden, not roasted)
1 gal. of water (enough to cover peanuts 1–2 inches in pot)
1/2 cup salt (your taste preference)
Smoked ham hock (optional, for added flavor)
Sliced pickles (optional, for added flavor)

Rinse unshelled peanuts well, then place in large pot, cover with water. Add salt and ham hock. Bring to a boil. Cover pot and continue cooking on medium heat for 2 – 3 hours, more a gentle boil than rolling boil ~ length of time will depend on how "green" your peanuts are to start. After 2 hours, check. Peanuts should be soft to chew, but not over-mushy. Continue to cook until desired doneness. When done, remove from heat and cool, then drain. Eat warm or room temperature.

You can alter recipe by adding Cajun seasoning, adjust salt content—your choice! Just be sure to enjoy this southern tradition. Despite what Lacy thinks, these are *gems* from the kitchen.

About the Author:

Dianne Venetta lives in Central Florida with her husband, two children and part-time Yellow Lab Cody-boy! An avid gardener, she spends her spare time growing organic vegetables, surprised by what she finds there every day. Who knew there were so many amazing similarities between men and plants? Women, life and love and her discoveries along the way provide for never-ending fun on her garden blog: BloominThyme.com.

You can also find her on twitter @DianneVenetta and facebook.com/DianneVenetta. Plus, learn how you can become a member of her street team, Bloomin' Warriors, where you'll be eligible for special discounts, advance excerpts, author swag and unique gift items throughout the year. For full details, be sure to check out her website, DianneVenetta.com.

Other novels by Dianne Venetta:
Romantic Women's Fiction
The Gables Trilogy:
JENNIFER'S GARDEN
LUST ON THE ROCKS
WHISPER PRIVILEGES

Women's Fiction
CONDEMN ME NOT

Mystery/Romance Fiction
Ladd Springs Series:
LADD SPRINGS #1
LADD FORTUNE #2
HOTEL LADD #3
LADD HAVEN #4
LOSING LADD #5

Read an excerpt from Ladd Haven...

Chapter One

"So they can't take a honeymoon?" Seated across from Casey Owens in a red-vinyled booth at Fran's Diner, Jimmy Sweeney shook his head. Bright light flooded in through the pane of front windows, red-checkered curtains serving to cast his fair complexion in warm shades, accentuating the naturally red highlights in his brunette hair. Casey noted most of the black hair dye had grown out, the dark ends the only visible hint of Jimmy's Goth stage. He refused to cut his hair short which would have eliminated the color altogether, claiming he wasn't comfortable with short hair. Too mainstream. At least it was only the tips, Casey mused. The brown hair made him appear semi-normal and not half-bad looking, no longer sullen, brooding and rebellious.

Jimmy was a loner at school, torn between his desire for attention and his debilitating shyness. He couldn't make the first friend yet it was all he longed for. Friends, people who understood him, accepted him. He was a little on the quirky side, but Casey had come to learn it was due to his extreme intelligence. Jimmy was a brainiac born to a family of dysfunction. His aunt Candi was Casey's best friend, a thirty-eight-year-old woman who still lived at home. His Uncle Clem was a no-good bum, a man who tried to loot gold from Ladd Springs, land that now belonged to her thanks to her mother's vigorous battle to prove paternity. A victory Casey had only recently come to appreciate. While she was glad to own part of Ladd Springs, Jeremiah Ladd was a dirt bag. Could anyone expect her to celebrate the fact he was her father?

Her change in attitude was due in large part to Jimmy. He'd convinced her to see the positive in owning half of Ladd Springs, as opposed to the negative. Forget the reason she had the land and focus on what it meant going forward. But that was Jimmy. He was her constant. The guy who'd been there for her when everyone was else was too busy with their own lives. The two struck up conversation one night while rolling silverware after working a shift at the diner. Going through troubles of her own at the time, she'd needed a friend and was willing to chance a conversation with the extremely odd Jimmy Sweeney. Turns out, he wasn't so weird once you got to talking to him. He was smart, generous, and a good listener. They even had a few things in common. Peering into his dark eyes, eyes that held affection, friendship, she sighed. If it hadn't been for Jimmy and his friendship, Casey would have lost her mind. Lost her life, really.

"It doesn't seem right," Jimmy said. "If I were newly married I'd want one."

Staring at him, a part of her knew Jimmy wouldn't mind that marriage to include her. Only she wasn't interested. "They're too busy with opening the hotel," Casey replied, picking at a biscuit on her plate, one of two her Aunt Fran had delivered along with a cheese sandwich, none of which she'd ordered. She didn't want biscuits or sandwiches or her customary cheeseburger and fries, but if she didn't eat, Fran would get on her and she wasn't in the mood for another lecture. *Now fill up, sugar, you're eatin' for two. Don't go starvin' that baby or I'll report you to your doctor.* With the amount of food Fran was trying to pile down her throat, one would think Casey was eating for two hundred! She was pregnant, not vying for an eat-a-thon.

"But no honeymoon?" Jimmy pressed. "I thought that's what newlyweds were supposed to do."

"Eventually they will." Swiping a finger against a thick drip of honey, Casey sucked the sweet substance from her fingertip. "My mom wants to go to Bermuda for her honeymoon."

Jimmy gaped. "Bermuda?"

Casey nodded. "Says it's the closest exotic destination she could think of."

"What—she afraid to go far?"

"She's not sure about flying." Annie Owens was almost forty years old and had never been on an airplane. Casey would say that was weird, except she hadn't been on one either. Growing up in a small town with little money to their name, they never had reason. Now that her mom had married Cal Foster, things were different. He had money—lots of it— and he was more than willing to share, offering to build her a small house of her own on the land her mother had secured for her. Warm feelings washed over her. Mr. Foster was a good man. A loving man. Casey was glad her mother had married him. Better yet, the marriage came with a new stepsister, one she hadn't met yet. Cal's daughter, Emily, was eleven and lived in Arizona with her mom. Unable to attend the wedding, Emily was scheduled for a visit later in the summer and Casey couldn't wait. With no siblings of her own, Casey thought it would be neat to have a kid sister. Cal said if things went well, Emily might be able to spend summers here. Well, if Casey had anything to say about it, Emily's first trip to Tennessee would be memorable.

Jimmy nodded, as though flying anxiety were completely normal. "Cool."

Casey smiled. So easygoing. Jimmy accepted life as it came. He was smart, wise. It was Jimmy who was able to convince her of the futility in taking drugs. There'd been a time when she was so unhappy, so miserable, life didn't seem worth living. But he made her see there was hope over the horizon. Change, freedom. Despite the people around you, life could be enjoyed. And Jimmy knew what he was talking about. His parents fought non-stop. They were loud and obnoxious but refused to get a divorce. His grandparents took him in but they weren't much better. They were miserable. Yet throughout it all, Jimmy said he never gave up hope. He hid behind a wardrobe of black for a while but said he always believed in himself and his future. Today he lived on his own in a cute apartment downtown, drove a nice car and was taking classes to earn his degree. He didn't know what he wanted a degree in yet. Only that it would be something that would get him a good job and get him out of this town.

Unfortunately, Jimmy wasn't her type. He was too tall, too skinny, but he was nice and he was her friend. Casey set a hand on the enormous swell of her stomach. Two things she had come to appreciate after Troy Parker left town. The love of her life, and father of her child, had deserted her. By the time he finally got around to telling her what he'd done, where he'd gone, she'd been so mad she refused to take his calls. He'd moved to Kentucky. Took a job on a ranch there and planned to settle down. Troy didn't ask her to come with him. He didn't insist they never spend another night apart. Nope. He up and left and didn't call her for a week.

A strange sensation pushed into Casey's stomach. It wasn't nausea, it wasn't a cramp. Pushing back in her seat, she slid a hand over the rise of her belly, rubbing in a circular motion as she allowed the feeling to pass. They seemed to be occurring more often these days, feelings in and around the baby inside her. They were physical sensations, but she was beginning to have emotional ones too. An intuition she never had before. Too bad it didn't exist before she started dating Troy. Maybe then she would have seen him for the train wreck he was.

Jimmy looked down at her stomach as though it were a ticking time bomb. "Are you all right?"

"Fine."

"Are you sure?"

She nodded. Like everyone else, Jimmy was a worry wart when it came to her condition. There was nothing wrong with her. It was just a feeling. Continuing to caress her belly in a rhythmic motion, calming, Casey wondered if it could be indigestion. Staring at the tall glass of half-drunk coke, she wondered if it might be the carbonation unsettling her stomach. Or maybe the biscuit drenched in honey butter. Strange how pregnancy changed things. Not only was she experiencing new sensations and feelings, but her tastes had changed. She used to love French fries, but now they soured her stomach. Too greasy. Same with cheeseburgers. She could no longer eat the two staples of her diet. She glanced around the restaurant, her gaze landing on a waitress carrying a heavily loaded tray of food through the diner. Circling a table, she delivered fried chicken, fried okra, fried tomatoes and cornbread. Casey frowned. Practically everything in the restaurant was fried, which made her cringe. Good thing she only had another two months or so. She wasn't sure how much longer she could tolerate it!

The front door opened, the clang of bells reverberated in her heart.

"Casey?" Alarm careened into Jimmy's gaze. "What's a matter?"

Panic closed her throat. She couldn't speak. She couldn't move.

Troy Parker, in the flesh, was standing by the hostess stand.

Jimmy whirled around at the same moment Troy spotted them. Removing his black hat as they made eye contact, his familiar brown eyes latched onto Casey like a bee on a blossom. Her heart squeezed, her legs dissolved beneath her. Troy was here.

But why?

He hesitated, glanced around tables and booths in the crowded diner. Even from ten yards away, partially concealed beneath those long brown bangs of his, she could see his anger flash hot. Troy clenched his jaw and headed straight for them. Instinctively, she jammed elbows to the table and leaned forward, crossing her arms protectively over her stomach, catching the edge of her plate which toppled, then spun loudly back in place. Casey's pulse shot wildly out of control—thudding so hard—she feared it would break loose from her chest.

Troy's long jean-legged strides closed the distance in seconds. Jimmy turned back to face her, the full impact of what was coming gripping his expression steps before Troy made it to their table, arriving in a sweep of tension, emotion churning the air around him. He stared down at the two of them, eyes darting between her and Jimmy, hostility pulsating beneath his surface of calm. Casey gulped. "Casey," he said tersely.

"Troy," she returned, scratching out the single word.

Jimmy sat pensive, clearly unsettled by the surprise appearance of her ex-boyfriend, a position he'd been vying for himself of late. Jimmy wanted to give her baby a name. He wanted to support her, be there for her where this man had not. It was a gesture she appreciated but declined. She couldn't be with Jimmy. She wasn't interested.

There was only one guy who held her interest and he was standing before her very eyes, glaring at her like she was a traitor or something. He stood bolted in place, looking between the two of them, as if waiting for Casey to fill the void. "I thought you were in Kentucky," Casey sputtered, even as she battled a chest full of nerves and her heart sang, *Troy's home.*

"I'm not," Troy replied. "I'm here."

"We can see that," Jimmy wisecracked, swiping Casey with a sidelong gaze.

Troy's hand flinched, giving Casey a start. "Why are you here?" she asked quickly, diffusing the powder keg between the two. Troy didn't care for Jimmy and the feeling was mutual.

"I quit."

Her spirits burst like a balloon. Troy quit. *Of course.* It's what he did.

"It's not what you think."

"We don't have to *think*," Jimmy said, surprising Casey with his show of nerve. "It's what you do. It's expected."

Troy turned on him. "Why don't you hold your tongue before I rip it out of your mouth?"

Casey jumped at the sheer nastiness he was displaying. "Troy!" He could break Jimmy in two and probably love the chance to do just that. "Please!" she cried. A few nearby diners were taking in the trio, but none with any knowledge as to the significance of what was happening.

"Why don't you get lost?"

Casey stared across the table. This was a side to Jimmy she had yet to see. Usually he preferred to hang on the sidelines, avoid confrontation altogether. He did it the last time he and Troy faced off, did it with their professor at school...

"You first," Troy spat.

"Stop it," Casey thrust between them.

Troy tossed a fiery glare her way but quickly extinguished it. "I don't need him interferin'."

"Interfering with what?" she asked, annoyed and disconcerted at the same time. Troy was back. He was fighting with Jimmy. Continuing to conceal the round of her stomach, she smacked, "You're the one who walked up on us, remember?"

Taken aback by the edgy response, he gave her a double-take—which gave Casey a warped pleasure. *That's right, Troy. You're the one interfering. We don't want you here.* But for some reason Casey couldn't give voice to the first word. She was too happy to see him.

Troy straightened. He pushed back his muscular shoulders and announced, "I came by to tell you I'm back. For good."

Casey laughed, but it was strangled, ineffective. What she intended to be hurtful fell short. She couldn't look at Troy and instead sought refuge in the safety of her friend and supporter, Jimmy Sweeney. His Adam's apple rose and fell as he accepted her lead. "Sure you are," she muttered, wishing his return wasn't on public display. There were so many things she wanted to say, to know. Troy was home. He'd quit. What would he think about the baby?

"I am, Casey." Appearing to dull the blade of his attack, Troy shifted weight from heel to heel, holding her steadily in his gaze. His eyes were molten with emotion, his surprise discovery of the two of them together surely unsettling. Troy was the jealous type and, worse, had always suspected Jimmy of being interested in more than friendship. To find them together had only underscored that suspicion. "I made you a promise when I left here and I aim to keep it."

"Too late. You already broke it." Uttering the words broke her heart all over again. On their last night together, the most beautiful of her life, Troy had promised they'd be together forever. He was talking future and family. Her heart pinched at the memory. Stupidly, she'd believed him. Tearing her gaze from his face, she sought the safety and security of Jimmy.

"I didn't break anything," Troy countered. "I quit drinking, I'm on a better road..."

But the fight had left him. From the corner of her eye, she could see him waver. Troy wasn't sure what to do. She understood his instinct was to stay and argue, but her voicing her position in no uncertain terms seemed to undermine him. He wasn't sure how to proceed.

From across the table, she could feel Jimmy's displeasure. He was mad—at her, at Troy—at the whole situation. He'd been warning her about this day, warning her that Troy might come back and try to convince her to give him another chance. As if she'd forgotten, Jimmy constantly reminded her how Troy had run around with Jeremiah Ladd's girlfriend, flirted with Jillian Devane, all while professing he cared for Casey. Then dumped her, ran off and left her pregnant.

Casey didn't need reminding. She lived with the pain every day of her life. At the moment, it was dulled in comparison to Troy realizing she was pregnant. That conversation was sure to stir up a hornet's nest of trouble. Glaring at Jimmy, she needed Troy to be gone. She could only sit hunched over the table for so long before it became awkward and he saw the size of her stomach beneath the flimsy cotton dress.

"I'm finished with it all," Troy said. "No more."

"Yeah," Jimmy replied snidely, "until the next eighteen-wheeler pulls into the lot with a case of Jack Daniels."

"Jimmy!"

Troy glowered. "Why don't you shut your mouth before I knock your skull into next week?"

"It's the truth," Jimmy continued, angling his shoulders to face Troy. "You're a waste of breath."

Ignoring him, Troy thrust angrily to Casey, "We need to talk. This isn't over 'til we do."

"What isn't over?" Jimmy asked. "You already dumped her. What more do you have in store?"

Troy stood rigid, his wrath aimed squarely at Jimmy. "This ain't none of your business."

"It is my business when you're standing here talking to my girlfriend."

Casey gasped. Troy froze. He locked onto Jimmy. "*What did you say?*"

"You heard me," Jimmy repeated.

Gawking at Jimmy, Casey was met by a challenge. *Tell him the truth.* Fastening his gaze to hers as though daring her to say otherwise Jimmy hitched his chin toward Troy. *Go ahead. Tell him you're pregnant.*

Casey freaked. Did he think he was helping? Did he think taunting Troy with a statement like that was going to settle the matter?

Troy pounced on her, his brown eyes searching. "Is this true? Is what he said true? You two are dating?"

Fear zipped up and down her spine as she evaded his question. No—it wasn't true—but maybe Jimmy was right. Judging by Troy's reaction, maybe this was *exactly* what he needed to hear to get a taste of how it felt to be dumped—flat on his face.

"Answer me."

"I don't answer to you," Casey defied. Drawing strength from Jimmy's presence, Troy's anger, she flipped her gaze up to meet his and nearly fell out of her seat. Instead of angry, the upheaval in Troy's gaze undid her. He wasn't angry. He was crushed. Guilt washed over her in a flood of surprise. But if he was here because he quit, he sure as heck wouldn't be happy to hear she was pregnant with his child!

Nerves pushed in at her stomach. Uncertainty flapped in her breast. Pregnancy changed everything. Things were different. She couldn't dash out on a last minute picnic or hike along the river's edge. They couldn't lie around in a field late at night, stargazing until the wee hours of morning. Pregnancy meant bills, diapers, a screaming baby... It meant responsibility. Stability. Troy couldn't quit work on a whim or get fired for impulse decisions. Being a father meant a whole new lifestyle, one that didn't suit Troy's temperament. No matter what he promised that night, that beautiful, wonderful night, reality would prove different. Casey struggled against tears. It was *her* reality now. Something he was going to have to get used to. "When you left me, Troy, you gave up your right to have a say over what I do, or don't do."

"I never left you!"

The outburst drew curious stares as Jimmy retorted, "Could'ave fooled us."

Troy plastered his hat onto his head. Without making a move for the door, he stared at Casey for the longest minute. It was a look that erased people and time, months and doubt, and replaced it with longing. There was so much left to say, so many questions, feelings, but neither uttered the first one. Too much needed to be said. Jimmy was wedged between them. It was awkward. Troy turned on his heel and strode out of the diner, dragging Casey's heart behind him. Her gaze trailed him as he shoved open the door and disappeared from her sight. He was gone. It was over. In a rush of rage, she turned on Jimmy, smacking a hand to the table. Silverware bounced as she demanded, "What the heck was that about?"

"What?" he asked dully.

"You telling him we're boyfriend and girlfriend!"

"Well, we should be," Jimmy mumbled.

"But we aren't, Jimmy! Now he thinks we are!"

Met by a vacant stare, Casey could kill him. With one stupid statement Jimmy ruined her opportunity to understand what had happened. Why did Troy leave? Why was he back home? What happened between them? Was it her fault? His? At this rate she'd be lucky to ever see him again, let alone speak to him.

"What am I going to do?" she wondered aloud.

"I thought you said he was a thing of your past." Dark brown eyes grew still. "Sounds to me like you want to pick up where you left off."

About to tell him exactly what she thought, Casey stopped herself. It was clear how she felt—to Jimmy, herself—to everyone but Troy. A ripple of spasm crawled slowly across the side of her belly, reminding Casey of someone else who didn't know, might never know, especially now that she had just run him off. Troy was probably gone for good this time. Knowing his obstinate temper as she did, he wouldn't give her a chance to explain about Jimmy. He hated the guy. Troy would assume it was true and cut her from his life.

"I was only trying to help you," Jimmy said. Sliding his glass of coke to him, he pulled a long sip from his straw. He didn't look at her. He drank. Purposefully, mindfully, he ignored her.

Dropping her gaze to the table, Casey was torn. She couldn't be mad at him. Jimmy was only acting based on what she'd told him. She never wanted to see Troy again. Never wanted to hear his name. She'd never expected to see him again, especially not making statements like he had. *I made you a promise when I left here and I aim to keep it*. Did he mean it?

Visions of him storming out tumbled through her. Angry, hurt, Troy wasn't interested in explanation. Consumed with thoughts of him, she tried to convince herself it was for the best. Men disappeared when they heard their girlfriend was pregnant. It meant obligation, commitment, two important traits Troy lacked. *I quit.*

He couldn't even hold down a job. How was he going to support a family?

At a quiet slurp, Casey's thoughts reverted back to Jimmy. Unlike him. He worked two jobs to pay for his apartment and college classes, plus the occasional money he slid to his mother on the sly because his dad was a bum. Jimmy didn't run from responsibility. Casey's spirits slumped. He begged for it.